THE MOONSHINE MESSIAH

ADVANCED PRAISE
THE MOONSHINE MESSIAH
by Russell W. Johnson

"Like the illegitimate child of *Justified* and *Sons of Anarchy*, *The Moonshine Messiah* leaps off the page with a rarified air of gritty, hillbilly realism. The legitimate part is the voice author Russell Johnson uses to tell this no-holds-barred, Appalachian assault of avarice and antagonism."

—**Craig Johnson**, author of the *Walt Longmire Series*

"Russell Johnson hits the ground running with a novel so explosive you might not be allowed on a plane with it. Appalachian sheriff Mary Beth Cain heads up a cast of characters so well-rounded, they might well have been written by Carl Hiassen, Elmore Leonard or Ace Atkins. *The Moonshine Messiah* is the kind of book that will make you miss work to finish reading."

—**Eryk Pruitt**, author of *Something Bad Wrong*

"Russell Johnson performs an incredible magic trick with *The Moonshine Messiah*, pivoting between laughs, thrills, and tugs on the heartstrings just as fast as you can turn the pages. And he has created a compulsively readable character in Mary-Beth Cain, a small-town West Virgina sheriff as gutsy as Michael Connelly's Rene Ballard and as irreverent as Elmore Leonard's Raylan Givens. Everyone will find something to love in this unforgettable debut."

—**J.G. Hetherton**, author of *Last Girl Gone*

"Russell Johnson really brings the heat with his debut Southern mystery, *The Moonshine Messiah*. With this intricately woven tale of crime, conspiracy, and corruption, you'll think you've discovered a lost season of Justified. It's witty, action-packed, and filled with unforgettable characters, headlined by badass sheriff, Mary Beth Cain. My fingers are crossed for a sequel to this winner."

—**Scott Blackburn**, author of It *Dies with You*

"Russell Johnson's *The Moonshine Messiah* is *Justified* meets *Fargo* and with as many twists and turns as a Blue Ridge Mountain pass you won't put this book down. It's one I wish I could read again with fresh eyes."

—**Mark Westmoreland**, Author of *A Violent Gospel*

More Praise
FOR THE MOONSHINE MESSIAH

"Readers seeking thematic depth with heavy doses of thrills and suspense will not want to miss Russell Johnson's *The Moonshine Messiah*. The novel engages the current sociopolitical conversation without skimping on the action. An array of distinctive and sympathetic characters—including a remarkable female lead—lock horns in a fraught family dynamic with the potential for national and personal consequences, keeping the stakes high, the twists dizzying and the outcomes explosive. A highly entertaining novel that makes a lasting impression, *The Moonshine Messiah* will leave readers eager to see where Johnson takes his talents next."

—**Bill Floyd**, award-winning author of *The Killer's Wife*

"While *The Moonshine Messiah* is a hell of a crime novel, it absolutely shines as a portrait of rural America striving for hope and relevance in a changing world. Sheriff Mary Beth Cain is a tough and determined protagonist, and perhaps the only character in the wide world of fiction capable of navigating such a fast-moving and explosive plotline. Johnson is at the top of his game—this is small-town Appalachian noir at its finest."

—**C.W. Blackwell**, author of *Hard Mountain Clay*

"*The Moonshine Messiah* is crazier than a Saturday night at Waffle House, spicier than Nashville Hot Chicken, and as surprising as snow in Savannah."

—**J.B. Stevens**, award winning author and critic

"A rural route odyssey of conspiracy and vice."

—**Coy Hall**, author of *The Promise of Plague Wolves*

RUSSELL W. JOHNSON

THE MOONSHINE MESSIAH

A MOUNTAINEER MYSTERY

SHOTGUN HONEY

2023

Published by **Shotgun Honey Books**

215 Loma Road
Charleston, WV 25314
www.ShotgunHoney.com

Cover by Bad Fido.

First Printing 2023.

ISBN-10: 1-956957-25-1
ISBN-13: 978-1-956957-25-9

9 8 7 6 5 4 3 2 1   23 22 21 20 19 18

For my favorite fierce mountain mamas:
my wife, Michelle; my mother, Jane Ellen; my sister, Sarah;
and the state where I was born, West--by God--Virginia

THE MOONSHINE MESSIAH

THEY STARTED COMING a week ago, roaring into Jasper Creek like some kind of Satanic cavalry charge, dressed in black leather with metal spikes and emblems of skulls and serpents and eagles and flame. More bikers had come every day since then, pouring relentlessly into the sleepy Appalachian town—and no one knew why.

Sheriff Mary Beth Cain had staked them out overnight at the KOA campground where they were living like hippies in tent cities, passing copious amounts of hooch around the campfires. The backs of their jackets said they were from Industrial towns. Places like Detroit, Pittsburgh, Milwaukee, Sheboygan, and Youngstown. Such a gathering might make sense in Sturgis or Daytona, or some other biker pilgrimage destination, but Jasper County was in southern West Virginia, the ass-end of the state, surrounded by nothing but worked out coal fields and hollers so deep you had to lie on your back to see the sun. Not exactly a tourist magnet.

The fuckers were up to no good. Mary Beth could feel it.

At seven-thirty that morning, she spotted the first to rise, one

1

of the older bikers walking around the KOA bathhouse. With binoculars, she watched him as he readied for an early morning ride, revved his engine and took off serpentining through the campground. When he made a left onto the road that led up to Highway 460, Mary Beth spotted something strapped to his back that gave her a chill. A long gun. She was pretty sure it was an AR-15, a military style semi-automatic rifle that had become the weapon of choice for mass shooters.

Mary Beth decided to follow.

Her car was unmarked, a black Camaro convertible she considered the greatest perk of her office, but she knew she'd soon be made for a cop, regardless. For days she had tailgated various bands of these guys, practically forcing them over the speed limit as a pretext to pull them over. But so far she hadn't found anything other than bad hygiene and good manners, the bikers always being all "yes ma'am," and "no ma'am" and "I'll be sure to watch my speed ma'am," before getting off with a warning.

The man she followed now was heavy set, wore dirty jeans and a puffy black coat without insignia. Long hair and beard were both bushy and gray, an outlaw Santa Claus in polarized shades. His motorcycle was a forest green Dynaglide, a comfort bike, and he was taking her nice and easy, cruising low and slow through town.

He knows he's being followed. Mary Beth was sure. Thought maybe he was trying to wait her out, see if she got bored enough to move on. But Mary Beth stayed the course for nearly an hour. A low speed, sirenless chase, like O.J.'s white Bronco, minus the hoopla, until she realized he was heading out of Jasper County into McCray.

"Why in the hell?" she said aloud.

This was the third or fourth time she'd followed a group of bikers out there. A place nobody in their right mind wanted to go, least of all, Mary Beth. She'd grown up in that former coal mecca that was now on its last legs, where only the most stubborn of locals remained by subsisting on welfare and disability scams and all manner of backwoods, black-market wheelings and dealings. The first time a group led her down those windy roads she assumed they were just trying to take her outside her jurisdiction. Little did they know that McCray County's population had dwindled to the point it was being annexed into Jasper. Her department was already getting calls for assistance with its near daily overdoses, and all too soon the entirety of McCray's dilapidated, drug-infested enclaves would officially be under Mary Beth's authority.

"Screw this."

Mary Beth hadn't had her coffee yet and wasn't in the mood for another trip through there. She flipped on the party lights flanking her rearview mirror and let the siren wail.

The motorcycle moved to the side of the road.

This was the first time Mary Beth had pulled over one of these guys alone. Policy mandated she use backup in such a situation, armed suspect and no exigent circumstances, but she was the sheriff, *goddammit*, and she was getting impatient.

She used her car's loudspeaker to issue a command. "Hands in the air. As high as you can reach."

The biker did as he was told, his back to her with the weapon of war laid across it at an angle.

Mary Beth dropped the mic, lowered her window, and opened the driver side door, swinging it out like a shield. She pulled her Glock 22 and trained it on the back of the biker's head.

"Take three steps towards me," she shouted. "And do it slow."

The biker dismounted awkwardly. He pivoted around to face her and took three slow, exaggerated steps, like a pirate walking the plank.

"On your knees!"

The heavy man wobbled, had difficulty dropping to his knees and lowered a hand to steady himself.

"Hands in the air! Now, motherfucker or I'll blow your head off!"

"Easy, ma'am. Yes, Jesus, God." The man reached for the sky like a Pentecostal at an altar call. "I'm complying here. You'll have no problems from me."

Mary Beth's heart battered her rib cage as she thought about that AR15. If there was a bump stock on that thing he could turn her car into Swiss cheese in about three seconds.

"Good." Mary Beth tried to slow her breathing. "You follow my commands and we'll get along just fine. Understand?"

"Yes, ma'am."

Mary Beth swallowed hard. "Okay. Slowly. And I mean, molasses in January, slow. I want you to lie down on your stomach with your arms out in front of you. Just like you've got them now."

Again, the man complied.

Once he was prone, Mary Beth approached. She placed her size seven boot on his lower back and tapped the barrel of her gun against his helmet.

"You hear that?"

"Yes, ma'am."

"That's my gun. I am going to pull this rifle off your back. If you make any sudden moves, I am going to use my gun to fire a bullet through your spinal cord. We clear?"

"Crystal."

Mary Beth seized the rifle with her left hand. She pulled it straight up from the man's back and wriggled the strap out from under him.

"Good." Mary Beth took a step. "Do you have any other weapons on you?"

"No, ma'am."

Mary Beth backed away ten paces and laid the rifle in the grass out of reach just as a station wagon of gawkers passed by. "Stay put," she said. Mary Beth approached carefully and frisked the man to ensure he truly had no other weapons. While he lay by the roadside, she also did a quick inspection of his saddle-bags, confirming there were no other weapons or contraband. The only thing of note she found was the man's ID and a permit for the gun.

"Okay, you can sit up."

The man rolled onto his back and propped himself on an elbow before eventually getting upright.

"Want to tell me what you're doing?" Mary Beth said.

"Just wondering and wandering."

The man's odd response was something Mary Beth had heard before and was beginning to recognize as some kind of code, maybe a biker way of saying "fuck you" to the cops, the way folks around Jasper said "bless your heart" when they were too polite to tell you to go to hell.

"I mean, what's with the rifle?" she asked.

"It's just for protection."

"Protection?" That rifle had a sixteen-inch barreled SP1 carbine with a collapsible buttstock and a high capacity magazine. It was what police departments with budgets far greater than Mary Beth's issued to their SWAT teams. "You expecting a zombie apocalypse?"

"You can never be too careful, ma'am."

Mary Beth gave him an ugly look. Then she made him wait there, sitting in the dirt, while she ran a check to make sure he didn't have any outstanding warrants, or better yet, felonies, but to her disappointment, his record came back clean.

"I was told West Virginia was an open carry state," the man said when she returned his ID.

"Uh, huh. Yeah, that's right."

"Can I ask why you pulled me over then? I don't think I was speeding."

Mary Beth maintained a bland expression. "I pulled you over for that busted taillight."

The biker removed his sunglasses, revealing white, unburned circles on an otherwise ruddy face. "I don't have a busted taillight."

Mary Beth bent over so they were eye-to-eye. "Want to keep it that way?"

The biker nodded. He remained compliant while Mary Beth retrieved a tape measure from her car. She'd spent the last couple days researching every conceivable motorcycle regulation she could find, dreaming up new ways to harass these guys into moving on. Now she took her time inspecting the Harley, eventually coming up with citations for a seat that was too low, handlebars too high, and the lack of a passenger handhold.

"Y'all don't really want to keep hanging around this little hillbilly old town, do you?" she asked, as she handed over the ticket. "Can't be any fun getting harassed by the local fuzz every day."

"It's a beautiful part of the country," the man said. "Especially this time of year with all the leaves changing colors."

Mary Beth frowned. She pulled back the citation. "You know, I'm not sure I measured right. Think maybe I might need to start all over. Maybe disassemble a few things while I'm at it."

The man gave her a shit-eating grin, a mischievous glint in his eye. "Don't mind at all, ma'am. Take *all* the time you need."

That's when Mary Beth finally got it. Flaunting the AR15. The slow going drive, and patient compliance no matter how ornery she got.

He wanted her there. Wasting her time. Not watching what all the others were doing.

He was a diversion.

02

MARY BETH TORE-ASS back to the campground. Empty. Not a single sleeping bag or hung-over biker in sight.

"Shit."

She kicked herself for not ordering eyes on the pack while she followed her lone gunman, but the truth was, her department was spread so thin with the whole McCray County annexation thing, she really couldn't spare it. She'd wasted enough resources on these bikers already.

Maybe they've finally headed out of town, Mary Beth thought. That was a pleasant notion, but no such luck. Within ten minutes patrolling she found a swarm of at least fifty of them parked outside a wood-paneled roadside bar called Lucky's. It was a rough watering hole, well known by law enforcement. The kind of joint with bars on the windows, where the band played behind chicken wire and the patrons feet stuck to the beer-drenched floor.

Lucky's sat near the exit ramp for Highway 52, catty-corner to the Waffle House where Mary Beth parked and called in a code seven for a meal break. She switched off her radio and commandeered a window seat inside so she could caffeinate while watching the bikers and deciding what to do next.

"Usual, Sheriff?"

Ralph Sherman, the portly proprietor of the Waffle House, rolled greasy white sleeves above his thick, hairy forearms. He didn't normally wait tables but often insisted on serving Mary Beth, personally.

"What's that?" she asked.

"Do you want your usual?"

Mary Beth hesitated. She really could go for her normal biscuits and gravy but had recently decided to try and lose a few pounds. "Just a veggie omelet today," she said.

"On a diet?"

Mary Beth shot Ralph a look. Though she was tall and relatively trim, Mary Beth had recently turned forty, and her slowing metabolism bothered her enough she'd stopped wearing a bulletproof vest under her uniform.

"Not that you need it, of course," Ralph said, scratching nervously at his hairy arm.

"Just trying to get healthy," Mary Beth said.

Ralph smiled, relieved. "One veggie omelet, coming up."

"Thanks. Oh, hey Ralph, how many of them do you think there are now?" She pointed to the rows of motorcycles parked across the street.

"Hard to say. They aren't all one group. But it's gotta be close to a hundred now, all together."

A hundred. That's what Mary Beth thought too. "What do you think they're up to, Sheriff?"

Mary Beth sighed as a group of ten more bikers stormed down Jefferson.

"Wish I knew. My first thought was crank. Bikers have been known for that. And we worked so hard to clear out the meth dens around here, I thought maybe they were moving in to fill the void. But there's been no signs they're cooking."

"Could just be bringing it in."

Mary Beth shook her head. "I'd have caught wind if they were selling around here."

"I bet," Ralph said, then caught himself, suddenly looking as embarrassed as if he'd just farted in church.

Mary Beth didn't have to ask why. She and everybody else in creation had read the Charleston paper's recent exposé, *Rough Justice*, chronicling what they called her "extra-legal" methods—evidence tampering and coercive interrogations, as well as an unseemly connection to the so-called "McCray County Mafia," a country-bumpkin crime syndicate *allegedly* helmed by Mary Beth's very own mother, Mamie.

"You know, it could be Oxy," Ralph suggested, trying to ease past his faux pas. "That'd explain why they keep riding into McCray. Maybe they're picking it up there and running it."

Mary Beth had thought about that too. McCray had more than its share of hillbilly heroin, thanks to a crooked doctor who rained pain pill prescriptions into the hollers like confetti. "But they aren't running anywhere," she said. "If they were picking something up, they'd have taken it off somewhere by now. If they were bringing something in, they'd have left to go get more. These guys act like they're sticking around."

"Well, they're making folks awful nervous. A pack of them were in here the other day. Every one of them armed. Just carrying it right there in the open."

Mary Beth frowned. "Did you happen to ask any of them what they were doing here?"

"Yeah, sure." Ralph scratched at his arm some more. "It's kind of weird. They all say, 'Wanderin' and wanderin.'"

"Wandering and wondering," Mary Beth corrected.

Ralph stared at her blankly. The way folks around Jasper Creek talked, wandering and wondering sounded the same and were used interchangeably, but the first person Mary Beth heard use the odd phrase had been from Detroit, and his accent made the difference clear. Plus, she'd asked him to spell it to be sure.

"Wander, w-a-n-d-e-r, means to move around aimlessly. Wonder, w-o-n-d-e-r, means to be curious about or in awe of something."

Ralph shrugged. "Well, after they told me they was just wanderin' they stared at me like they were expecting me to say something back. And when I didn't, they just went back to casual conversation. Real polite like. Almost too polite. It's just weird, Sheriff."

Mary Beth's experience had been much the same. "Just wanderin'," she repeated, adopting her, and Ralph's, natural pronunciation.

Just then four more bikers pulled up to Lucky's and Mary Beth decided she was tired of not knowing what in the hell was going on.

"You know what, Ralph? Cancel the omelet."

Mary Beth stood, buttoned her brown jacket and retrieved her beloved floppy brimmed Stetson from the cracked pleather bench. She took her time positioning the hat just right, checking her reflection in the window and wondering why she'd even bothered trying to straighten her hair that morning. It was already kinking up like strawberry blonde corkscrews.

"Do me a favor, will you Ralph?" she said. "I'm gonna take a walk across the street. If I don't come back out of Lucky's in fifteen minutes, give a call down to the station and let them know where I am, would ya?"

03

AN OCEAN TIDE OF FOG was rolling down the Old River Mountains as Mary Beth crossed the parking lot, giving her a foreboding feeling. That night, Jasper Creek's football team would play their chief rival, the Perry Town Panthers, and virtually everyone from the two towns would cram inside Yeager Stadium for an event that would occupy most of her deputies. She knew that if Hell's Angels was going to pull some shit, that'd be the time to do it.

Mary Beth popped the trunk to her Camaro. She already had her Glock 22 holstered to her hip, and a subcompact Beretta, that she called her Hummingbird, strapped to her left ankle, but wanted something that would make a bigger impression. There were at least sixty bikers over at Lucky's and Mary Beth would need to do something dramatic to take control of the situation right from the start. She retrieved a pump-action, Remington shotgun and pondered whether it would be best to fire a round into the ceiling or maybe just rack a load, nice and loud, then walk up to the biggest, baddest looking guy in there, ram the barrel of the Remington against his testicles and tell him she had some questions she'd like answered.

"This is crazy," Mary Beth admitted. But something needed to be done, dammit, and with the scrutiny she'd been under since the *Rough Justice* expose, she didn't want to involve any of her deputies. The unflattering news coverage had prompted a Justice Department investigation that was already worrying her chief deputy, Izzy, so much he wasn't sleeping at night.

As Mary Beth contemplated her next move, a vehicle jumped the curb into the Waffle House parking lot. She wheeled around, shotgun instinctively raised to her shoulder until she recognized the SUV. It was a two-tone, brown Chevy Blazer with a jacked-up suspension to allow for monster-truck size tires, and had the sheriff's department emblem painted on the door, along with the word: CHIEF DEPUTY ISAIAH "IZZY" BAKER.

"Speak of the devil," she said.

Izzy swung open the door and kicked a metal-runged rope ladder clanging to the ground.

"You always did know how to make an entrance," she said. And meant it. Izzy stood out wherever he went, in part because he was the only Black officer on the force, but more so because he stood just shy of five feet, even with boots on.

"Thought I'd find you here," Izzy said, as he began an awkward, painfully slow descent.

"You should fix up an inflatable slide for that thing, like they have on airplanes. It'd be a lot faster," Mary Beth said.

"Ha, ha."

Mary Beth was the only one Izzy would take short jokes from. They'd been tight since high school. Ever since her dad died and she moved from McCray County to live with her grandparents in Jasper Creek.

"You forget to charge your phone again?" Izzy asked. "I've been trying to call you all morning."

Mary Beth felt her pants pocket and realized she'd left the phone in the car.

"Why? What's up?" she asked, just as Izzy was finally reaching the ground.

"You tell me." Izzy nodded toward the shotgun.

"Oh this? This is nothing. Just thought I'd mosey across the street and welcome our visitors."

Izzy frowned. "You think that's a good idea? With all the—"

"Relax, Jiminy Cricket. I'll be totally professional."

"This is not a joke, MB. You're under a microscope now. You've got to be on your best behavior."

Izzy always did have a way of looking up at Mary Beth that felt like he was looking down.

"Well, I've got to do something," she said. "There's more coming every day. They're up to something."

"Maybe, but it's gonna have to wait. Your lawyer's been calling down to the station, all in a panic. Says he needs to see you right away."

Your lawyer. God, how Mary Beth hated those words. The federal investigation had forced her to hire Alexander Pomfried, the biggest shitbag defense attorney in town. It had been Izzy's idea, and a prudent one, but still, the notion that she'd "lawyered up," made her feel sick to her stomach. People could say what they wanted about her criminal family, but everything Mary Beth had ever done – whether technically proper or not – was well-intentioned. Part of her *wanted* to be judged for it. But the other part, the part that listened to Izzy, knew how these things could go. And there were things the feds could try to pin on her that weren't really her doing but she'd been loathe to disavow, like all the dead folks who rose from the grave to cast a ballot for her in the last election.

"Pomfried can hold his horses," she said. "This should only take a few minutes."

Izzy shook his head like the parent of an incorrigible child. "You know what your problem is?"

"I've only got one?"

"No, you've got a lot of them. I can list them if you like. But the problem rearing its ugly head right now, is that you always think the rules don't apply to you."

"Is this a racial thing?"

"No. It's an idiot thing. It's about arrogance. Thinking you know better than everybody else. Acting just like your—"

"Don't say it!" Mary Beth knew where Izzy was heading. All her life, people had told her how much she favored her villainous, sociopathic, arch criminal mother—the infamous Mountain Mamie. "I'll go see the damn lawyer, okay?"

"Good. That's all I ask." Izzy threw the rope ladder into the cab of his Blazer, then jumped surprisingly high to grab the bottom of the door and slam it shut before walking around to the passenger side of Mary Beth's car.

"Where do you think you're going, Tonto?"

"With you."

"What on earth for?"

"So, you don't just circle the block and come right back here after I leave."

Shit. Mary Beth had planned on doing exactly that. She was scratching around for another idea on how to ditch Izzy and get back to the bikers when the car radio went off: "Sheriff, we've got an urgent request for an assist out of McCray."

Deputy Tucker.

"Okay, so assist," Mary Beth snapped back. With the pending annexation and McCray's threadbare police force, they'd been getting assistance requests for weeks.

"We've tried, Sheriff. Request came in nearly thirty minutes ago: shots fired on deputies responding to a domestic. Some old coot has them pinned down."

"Well, what are you waiting for? Get somebody out there!" Mary Beth barked.

"I'm telling you, we've tried, Sheriff, but they can't give us an address. All we know is it's some shack a few miles off Rural Route 4. We've had two cars circling around all over who can't find it. You know what it's like in McCray. All those hollers and mountain roads are like a maze."

"Get the GPS coordinates," Izzy suggested

Mary Beth shook her head. That wouldn't work. You could never pick up a consistent satellite signal in McCray. Her Sirius XM cut off every time she drove through there.

"They said you'd know how to find it, Sheriff. The old guy who's raising hell is supposed to be some relation of yours. Name is James Logan."

A chill rippled up and down Mary Beth's spine. "Oh, shit," she said. Uncle Jimmy. This was urgent. "Sorry, Izzy, but Pomfried really is gonna have to wait."

Before Izzy could protest, Mary Beth said she was in route and they both piled into her Camaro. Mary Beth flipped on the lights and hit the gas. She gunned it up past seventy down College Avenue, where the speed limit was thirty-five, then hit the brakes and fishtailed onto Sycamore. From there she got on Highway 123, which would have taken her all the way into McCray but she veered onto Rural Route 6, down toward Crawdad Holler.

"What are you doing?" Izzy asked.

"If we're going to see my Uncle Jimmy. I want to take him a present."

"I hope you're joking?"

"Nope," Mary Beth said as she swung onto a backroad.

"We don't have time for this, MB. Officers are pinned down."

"They've been pinned down for half an hour already. Five more minutes won't kill them."

"It might."

"Trust me," Mary Beth said. "I know my Uncle Jimmy. He'll be a whole lot more pleasant to deal with if he has his medicine."

She pulled to a stop outside a double-wide trailer surrounded by the decaying corpses of vehicles too rusted to tell the make.

"This is your uncle's pharmacy?" Izzy asked.

"In a manner of speaking."

Mary Beth hopped out and went and banged on to the trailer's rickety screen door until a thin, shirtless man with full sleeve tattoos answered.

"Morning, Sheriff," he said after releasing a belch that assaulted Mary Beth with the aroma of Spaghetti-Ohs.

"Colby, I got a situation and need to commandeer a jar of your blueberry moonshine. Bring me the strongest stuff you got."

The man disappeared for a minute before reemerging with a mason jar he placed into a brown paper bag. "Normally charge forty bucks for the Blue," he said, "but I'll give it to you for twenty."

"How about you give it to me for free, and we both forget we had this conversation about your illegal liquor operation?" Mary Beth said.

Colby sighed. "Suppose that would work too."

"You're a good Samaritan, Colby."

"Some say it so, Sheriff." The shirtless man scratched himself. "Some say it is so."

Mary Beth smiled. She liked that line. She'd have to use that sometime.

04

THE SPEEDOMETER LOOKED like an arm wrestler giving way as Mary Beth drifted down the twisty mountain roads—thirty, forty, fifty–ridiculous speeds through those switchbacks. She expertly straightened the curves, liberally swerving into the opposite lane to avoid careening into the rusty guardrail.

"Look out!" Izzy yelled as a battered sedan appeared behind a blind hairpin turn.

A head-on collision seemed imminent until Mary Beth yanked the wheel. She barely avoided the car and a jutted rock formation as the Camaro skidded onto the shoulder of the road, sending a shower of gravel raining down the mountainside.

"'You trying to give me a heart attack?" Izzy said.

"Relax," Mary Beth told him. "I know these roads. I was born in McCray County."

"I know, but I'd rather not die here, if you don't mind."

"Quit your bitching," Mary Beth said. "We're almost there."

They continued down the mountainside, over pockmarked pavement, until the road leveled out near Honeysuckle Pass. That's when the Sirius XM cut out and Mary Beth switched the radio to 850 AM, the station where her brother broadcasted. Sure enough, there was Sawyer, her dumb brother, all riled up in full-on, foaming-at-the mouth sermon mode.

What's happened to us out here—we're just the canary in the coal mine, so to speak. You're already seeing it throughout the rust belt. Manufacturing jobs all gone there too. And I know y'all wanna blame trade. But I'm here to tell you that's a red herring, people. Just like folks blaming coal's problems on environmental regs. Sure, that hurt, but it's a drop in the bucket compared to what modern technology's done. Now you can mine a seam with twenty men, when it used to take five hundred.

"Sounds like your brother's still on his Luddite kick," Izzy said, Mary Beth rolled her eyes. Sawyer continued his deep baritone voice that was alternately playful and dramatic.

Let me ask you this, as you're listening on your radios: Do you drive for a living? Well, we're about 30 seconds away from drones and driverless cars taking your job. Or maybe you're working at McDonalds? Guess what, in Europe they already got robots making those Happy Meals. Just a matter of time before they're here. Try supersizing that Welfare check. And you can always get a job waiting tables, right? Ha! You seen those touch screens they're putting in restaurants now? They're taking orders and taking credit cards and taking your job, Jack.

"He sounds like the damn Unabomber," Mary Beth said. "The last time I listened to him he was—"

"Hang on," Izzy interrupted. He turned up the volume.

And all you white-collar workers think you're safe in your cubicles, typing away on your computers. Well guess what? Whatever it is you do that you think's so special, there's an app for that. I guarantee you. And if there ain't yet there will be soon. Just wait till technology comes for you.

Cause is doesn't matter what you do. Somebody will build a machine to do it just as well, and then they'll straight shitcan your ass. Won't be happy till the only people making money are a handful of fat cats.

Mary Beth brought the Camaro to a hard stop when the pavement gave way to a dirt road that led up onto Cottonmouth Ridge. The path was way too rough for her low-riding car so they'd have to walk it from there.

"Somebody should tell Sawyer, can't nobody outside these hollers pick up his little radio show," she said.

Izzy gave her a sideways look. "You're joking, right? He's all over the internet. Just Google him."

"Whatever." Mary Beth didn't believe that for a second. "Sawyer couldn't spell Internet—even if you spotted him the I-N-T."

"Oh yeah? Take a look." Izzy pulled out his smartphone and tried searching up Sawyer Thompson, "The Moonshine Messiah," as he was often called, but couldn't get a signal. "Damn, boonies. Well, wait till we get back across the county line and check it out. Sawyer's got quite a following. Actually makes some good points, every now and then."

Mary Beth huffed. Sawyer was crazier than a shithouse rat. A worthless two-bit grifter just like most of her cousins and all the other people she'd grown up with in McCray.

"Come on," Mary Beth said, grabbing the moonshine. "We've still got a long hike ahead of us."

She and Izzy both were breathing heavy from the steep climb, and were about a hundred yards from the clearing leading up to Uncle Jimmy's cabin, when they heard the crack of a high-powered rifle.

A bullet grazed past Mary Beth's left ear and a rotted-out birch tree exploded behind her, sending wooden shrapnel flying everywhere.

"Get down!" a man's voice called from somewhere up ahead.

Mary Beth and Izzy both dropped to the ground just as another bullet took down a large branch from a sycamore. It fell to the ground in front of them, providing enough cover to slither off the road, as shots continued to rain.

"Keep your head down! The old bastard's crazy!" Mary Beth's eyes tracked left until she spotted where the voice was coming from. There was a gray McCray County Ford Explorer pulled off-road behind a semi-circle of scrub pine and evergreens that made a screen between them and the madman on the hill. At least one of the vehicle's tires had been shot out and it was riddled with bullet holes.

"This is Sheriff Cain and Deputy Baker from Jasper County. Who's over there?"

"Deputies Hawlings and Jenkins," the man yelled back. "And one of the old man's daughters is with us too."

Mary Beth raised an eyebrow. "Which daughter? Janice or Raelynn?"

After a slight pause the man called back, "It's Raelynn."

"No shit? How you doing Rae?"

"Okay, Mae B," came a shaky female voice. "How you?"

"Well, I just got shot at a couple of times but other than that, I'm doing fine."

"I know, right?"

Mary Beth hadn't seen Raelynn in a few years. They were the same age so there'd been a bit of a rivalry between them growing up, in which Mary Beth competed by being good at sports, while Raelynn's talent was sleeping with every guy Mary Beth ever dated.

"Hang on," Mary Beth said, "I'm coming over there."

She ordered Izzy to hold his position then made a hunched-over dash across the dirt road. She squeezed behind a scrub pine just as a bullet struck a rock behind her, making a sound like a church bell. Mary Beth crouched near the Explorer's tailgate and scooted around to the side where the two deputies and her cousin Raelynn were cowering.

"That was close," said the deputy whose name tag identified him as Hawlings. The older of the two, mid-fifties, was leading man material, with a strong square jaw and hair that was more salt than pepper. Raelynn was sitting awfully close to him, rubbing shoulders as she did her damsel in distress routine.

"He's had us pinned down here for over an hour," Jenkins, the younger, more nervous looking deputy said. "You know this guy?"

"Sure, Uncle Jimmy's a peach," Mary Beth said. She was staring at her cousin, and had to admit that Raelynn looked good, like she went on a revenge diet to let her ex-husband know what he was missing. Hawlings' coat was wrapped around her shoulders and when she shivered, it revealed a skimpy little outfit underneath, like she was a waitress for one of those breastaurants.

"He's off the deep end," Raelynn said. "Won't take his medicine. Totally paranoid. Was planning to go into town shooting people he thinks are out to get him. I tried to hide his keys, but when he heard the police pulling up, he went off in a rage. I ran down here to try and warn these guys not to come no further, and he started firing on us."

"Are his keys still in the house?" Mary Beth asked.

"Yeah, his are. I got mine."

"How well hid are they?"

Raelynn frowned. "I did my best, but I was moving quick, Mae B. It's just a matter of time till he finds them."

Mary Beth heard some branches break and peered around the Explorer. Izzy was still on the opposite side of the dirt road but had advanced his position, finding a good spot to hide behind a hickory stump.

"Izzy?"

"I'm here, Sheriff."

"We got a wild one up there, threatening to head into town, guns blazing. I'm gonna go and distract him."

"How?"

"Don't you worry. I've got a plan. But while I'm distracting him, I need you to creep around to the barn and disable his truck."

Izzy pulled his gun, a massive .44 Magnum with an extended barrel as long as his forearm. "You want me to shoot out his tires?"

"I was thinking of something a little more subtle. Like maybe pull out the distributor cap."

"Right." Izzy holstered his weapon. "Roger that, Sheriff. I'll take care of it."

"Good. Oh, and Izzy…"

"Yeah, Sheriff?"

"Stay low." She winked as Izzy gave her a middle-finger salute.

"You got a loudspeaker in there?" Mary Beth asked Hawlings.

"Sure. What are you gonna do?"

"Just talk some sense into him."

Mary Beth opened the driver-side door of the Explorer, switched on the loudspeaker and stood on the running board so she could peer over the vehicle.

"Uncle Jimmy!" Her amplified voice reverberated off the mountainside. "This is your favorite niece. Your sister Mamie's girl, Mary B—"

A shot tore through the evergreens right above Mary Beth's head. It sent her reeling and she landed flat on her back. All the air left her lungs as Izzy started yelling.

"I'm okay," Mary Beth yelled back when she was able to catch her breath. She sat up and shook her head. "Where's my hat?"

Raelynn handed over the Stetson. Mary Beth snatched it jealously and examined to make sure it was uninjured.

"His memory ain't good, Mae B," Raelynn said. "He'd probably know you by your nickname, though."

Mary Beth groaned. She found the CB mic hanging out the door and crouched safely behind the Explorer this time as she said, "Uncle Jimmy, I'm the one you used to call Strawberry Shortcake."

A wicked laugh cackled from the opposite side of the dirt road until Mary Beth picked up a small rock and whipped it, side-arm, in Izzy's direction.

"Now listen, Uncle Jimmy," Mary Beth said, slipping into her deepest McCray slang. "I done brought you some of your favorite blueberry moonshine. And I'm gonna walk it down this here dirt road and bring it to you. But first, I'm gonna take the lid off."

Mary Beth pulled the jar from the paper bag and unscrewed the gold-colored lid, catching a whiff of ethanol so strong she could already feel a contact buzz. "So, you be a good ole boy and don't shoot me. Cause if you do, I'm gonna spill all this good 'shine. And that'd be a tragedy."

05

IZZY HELD HIS BREATH as Mary Beth stepped out from behind cover onto the dirt road, holding the moonshine above her head like a flag of surrender. "I swear she won't be happy until she gives me a heart attack," he muttered.

Mary Beth was brave, no doubt. Some said, fearless. But reckless was the word that came most often to Izzy's mind when thinking of his best friend. He peered through the trees toward the cabin and tried to get a fix on the old man, but all he could make out was a shadowy form on the porch.

Mary Beth coughed loudly to mask her instruction for Izzy to, "Move your ass."

"Shit," Izzy said. "Here we go."

He hated the fucking woods. *Hated.* If he came within a country mile of poison ivy, he'd have a rash for weeks. Yet there he was, crawling through leaves and briars, and shit, hoping not to get shot. He maneuvered wide to his right, wanting to safely flank the house without alerting the old man, but there were so many damned leaf-concealed twigs and pine cones that kept cracking and snapping no matter how gingerly he stepped.

Izzy pressed down on a branch that cracked like a glowstick. It was loud enough he expected to hear a gunshot any second but, instead, the sound that filled the air was Mary Beth, singing *Country Roads*, West Virginia's unofficial state song, at the top of her lungs.

Lean on Me would have been a better choice, in Izzy's opinion, since Bill Withers was actually from the mountain state, a place not too far from there, actually, called Slab Fork. But under the cover of Mary Beth's pitchy vocals he was able to make it all the way to the rear of the cabin without a shot fired. Izzy lost sight of Mary Beth just as she was hitting the line about the misty taste of moonshine.

Uncle Jimmy's detached garage had heavy barn-style doors that opened with the screech of a rusty hinge. Izzy froze, but Mary Beth could still be heard singing in the distance and Izzy realized the old man was actually singing along with her now, and kind of getting into it as they hit the chorus.

Izzy slipped inside where he found not one truck but two. A little white Chevy S-10 and a big black Ford F-150, both older models, with plenty of wear. Izzy took a guess that the big truck belonged to the old man.

Fortunately, the F-150 was unlocked, so popping the hood was no problem. But reaching it would be. Izzy needed something to stand on. He borrowed Uncle Jimmy's large, red, Craftsman tool chest that he rolled close enough to climb upon and reach under the hood. The blue distributor cap that housed the spark plugs wasn't hard to locate, but it was protected by some type of exhaust tube that made it difficult to access. Izzy made a brief effort to remove the tube before deciding on a more expedient course. He fished a pair of snippers from the tool chest and simply cut the wires. It would be a lot harder to restore power that way, but at least the truck wasn't going to town any time soon.

Izzy hopped down and rolled the toolbox back to the rear

of the garage before noticing for the first time the two stickers on the rear bumper of the F-150. REDNECK PRINCESS and WARNING: MY BOOBS ARE BIGGER THAN MY BRAINS.

"Son of a bitch," he said. He'd just disabled the wrong truck.

Izzy strained to hear if Mary Beth and Uncle Jimmy were working on an encore. The singing around front had stopped so he had no way of knowing what was going on over there or how much time he'd have. He quickly retrieved the snippers and went to work on the S-10, slicing through wires like he was Edward Scissorhands.

He'd just closed the hood when he heard Mary Beth shout, "Uncle Jimmy! No!" Then a gunshot exploded, followed by an awful, primal sound, like a woman howling in pain. Izzy pulled his gun and started for the door when he heard another blast of gunfire and the howling stopped.

06

MARY BETH WAS DOING John Denver proud, singing *Country Roads* with gusto as she approached the house, not knowing if her subterfuge was working until Uncle Jimmy started singing along as he sawed back and forth on his wooden rocking chair.

She was a few steps short of the porch when the song ended and Uncle Jimmy said, "You got a good voice, Strawberry." He was a wiry little man with snow white hair slicked back with too much pomade and wore black-framed sixties-style glasses.

"Thanks," Mary Beth said. "You know you ought not shoot at people who are trying to come visit you, Uncle Jimmy."

Jimmy shrugged. He had an old M40 rifle laid across his lap and cases of ammo stacked up next to him. "Those were just warning shots, Strawberry. If' I'd wanted to hit you, I'd a hit you."

"Well, what do you want to go scaring me for?" She was still pouring on the McCray accent, extra thick.

"I thought you was with them." Uncle Jimmy pointed his rifle toward the stand of evergreens where the deputies and Raelynn were holed up. "When you told me your name, I thought too that maybe your Mama sent you up here to convince me to sell

27

out to them prospectors. But then I remembered, you don't much care for your mama, do you?"

"You could say that."

Mary Beth was doing her best to maintain eye contact with her uncle, but was distracted by the snarling pit bull tethered next to him. As she took the first step up to the front porch, the dog barked ferociously until Jimmy quieted him with an angry swat.

"Whatever happened to you?" Uncle Jimmy asked. "Ain't seen you around in quite a spell."

"After my daddy died, I went to live with my grandparents in Jasper Creek. Didn't get back here as much as I'd have liked."

Mary Beth hazarded another step. The pitbull barked and yanked at his chain until Jimmy boxed his ears.

"Always liked your daddy," he said. "Never quite did get what he saw in your mama, to be honest with you."

"Often wondered the same thing," Mary Beth said. Her daddy may have been a drug dealer, but he'd also been a kind, simple man who she believed would have been content with an honest life had he not felt obliged to satisfy her mother's ambitions. She, Madeline "Mamie" Logan—who'd gone through too many subsequent husbands and last names for Mary Beth to keep track—had grown up dirt poor and determined to better her situation, but also came from a time and place where a woman's way to advancement was to cajole what she needed out of a man. And Mamie was plum awesome at it.

"Your mama's always been a wily one," Uncle Jimmy said. "But I guess your daddy's the one who took a bullet for it, didn't he?"

"Guess so," Mary Beth agreed. She started to take the final step up onto the porch but hesitated. "Say, Uncle Jimmy, does your dog bite?"

Jimmy looked down at the powerful mastiff like it was a harmless little yapper. "Nah, Two Dogs won't bite unless I tell him to. Lie down Two Dogs! And shut up!" The dog whimpered and bellied up next to Uncle Jimmy like a dragon nesting in a pile of gold.

Mary Beth looked around to see if there was another dog on the porch she'd missed somehow. "Why do you call him Two Dogs?" she asked.

Jimmy gave her a look. "Cause it's his name, I reckon."

"Yeah, but why'd you name him that, seeing as there's only one of him?"

"Cause there used to be two. One got killed, tussling with a black bear. After that I kept hollering 'Two Dogs' and this one kept a'coming, so no need to change it. Your name's whatever you answer to."

Mary Beth had to admit that made some sense. Uncle Jimmy had always been full of little nuggets of hillbilly wisdom like that.

"So how about that bottle of blue?"

"Right." Mary Beth took the final step onto the porch, staying as far as she could from the dog and handed her uncle the jar.

He wasted no time getting into it.

Mary Beth took a seat in an empty rocking chair that backed up to the mountainside and gave Uncle Jimmy a few minutes of quiet sipping while they enjoyed the view.

A strong gust of wind whipped around the porch. Mary Beth buttoned the top button of her coat and noticed Uncle Jimmy was only wearing a flannel.

"Sweet Jesus, Uncle Jimmy. It's colder than a mother-in-law's love up here. Don't you wanna put on a coat?"

Uncle Jimmy offered her the Mason jar. "Have a hoot," he said. "That'll warm you up."

"I'll pass." Mary Beth had already smelled enough of that poison.

Uncle Jimmy gave her a mean stare. "I said, have a hoot."

Mary Beth didn't think it wise to argue. She took hold of the jar, eyeing the fermented blueberries that floated like dead flies. "What should we drink to?" she asked.

"Let's drink to the Flash."

"The Flash?"

"Elwood Gray."

It took Mary Beth a second to get the reference but she knew Elwood Gray was a local legend, the first Black man to play for McCray County High School after integration, who led the team to back-to-back state championships in sixty-five and sixty-six. Some said he was a direct descendant of John Henry, the steel driving man who died outperforming a machine designed to replace him. But Mary Beth mainly knew Gray as the McCray County Commissioner who had most vigorously opposed the annexation into Jasper. An opposition that ended a couple of weeks earlier when the Flash went up in flames—literally—having died in an accidental fire at his Mapelton apartment after he got drunk and passed out with a cigarette in his hand.

"To the late, great, Elwood Gray," Mary Beth said. She took a tiny sip and the liquor hit her hard, burning down her chest, causing her to gag.

Uncle Jimmy slapped his knee. "Goddamn. That's good, ain't it?" He smiled with a mouth full of teeth as yellow and sharp as Two Dogs'.

"Sure is," Mary Beth said, still coughing. She handed the jar back to Uncle Jimmy who helped himself to a few more sips.

She just needed to keep Jimmy talking long enough for Izzy to finish his mission. Plus, she figured if she could get her uncle to down half of the jar of shine, he'd eventually have to go take a long alcohol-induced nap, and Raelynn could handle him from there. Just start mixing his meds in with his mashed potatoes and all should be fine.

"So, Raelynn says you don't want to take your medicine anymore," she said, just reaching for something to talk about.

"Raelynn," Jimmy said with disgust. "She's in it with 'em."

"With who?"

"All of 'em. Prospectors going around, wanting to buy up

everybody's land for nothing. Looking for clean coal. *Clean* coal. Dumbest Goddamn thing I ever heard. Coal ain't supposed to be clean."

"Well, you need your medicine, Uncle Jimmy. Every time you stop taking it you get yourself in trouble. Remember a few years back I had to come up here and smooth things out for you?"

Uncle Jimmy seemed to grasp for the memory but came up short. "I don't recollect," he said.

"Remember Buck Davis?"

Uncle Jimmy scowled and ran his gnarled hands through his hair, fluffing out the feathers of his duck-ass hairdo. Mary Beth could see the memory coming back to him. It was then that he took note of the star on her chest. "That's right. You're the law, ain't you? Over there in Jasper?"

"That's right," Mary Beth said.

Uncle Jimmy had a plug of chew crammed inside his jaw and spat. A trail of brown juice ran down his chin, clinging to his beard stubble. Mary Beth didn't know how in the hell anyone could chew that stuff and drink at the same time.

"Can't trust the law around here," he said. "They're all in on it."

"In on what, exactly?"

"They work for the coal companies. Always have."

Jimmy took another sip. He breathed real deep, enjoying the burn of that one.

"They want me to take my medicine to numb me out, see. Keep me from taking care of my business."

"What business is that, Uncle Jimmy?"

He gave her a hard stare, gripping the rifle he'd kept since his Marine days. "Revenge, little girl. Revenge for the Flash. I know they killed him."

"Now why would somebody want to do that?" Mary Beth asked carefully.

Uncle Jimmy leaned back in his chair. His eyes were already

glassy, and Mary Beth could tell the wheels were now turning more slowly.

"'Cause Gray took a stand against 'em. Against big coal. Telling it like it is. Tried to block the strip mining and get some new businesses in here. Made all kinds of enemies. You say something bad against coal and folks around here are on you like stink on shit."

Mary Beth had read a little about Elwood Gray's opposition to strip mining. The paper said he had some pie-in-the-sky ideas about attracting green energy companies to come in and revitalize the area.

"So, who is it you're seeking revenge against?" she asked, "Who's the bad guy?"

"They!" Uncle Jimmy shouted. "Them!" He shook his head angrily. "I don't know exactly who, but I'm gonna find out."

"The way I hear it, the Flash accidentally killed himself."

"Uh, uh. Ain't no way."

"That's what the paper said. They say he got drunk and fell asleep with a cigarette in his hand and caught his easy chair on fire."

Uncle Jimmy slapped the arm of his rocking chair. "The. Man. Didn't. Drink!"

"How do you know?"

"'Cause I just saw him this past April. We was both riding a car in the Easter parade and he told me he gave up the drinking."

Mary Beth shrugged. "So, suppose he lied?"

"The Flash don't lie."

"Okay, so, suppose he was telling the truth at the time, that he'd quit drinking, but then later he started up again."

Uncle Jimmy squinted, his expression morphing from simple anger into something truly frightful. His war face.

In one quick motion, Uncle Jimmy raised the rifle from his lap. Mary Beth barely had time to yell, "Uncle Jimmy! No!" before he pulled the trigger.

The sound was deafening from such a close range. Through the high-pitched whine of her wounded eardrums, Mary Beth picked up a kind of terrible, shrill howling noise. Then Uncle Jimmy squeezed off another shot. Mary Beth turned toward the ridge behind her where she saw a dead bear cub curled around the base of a tree.

"We're in the revenge business today, Two Dogs," Jimmy said.

The dog was licking his lips as Uncle Jimmy undid his chain. "Go on," he said. "Go and get you some revenge for what they did to your brother."

07

"I THOUGHT the old man had shot you," Izzy said, when Mary Beth finally returned to the clearing. "I came around the corner ready to fire, and I saw you up on the porch sipping moonshine, all casual, like you were just watching TV or something."

"When he fired that gun, I thought he was shooting at me," she said. "After that, I needed a drink."

"What's the old man doing now?" Deputy Hawlings asked.

"Sleeping. Damn near polished off the whole jar of moonshine." Mary Beth turned to Raelynn. "When he gets up, just mix his meds in with some food, okay?"

"I'll get my brother to do it," Raelynn said. "Jack should be on his way out here soon. But I got to get to work."

"Can it wait?" Mary Beth asked. After all the trouble she'd been through that morning, the last thing she wanted was for Jimmy to wake up and go back on the warpath before getting a good dose of his meds.

"No, it can't wait. I just started this job. Haven't been there long enough to start calling in sick. I've got to get."

"Uh, you may have some trouble getting there." Izzy

round-aboutly explained that he'd accidentally disabled her truck, in addition to her father's.

"I hope to hell you're joking," Raelynn said, planting her hands on her hips.

"I'm sorry, I didn't know which truck was the right one."

"So you just went and fucked 'em both up, huh?"

"Relax," Mary Beth said.

"Well, goddamn it, Mae B. How the hell am I supposed to get to work?"

"I'll give you a ride," Mary Beth said. "Just calm down."

"Calm down? I got a busted-up truck."

"We'll get somebody up here to fix it," Mary Beth assured her.

"When?"

"As soon as possible. Just chill your ass out."

Raelynn crossed her arms. "Okay," she said, nodding her head. "But I'm gonna need some recompense for my pain and suffering. Y'all have violated my rights."

Mary Beth grabbed her cousin by the arm and yanked her to the side. "What we did, is save your sorry ass. Which, given our history, is a whole hell of a lot more than I should've done."

Raelynn opened her mouth like she wanted to say something back but thought better of it.

"Where are you working these days, anyways?" Mary Beth asked.

Raelynn waved a hand, like she didn't care anymore. "Little bar out your way. Name of Lucky's."

Well ho-ly dog shit. Mary Beth pushed her hat back to make room for the light bulb that was going off. "You don't say." She'd been wanting to get back and deal with those bikers all morning. And now Mary Beth had a pretty good idea of just how she could do it.

The McCray County deputies changed their blown-out tire then gave Mary Beth, Izzy, and Raelynn a ride back to the paved road where Mary Beth's Camaro was parked. By that time,

Mary Beth had worked out a plan, but in order to carry it out she needed to ditch Izzy, who wouldn't approve. So she gave her chief deputy a job to do by explaining her Uncle Jimmy's theory that Elwood "the Flash" Gray's death was no accident.

"You said yourself, that Jimmy's crazy," Izzy said.

"Yeah," Mary Beth responded, "but like my daddy used to say: even a broken watch is right twice a day."

"So what do you want me to do?" Izzy asked.

"Hang out with the McCray deputies and see what you can find out?"

"Like what?"

"I don't know, police stuff. See if the Flash really quit drinking. Find out if he had any enemies. Ask if anybody saw anything. And while you're at it, check into these prospectors who are supposedly going around buying up land out here. Maybe there's a connection. McCray's about to be our jurisdiction, after all. We've got an obligation to follow up, don't you think?"

"We've got two current McCray deputies right over there. Just ask them," Izzy said.

Mary Beth lowered her voice. "My uncle says that the local law enforcement is crooked."

"The newspaper says the same about you."

"Yeah, but out here that's more than just Fake News. McCray cops have been in cahoots with the coal companies forever. Besides, even if there's nothing to it, you're the only one I can trust to check it out. Remember how we figured we must have a leak in the department somewhere? Somebody feeding information to reporters."

Izzy nodded. When the "Rough Justice" piece ran, it cited an anonymous source they figured was either a current or former deputy. Some even suspected Izzy since his wife, Princess, a former runway model, was now a local newscaster. But Mary Beth knew that was B.S. because Izzy would never rat on her. And, even if he did, Princess, who never liked Mary Beth much on account of how much attention she got from Izzy, would have done the story herself.

"Imagine if it gets out that we're checking into whether Elwood Gray's death was a murder covered up by local police. It'd be a huge scandal, probably all for nothing. You really want to put that kind of heat on me, on top of everything else I'm dealing with?"

"Okay, okay. Fine. I'll check into it," Izzy said. "But you promise me you're going straight to Pomfried's office, and you're gonna leave that biker shit alone, right?"

Mary Beth held up two fingers of her right hand, while crossing two fingers of the left behind her back. "Scout's honor," she said.

08

RAELYNN HAD HER CLEAVAGE jacked up even more than usual and was doing her best to balance a tray of thirty-four-ounce beer mugs, while walking with a switch so pronounced it would have made a porn star blush. Her efforts weren't lost on the bikers inside of Lucky's who all had a few hours' worth of drinks in them and were catcalling her every move. She deposited the tankers on a table at the center of the room where the biggest and loudest of the bikers were congregated. Guys who reminded her of Duck Dynasty or a ZZ Top video. Mostly white and middle-aged, with long beards, leathery skin, and tattoos as ubiquitous as freckles on a redhead.

It wasn't hard to pick out the alpha dog Mary Beth had told her to look for. Everyone laughed a little too loud at this guy's unfunny jokes. And he had a PRESIDENT patch sewn to his vest.

The man was tall, well over six feet and ridiculously muscle bound, with cut off sleeves that displayed his tree-trunk arms. His head was shaved clean but he had a long black beard, twisted into braids like a pirate and some type of serpent tattoo coiled around his neck.

Raelynn thought at first he was Latino, but the accent wasn't right. Like nothing she'd ever heard before, putting the emphasis on the wrong syllable. He was also younger than most of the other guys, mid to late twenties, and in better shape. Could probably kick any ten of their asses. A lot of the guys in there were tan and ruddy from long days riding under an unforgiving sun—not the types to wear sunscreen—but this guy was naturally tan. Olive-colored skin.

"Where are you from, sweet thing?" Raelynn ran a gentle hand across the man's broad shoulders.

"Corsica."

Raelynn liked the sound of it. Corsica. Sounded exotic. The most exotic place she'd ever been was Myrtle Beach. She'd always wanted to see Europe, or the Caribbean, but her ex-husband Rodney would never entertain the idea. He had that stoic, pessimistic, Appalachian way about him, like nothing good could never happen to nobody, and anybody who thought different was just plain stupid. Raelynn was so sick of that attitude.

The big man smiled at her, and all of a sudden, she saw there was actually something kind about his dark eyes. Like they were talking to her, telling her he was different than the others. Like all the tattoos and leather and the long facial hair was just a costume he could take off if he wanted to.

Raelynn's daddy, Jimmy, used to say she could walk into a room full of a hundred eligible bachelors and immediately zero in on the lone loser. And he had a point. Most of the men in her life had turned out to be real shitheads. But looking at Mr. Corsica, Raelynn couldn't fight the feeling that if she could just separate him from the herd, shower him down, dress him up, shave that crap off his face, get him to exfoliate and moisturize, floss, make him go to church on Sundays, he could be a real dream.

She flipped her bangs out of her eyes and made a sugges-
tive little pivot, sticking her butt in his face. Corsica smacked
it so hard Raelynn dropped her tray that clattered and spun to
the ground.

Fuck, that hurt. Raelynn wanted to turn around and slap
the guy, but remembered her assignment. *Goddamn you, Mary
Beth. We'd better be even after this.* She stooped to pick up her
tray while struggling to keep her top from riding down into
nip-slip city. Then stood and gave Corsica some duck lips, saying in a little girl voice, "Now, that wasn't nice."

Corsica smiled wide. His silver tooth gleamed. "Why don't
you take a load off? Come have a seat right here." He spread his
legs wide and rubbed at the crotch of his tight jeans.

"What have you got over there?"

"Come and find out."

The other bikers laughed. All eyes were on Raelynn as she
handed her tray to the old biker on Corsica's right and sat down
on the big man's left thigh. She flicked her hair again, and blew
softly in Corsica's ear as she began sliding her hand down his
chest, then nestled it between his legs. Once there, she probed
and groped to the delight of Corsica and the onlookers, then sat
up suddenly.

"Oh, my God."

Corsica smiled. "You like what you find?"

"My God," Raelynn said again. "It's…It's…."

"What?" Corsica asked. "Go on."

Raelynn looked at him with awe. "It's…the tiniest little
pecker I've ever felt."

The room erupted with laughter. Corsica's olive skin turned
crimson and his smile melted into something vicious. He stood
quickly and backhanded Raelynn across the room.

She fell to the floor, face stinging. Raelynn put her hands up
by her ears, fearing another blow. She could sense Corsica moving her way, about to kick her in the side or yank her up by her

hair. But before he could touch her, the front doors burst open. Mary Beth and a team of deputies came charging through, ratcheting scatter guns and telling everyone to "Freeze!"

09

"ANYBODY MOVES, shoot 'em," Mary Beth said. She used her shotgun to shove the big Corsican out the front door and nodded for Raelynn to follow, while her deputies panned the room with shotguns to keep the other bikers at bay.

The bright sun blasted them as they exited the darkened bar. Mary Beth pointed to a rusty iron bench and commanded her captive to sit. Then she threw a pair of handcuffs in his lap.

"Cuff yourself to the bench."

"What the hell is this?"

"It's for your safety, and mine, while we have a discussion. Do it!" Mary Beth raised her shotgun.

"This is fucking bullshit," the man said as he shackled his wrists to the bench.

Mary Beth ensured he was cuffed securely, then patted him down, taking a 9-millimeter Beretta from him.

"I got a permit for that."

"I don't really care," Mary Beth said. She unloaded the pistol and chucked it on the ground.

"Listen, it was just a little misunderstanding."

"Shut up," Mary Beth said. "We'll get to that in a minute."

There was a gleam of fury in the man's eyes but he controlled himself. "Yes, ma'am."

"You got a name, shithead?" Mary Beth asked.

"Nico."

"Got any ID?"

The man shifted his weight to show the bulge of his wallet in his back pocket. Mary Beth removed it and looked at his Pennsylvania driver's license.

"Nicola Antone."

"An-toe-nay," he corrected.

"What is that, Italian?"

"Corsican."

"Corsico's in Italy, ain't it?"

"Corsi-co is. But Corsi-ca is an island in the Mediterranean, it's actually part of—."

Mary Beth cut him off. "Yeah, yeah, yeah, whatever. I'm not here for a geography lesson, *paisan*." She snapped a picture of his ID with her cell phone, then said, "Smile, Nikky," before taking a picture of him too.

"What the hell's going on?"

"That's exactly what I want to know, Nico. What in the hell is going on? I had me a nice quiet little town here and now all of a sudden it's full of big uglies like you. And I'm wondering why?"

Nico gave Mary Beth a hard stare.

"You from Pittsburgh?" she asked, returning the stare. She pointed to the patch on his jacket.

The big man looked at her kind of hopeful. "No, I'm from...." He paused, thinking. "Quebec."

Mary Beth looked at his Pennsylvania driver's license. "Your ID says you live in Pittsburgh."

The man's shoulders sagged. "Uh huh. Yeah, that's right."

"What do you do out there?"

"Was a steelworker. Got laid off."

"So, you come all the way out here, looking for a job?"

"I'm just wandering and—"

Mary Beth raised her shotgun. "Nico, I swear to God if you give me that wandering and wondering line, I am going to shoot you in the fucking face."

Nico slumped on the bench. "So, what then? Am I under arrest for something? I didn't do nothing."

Mary Beth looked to Raelynn, still rubbing her cheek where Nico belted her.

"What, that? That was nothing," Nico said. "I got a room full of witnesses who'll say she assaulted me. I just defended myself. Look, it didn't even leave a mark."

Mary Beth pulled Raelynn's hand from her face. The cheek was slightly red, a touch swollen, but with a little ice, she'd be as good as new. "You're right," Mary Beth said. "Rae, I'm sorry but I'm gonna have to raccoon you."

Raelynn barely had time to get out the word, "What?" before Mary Beth cocked back and punched her cousin in the eye, dropping her to the ground like a rotted-out pine tree.

"Jesus Christ!"

Mary Beth stooped to pull her cousin's hand away from her eye. "Oh yeah, that's gonna blacken up nice. Give it a couple minutes and we'll get a picture of what he did to you."

"This is bullshit!" Nico yelled. "I didn't do that. You sent her in there to provoke me. This is...this is entrapment."

Mary Beth smiled. "Entrapment? That's a big word for you, Nikky."

Nico gathered himself as Mary Beth approached. "You know what, lady," he said, "go ahead and take me in. Little assault charge. My guys will have me bailed out before the end of the day."

"Oh, Nikky. Nikky, Nikky, Nikky. Sweetie, you just don't get what's going on do you?" Mary Beth sat down on the bench next to him and primly crossed her legs. "Rae, you change back to your maiden name after you and Rodney split?"

"What?" Raelynn asked, still lying on the ground.

"You change your last name back?"

Raelynn shook her head like a wet dog, trying to get her senses. "Are we even after this, you crazy bitch?" she asked.

Even? For everything Raelynn had done? All the backstabs, the double-crosses, the long line of boyfriends she'd bedded? That was worth a lot more than a shiner in Mary Beth's book. But she was in a magnanimous mood. "Yeah," she said, "this will make us even."

"Good."

"You didn't answer my question, though. Did you change your last name back, after you and Rodney split?"

"Yeah, why?"

"Then pull out your ID and show it to numb nuts here."

Raelynn looked confused by the request but did what her cousin told her.

Nico looked at the license and shrugged.

"You see that, Nikky? This here is Raelynn Logan."

"Yeah, so?"

"So, her father is James Edward Logan. You should do yourself a favor and Google him some time. Here, I'll help you out." Mary Beth pulled up a Wikipedia page on her smartphone and read:

Gunnery Sergeant James Edward Logan,
U.S. Marines, Retired.
Born: 1945, McCray County, West Virginia.
Spouse: Brenda Louise (Kenny) Logan, Deceased, 1950-2014
Children: Jackson (Born 1973), Janice (Born 1975),
Raelynn, (Born 1980).
James "Jimmy" Logan is one of the most prolific snipers in
American history, with seventy-five confirmed kills during

the Vietnam conflict and a suspected fifty more officially listed as unconfirmed. In addition, because much of Logan's service was highly classified, it has often been asserted that his true kill tally was well over 200, which, if true, would make him by far the deadliest American sniper of all time.

"Listen here," Mary Beth said, "you'll like this part."

Logan's feats are especially impressive because they were carried out exclusively in jungle terrain, where visibility is more challenging than other theaters of combat, and were accomplished with less effective weaponry than snipers utilize today.

Nico tugged at the cuffs, pulling away like the phone might burn him.

Mary Beth said, "You know, Nikky, one of the first things I learned about the law business in southern West Virginia, is we do things a bit different down here. Take my Uncle Jimmy as an example. He had what you could call, a little trouble adjusting to civilian life once he got back from the war. And his girls, they've never had real good taste in men. His daughter Janice, for instance—that's Raelynn's sister—she married a real son-of-a-bitch named Buck who'd never been any damn good and used to smack her around, something awful. After the last time he beat her up she moved back home with her daddy for a spell and Buck came knocking one day, looking for his wife. So old Uncle Jimmy met him at the door with an Ought Six, calmly blew Buck's head clean the fuck off, then went back inside, called the local sheriff, and told them to come clean that shit off his porch. And he never spent one day in jail 'cause there ain't a jury in West Virginia who would ever convict James Logan of anything. That man's a true blue American hero." Mary Beth scooted closer. "So that got me thinking, Nikky. Because every

now and then I'd run up against some real bad guys, drug deal-
ers usually, who I was having trouble making a case against.
And it dawned on me, all I had to do was let my Uncle Jimmy
know about how they'd harmed one of his girls, and wouldn't
you know it, those bad guys had a habit of turning up dead. You
know, you may want to Google me too, when you get a chance.
Sheriff Mary Beth Cain. See what you find out."

Nico struggled with his cuffs. "Look lady if you're going to
arrest me, let's go ahead and get this over with."

Beads of sweat popped up on his forehead that Mary Beth
wiped gingerly with a tissue. "Oh, sweetie. I'm not arresting
you. I'm just gonna email a picture of you to my Uncle Jimmy.
Along with a picture of what you did to his baby girl, of course."
Mary Beth pulled up the photo of Nico on her phone and made
a show of sending it off to a Yahoo address. Then she took a
photo of Raelynn, whose eye was already turning purple and
yellow, and emailed it as well.

"But I didn't do that!"

"Sure, you did, sweetie. Isn't that right, Rae?"

Raelynn nodded.

"This is bullshit!"

Mary Beth smiled at Nico, ever so sweetly. "You know, if I'd
wanted to arrest you, I could have just waited for y'all to leave
Lucky's and pulled a handful of you over for DUI. But most
of you'd get away, wouldn't you? No, instead, what I've done is
taken pictures of all your bikes out there. And I'll send those on
to my Uncle Jimmy, too. Tell him where y'all have been staying.
How many of you would you say there are now? Eighty? Ninety?
A hundred? That ain't nothing to Uncle Jimmy. So many places
to hide in these hills. So many good vantage points. You know
he's been real cranky ever since that American Sniper movie
about that boy from Texas who they're calling the best ever.
Jimmy's been wanting to increase his numbers."

"So what?" Nico asked. "You're saying this guy's gonna kill all of us?"

Mary Beth laughed and slapped Nico on the back. "Oh Nikky, you really are dense. That's the beautiful thing about snipers. It's not that they kill everybody. It's that they *can* kill anybody."

Ten minutes later, Mary Beth was giving the bikers a princess wave as they roared out of Lucky's parking lot and headed out of town. Nico was the last to leave. He'd regained his composure by that time and was looking ominous again behind mirrored sunglasses. "You may run us off," he warned, yelling over the growl of his engine, "but you can't stop what's coming."

"What's coming?" Mary Beth yelled back.

Nico made a fist like the old Black Power sign. "A revolution!"

Mary Beth smiled. She motioned for Nico to take off his helmet, then bend down to where she could speak directly in his ear.

"Well, Nikky," she said. "It's not coming today."

10

IZZY WAS PISSED when he first heard Mary Beth had gone to Lucky's, but by the time she finished the story he couldn't help laughing.

"I can't believe they bought that crap about your Uncle Jimmy."

"Well, half of it was actually true," Mary Beth said.

"Which part?"

"Jimmy was in Nam, obviously. And he did get off for killing Cousin Buck, though it was because Buck had broken in and was armed. But if Little Nikita had looked closely he probably would have figured out that bogus Wikipedia page was something I had the tech guys gin up."

Izzy started laughing again, then stopped. "But you never really got your uncle to..."

"Izzy! Of course not!"

"Just checking," Izzy said. With Mary Beth you never could be too sure.

"Where are you anyway?" she asked.

"Sitting outside the McCray County Police Station, enjoying

the only bar of cell service I've had the whole time I've been in this God-forsaken place."

"Learn anything about Gray?"

"Actually, yeah. Your uncle may not be so crazy after all. I talked to some of Gray's friends who said he'd been sober for a long time. They were shocked to learn the cause of death and don't believe it."

"Nobody'd want to believe that about a friend, though," Mary Beth said.

"One of those McCray deputies, says he thinks there's something to it, too."

"Which deputy?" Mary Beth asked. "Clooney or Fife?"

"What?"

Izzy could hear Mary Beth sigh. She always got frustrated when he didn't get her references.

"Which one of the deputies said that? The one who looks like George Clooney, or the little one who looks like Barney Fife?"

"Who the hell is Barney Fife?"

Izzy heard a smacking sound. "Duh. The little deputy on the Andy Griffith show. You know, Don Knotts?"

"No, I don't watch that show," Izzy said.

"Come on, everybody's seen the Andy Griffith show."

"Not me."

"You're serious?"

"Were there any brothers on that show?"

There was a long pause, then Mary Beth said, "Seems like maybe Opie's football coach was Black."

"Yeah, well, I wouldn't know, 'cause I didn't watch it."

"Regardless, you should know who Don Knotts is. He's from West Virginia. From Morgantown."

Now that she mentioned it, that did sound familiar. "Is he the guy who played Gilligan?" Izzy asked.

"No, that's Bob Denver. He lived in West Virginia too. In

Princeton. Actually got busted there back in the 90's because Mary Ann mailed him a package full of weed."

"Mary Ann from the show?"

"The very one. That's what was reported anyway. But it was never confirmed because Gilligan refused to testify against her."

"Good for him," Izzy said. "Gilligan ain't no snitch."

They were both laughing when Izzy saw Hawlings poke his head out the station and signal that he needed two more minutes. Izzy gave him a thumb's up, as Mary Beth made a bad joke about Mary Ann mailing a package of Mary Jane.

"So, did Raelynn give you any intel on who the prospectors are that tried to buy your Uncle Jimmy's place?" Izzy asked.

Mary Beth recounted the little she'd gleaned from her cousin. There were some investors going around trying to buy all they could in McCray at dirt cheap prices because everyone was so desperate to get out and there was nobody else you could sell to. In recent years, a lot of people had just let their homes go to the bank or set fire to them, hoping to collect some insurance money. But Uncle Jimmy wasn't interested. He threatened to shoot the prospectors if they didn't get off his property.

"You don't think your mother has something to do with them, do you?" Izzy asked.

"I asked Rae if Mamie was mixed up with the investors somehow, and she said she didn't think so. Though mom did suggest Jimmy take them up on their offer, because he was getting too old to live up on the mountain by himself. Said she'd take him in, but Jimmy wouldn't hear of it."

Izzy told Mary Beth he was planning to stop by the Register of Deeds office when he and Hawlings went downtown and said he would pull records on all the recent land transactions. Nobody new had moved into McCray County in years, so if there were any recent deeds in the county registry, they had to involve these prospectors, whoever they were.

"So, what else did Clooney say about the Flash?" Mary Beth asked.

"He said the sheriff here was acting real strange about the whole thing. Insisted on doing the investigation himself and resigned right after he closed it."

"Reeeeeeally?"

"Yep. Some said it was just grief. Everybody loved Elwood Gray, but Hawlings isn't so sure. He said that if I could stick around until about seven tonight, he'll take me out to where I can meet the old sheriff and ask him some questions, myself." Just then Hawlings exited the station and headed Izzy's way. "Hey, Clooney's coming now. I need to go."

"Wait!" Mary Beth sounded worried. "Where's he taking you to meet the sheriff?"

Izzy tried to think of what Hawlings had called it. "I forget the name. It was like Scar…Scar face. I don't know. Scar something. They're supposed to have some kind of girls fighting or something. Like mud wrestling, I guess."

"The Scarburry Hill Catfights?"

Izzy, snapped his fingers. "Yeah, that's it."

Hawlings opened the driver-side door. "Sorry, that took so long. You ready to go?" he said.

"Yep." Izzy made the chatty motion with his hand to let Hawlings know he was trying to get off the phone with someone who wouldn't shut up. "Okay, I gotta go," he said into the phone.

"Izzy, this is serious," Mary Beth told him. "Do not go there without me. I'll meet you, okay?"

Izzy was a little offended that Mary Beth didn't think he could handle the situation on his own. "I think I'll be okay," he said, as Hawlings fired up the engine.

"Izzy! This is an order. Don't go there without backup. I'll meet you in downtown Mapleton at 6:30. Just meet me by the big courthouse there in the center of town and we can ride up to Scarburry Hill together."

Izzy sighed. He often bristled when Mary Beth pulled rank on him but he knew not to argue. "You're the boss," he said. "Just don't be late."

11

MARY BETH WAS WAITING in her lawyer's office, wondering if she was already getting billed, when she heard that pompous, overly genteel voice that made her skin crawl.

"Feet off the desk, please, young lady."

Alexander Pomfried. God, how Mary Beth hated that son of a bitch. Just being in his office gave her a sick feeling, like when her mother used to make her swallow castor oil for mouthing off.

"At three hundred dollars an hour, I figured I could put my feet wherever I wanted," Mary Beth said.

Pomfried moved into her peripheral, wearing a seersucker suit and bow tie. He cleared his throat and dropped into his courtroom voice, a deep plantation drawl that managed to stretch the word "law" into two, and sometimes three, syllables. "Come on now, Sugar. Let's not get ourselves off on the wrong foot."

There it was. *Sugar*.

It was at that moment Mary Beth realized what bothered her so much about the man. It wasn't that Pomfried had won six acquittals in the last three years. No, as annoying as that was,

Mary Beth could handle competition. The thing that she could not countenance, however, was Pomfried's insistence upon calling her Sugar.

There she'd be on the stand, armed with weapons of lethal force, wearing a utility belt that would make Batman jealous—replete with a Glock, pepper spray, baton, and taser—and still he'd talk to her like she was a little girl.

"Now, Sugar, when you first got to the crime scene, there'd already been bystanders, trouncing all through there, hadn't there?"

"Well, Sugar, this isn't the first time a piece of evidence has gone missing from the sheriff's office, now is it? Oh, I'm sure your investigation was *very* complete, Sugar, but you would admit that you never bothered to follow up with this witness?"

Mary Beth slowly removed her boots from Pomfried's desk, giving him some serious stink eye as she smoldered from the memories of cross-examinations past.

"You know, you might want to give us your cell number so it's easier to reach you in emergencies," Pomfried said. "We've been trying to get in touch with you all day."

"Nah, that's okay," Mary Beth told him. "You can keep calling down to the station. They always know how to reach me."

Pomfried gave her a befuddled look as he rounded his desk, not used to clients talking to him that way. Mary Beth noticed he'd gained a considerable amount of weight since the last time she'd seen him but hadn't given in and purchased a new wardrobe yet. His pants looked like they could burst from the strain they were under, stomach drooping way down over the waistline.

Pomfried plopped his full heft into his leather chair making it rock back and forth. "This is serious," he said. "We don't have much time and we've already lost most of the day."

Mary Beth sat up and gave Pomfried her full attention.

"On Monday morning, you're gonna be indicted." Pomfried

said it matter-of-factly, dropping the pronouncement like a blacksmith's hammer. Her worst fear confirmed.

"Shit," Mary Beth said. She removed her hat and sat it in her lap, taking a less recalcitrant posture.

"Unless..." Pomfried said, raising a finger. "You take the deal the government's offering. They called this morning and said they were gonna give you one chance to resolve this thing before the indictment comes down and it all hits the papers. Word is, the very head of the U.S. Attorney's office in Charleston, John Jacobs, himself, is steering this investigation. Has got a real bug up his ass for you. But he's empowered an Assistant U.S. Attorney from DC to come down here and try to strike a deal."

That sounded hopeful. "What's the deal?" Mary Beth asked.

Pomfried looked bothered. "That's just it," he said. "I don't actually know the details. The AUSA I spoke to insists on delivering it to you personally. *Alone*. Is planning to be at your office at five o'clock this afternoon. Just over an hour from now. Said he was coming at the end of the day as a courtesy to you, when there'd be less staff around, to save you some embarrassment."

Mary Beth furrowed her brow. None of that sounded right, especially the part about meeting without her attorney—asshole though he was.

"I know," Pomfried said, reading her expression. "But he says he knows you. Knows you aren't gonna like what he's proposing, but says you'd be a damn fool not to take it, and thinks there's a better chance of that happening if he can present it to you without, *moi*, getting in the way."

"Who is this, now?"

"The Assistant U.S. Attorney? Name is Connelly. Patrick Connelly. Says you two go way back."

Well, shit my britches, Mary Beth thought. That was a blast from the past. Patrick Connelly. Her old high school flame. She'd heard he was some kind of bigwig U.S. Attorney in D.C. but he was supposed to be in the Land Use department or something, dealing with things like condemnations and environmental regulations. Why in God's name would he be involved in a public corruption case in Southern West Virginia? Mary Beth's public corruption case, no less? Did he ask for the assignment? And, if so, did that mean he was trying to help her, or get back at her? Mary Beth wondered. They hadn't exactly parted on good terms.

"So, you know this Connelly?" Pomfried asked.

"We went to high school together," Mary Beth said, not mentioning she'd also lost her virginity to the guy and he'd pretty much been the love of her life—until her husband, Bill, of course. God rest his soul.

"Well, whether he's an old friend or not, I'd normally never let a client meet with a prosecutor outside my presence. But he said I could either consent to the meeting or they'd go ahead and indict. And, *since I couldn't get you on the phone*," Pomfried said, staring accusingly over his half-lens glasses, "I reluctantly agreed. Provided—and this is important now, Sugar, so listen up—all you have to do is hear him out. You're not to say anything at all or discuss the case in any way. Understand?"

Mary Beth nodded.

Pomfried looked slightly relieved. He eased back in his chair. "I figure you've done enough interrogations and are savvy enough to know to keep your mouth shut. You'll be able to confer with me afterward. But he expects an answer by 9:00 am, Monday morning."

"Not a lot of time."

"No, it's not. And to make sure we understand the urgency of the pressure they're putting us under, he went ahead and previewed much of their case against you."

Pomfried shuffled some manila folders on his desk until he found a legal pad with copious notes scribbled on it. "Here it is." Pomfried was preparing to read off the parade of horribles when Mary Beth gave him the hand.

"You know what, Pomfried, save it." She checked her watch. It was already three-fifty pm. If she was going to meet with Patrick at five o'clock, she'd like to go home and freshen up. "Let me just ask, this deal they're offering, will it allow me to stay in office?"

"Connelly said it would."

"Then I'll take it."

The lawyer looked at Mary Beth like she'd just sprouted a polka-dotted horn in the middle of her forehead. "Don't you want to know what it is first?"

"Don't care. My whole goal was to stay in office. If this deal will let me do that, then I'll take it."

Pomfried sat the pad down and removed his glasses. "Sugar, you need to exercise some restraint here. Whatever this deal is, it's their first pitch offer. Which means, we can probably do better. That's why they're putting this time pressure on you. We need to negotiate over the weekend. Really consider our options. It might even be worth risking the indictment. Public corruption cases are hard to prove, Sugar. They've got a truck load of allegations against you but from what I've seen so far, not a whole lot of admissible evidence. Mostly hearsay, which they can present to a grand jury but they're gonna need a lot more to actually convict."

Mary Beth leaned forward, placing her hands on Pomfried's desk. "You don't understand, Pomfried."

"Understand what?"

"I can't defend this case. I—"

Pomfried recoiled like she might strike him. "Stop right there, Sugar. I don't want to hear this. If you're about to confess something to me, I do not want to hear it. If I know you're guilty, that means I can't put you up on the stand. Don't tell me. Do. Not. Tell. Me."

Mary Beth smiled. *Men.* She was always one step ahead of them. It was almost boring. "The problem's not that I'm guilty, Pomfried. The reason I can't defend this case is because I'm not guilty. Not of three-fourths of the stories that have been told about me, anyway."

"Come again?"

"Do you have any idea how hard it is for a woman to be sheriff in West *By God* Virginia? Half the legends and tall tales circling around about me, are things I made up myself. Others are half-truths and innuendo I never bothered to correct because it made my job easier."

"I don't understand, Sugar. Why would you do that?"

Mary Beth was surprised it wasn't obvious. "When my husband died eight years ago and I stepped in to finish out his term, the men went nuts. 'Ain't no woman, can keep the people of this county safe.' That's what they all said. But once I got a reputation for busting heads and cutting corners to get the bad guys, that all went away. And people thinking I've got the backing of my crime family relatives gives me street cred in the world where I have to operate. You know how many confessions I've got because crooks think I don't give two shits about the rules? If I had to defend this case and pull back the curtain on all that, everyone would know it's all been smoke and mirrors. A big bluff."

Mary Beth could tell she was blowing Pomfried's mind. Before she hired him, he'd been one of her biggest detractors, inside and outside of the courtroom. "I have to be crafty, Pomfried. It's like my mama used to say. 'It's okay for men to be stupid, because they can get by with their muscles. But women have to use their wits.'" Mary Beth left off the last line of her mother's favorite witticism that ended, "And sometimes, their tits."

Pomfried scratched his head. "Well, Sugar, I hate to tell you, but you've wasted your money. If all you wanted to do was take the government's first pitch offer then you could have hired a number of less expensive lawyers in town."

Mary Beth had to suppress a laugh. She put her boots back

up on the old barrister's desk. "Don't you worry about that. I think I've got more than my money's worth."

"How's that?" Pomfried asked, glaring derisively at her boots resting on a stack of discovery responses.

"Because now that you know my secrets, Mr. Lawyer. I'd say, we just created a disqualifying conflict, should you ever try to defend another criminal case in my county."

"What in the name of Hades are you talking about?"

"Conflict of interest," Mary Beth repeated. "If you were to ever defend another criminal in my county. I plan to have you disqualified."

Pomfried shot up from his desk. "That's ridiculous! I haven't learned anything about any current or future cases."

"Doesn't matter," Mary Beth said. "You've learned my methods. Something no other criminal or defense attorney knows. And, you've learned it because of your representation of me. So, I'd say, you've got a conflict that will pretty much put you out of the criminal defense business. At least as long as I'm in office."

Pomfried threw his notepad on the desk. "I'll withdraw," he said, folding his arms.

"Too late. Withdrawing now won't make a difference, and you know it. The conflict's already been created."

"No judge would do that to me."

"You sure?" Mary Beth could tell by Pomfried's face that he was anything but sure. "Besides," she said. "Even if you don't get disqualified, what criminal is going to hire you one they find out that you're my—" Mary Beth winked twice—"attorney."

That was the real kicker. Mary Beth didn't really know whether she could disqualify Pomfried or not. But now that he'd publicly represented her, she could easily manipulate the rumor mill throughout the jails and the county's seedier enclaves, to convince all potential perps that Pomfried was her boy and not to be trusted.

Pomfried knew it, too. The realization was written all over

his face as he brushed back his bushy white hair and blew out his cheeks.

Mary Beth stood to leave. "Just draft a few more wills, Pomfried. Take on a few more car wreck cases. There's plenty of other things you can do. You'll be okay."

She took her time strolling to the door, enjoying the stunned silence.

"You are one crafty woman," Pomfried said. "One devilish, crafty woman."

Mary Beth turned back and tipped her hat. "Some say it is so, Pomfried. Some say it is so."

12

IZZY WAS GLAD Deputy Hawlings was driving. McCray's
windy roads were like rollercoasters and the way Mary Beth
had whipped them around that morning left Izzy pining for
Dramamine. But Hawlings was taking things nice and slow.
Enough for Izzy to take in the sights of the insular, coal community with its rows of cookie cutter homes with their peeling
white paint, collapsing front porches, and tiny square yards surrounded by chain-link fences. Izzy could see how it was once
like a little pristine, communist community, with everybody
working for the same employer, living in identical homes, and
shopping in the company store using scrip—the pseudo money
coal barons gave out in lieu of cash. But now the houses were
all in serious disrepair. Every fourth or fifth one burned to
the ground.

"Does anybody still live in these?" Izzy asked.

"Some," Hawlings said. "Believe it or not. But most are empty."

They passed a corner lot where a number of people congregated around a metal drum full of burning leaves. Hawlings
made a comment about all the able-bodied adults there in the

middle of the day with no jobs to go to. Then they passed an abandoned Walmart where someone had spray painted "Fuck You" over the OUT OF BUSINESS sign.

"Guess somebody's not a big Walmart fan," Izzy said.

Hawlings scowled. "Wally World was great while they were here. One of the largest employers in the county. But it destroyed two jobs for every one it created, putting the mom and pops out of business. So, when they decided to pull up stakes and leave last year, we were really in the lurch. All the stores they shuttered aren't coming back. And people got to where they depended on Walmart. With all the pharmacies out of business, it was the only place to get medicine. And we got some real sick folks out here—silver hairs and shut-ins on oxygen. Now they have to get somebody to drive them all the way to Jasper Creek to get basic necessities. Shoot, there's only two grocery stores left and they run short of stuff all the time."

Izzy shook his head. He didn't get why anyone would hang around such a dying, depressing place. "Why does anybody stay?" he asked.

Hawlings looked wistfully out the window, like that was something he'd considered a thousand times. "It's home," he said. "It's what they know."

"I'd get out if it were me."

"That's easy to say, but a lot of these folks are old. A lot of them are sick. And most don't have any education. They don't have the skills to go start some new career somewhere. They built their lives around something that just doesn't exist any-more. It's like the earth got pulled out from under them."

Izzy could tell Hawlings really cared about the place, and its people. That's what made for a good cop in his book. It was the reason Mary Beth was so good.

"What about you?" Izzy asked. "You seem like a smart guy. You've got experience. I'm sure you could get a cop job some-where else."

Hawlings shrugged. "I've thought about it. But the truth is, I don't want to live anywhere else. This is my home, too. I did a tour in the army right after high school, got to get out and see the world. And there's some great places out there, don't get me wrong. Culture and conveniences and whatever. But there's just something about a coal town. Way folks all look out for one another. The pace of it. Up with the sunrise, work hard all day, then kicking back in the evening on the front porch, shooting the shit with your neighbors or just listening to the crickets as the dark settles in. It gets in your blood."

Hawlings got quiet after that and an awkward silence followed until Izzy asked if it would be okay to turn on the radio. "Sure." Hawlings hit the power button and out came Sawyer Thompson, Mary Beth's brother, still preaching away about the evils of technology:

Y'all heard of the IBM supercomputer, Watson, right? Went on Jeopardy and beat all the best that mankind had to offer. Well now it's diagnosing patients—doing the work of doctors. It's performing legal research—doing the work of lawyers. Shit, not long ago, it wrote a damn song. No one even asked it to. Just did it all on its own. Figured, songs are just combinations of words and sounds. It studied the most popular ones, dissected what made them work and put one together. Pretty, fucking catchy too. Probably working on a novel as we speak.

"You listen to Sawyer Thompson?" Izzy asked Hawlings. "The Moonshine Messiah? Shit, yeah. That guy's the truth." They passed a sign announcing they were two miles from downtown Mapleton, McCray's county seat, as Sawyer started going off on how Amazon was delivering packages by drone.

Which will make for some pretty interesting skeet shooting, should they ever be bold enough to try that shit in McCray County.

"Can I ask you something?" Hawlings said, in a way that put

Izzy on edge. It reminded him of the way folks would preface a comment with, 'Not to sound racist, but—' before saying the most racist shit he'd ever heard.

"Sure," Izzy said, hesitantly.

"What's it like? You know, taking orders from a woman?"

Izzy'd dealt with these kinds of questions for years and lost patience with them a long time ago. "What do you mean?" he said, like the question didn't make sense to him.

"You know," Hawlings said. "I'm not trying to sound sexist or nothing but come on, a woman sheriff, taking over McCray County? I mean, we ain't exactly baking cookies out here, if you know what I'm saying? If she—"

"Let me stop you right there," Izzy said. "Because the last thing you need to worry about is whether Mary Beth Cain is tough enough to be the sheriff of this, or any other county. I worked for her husband too, Big Bill Cain, who everyone considered a shit kicker, and she's twice the cop he was. An absolute crack shot and can solve crimes like nobody's business."

Hawlings smirked like he didn't believe it. "Oh yeah? So, how'd she get to be such a badass?"

"Comes by it honestly," Izzy said. "Grew up with criminals, so she knows how they think. Her daddy was a big hunter who had her out shooting deer when most girls were playing with baby dolls. And the craftiness and iron will she gets from her mama, of course, only don't tell her I said it. She's a little sensitive about any comparisons with the old lady."

Hawlings stared blankly. "Who's her mama?"

With all the press coverage in Jasper Creek of late, Izzy assumed everybody knew who Mary Beth's mother was, but apparently not. "You know Mamie who runs that strip club, Mountain Flowers? You know, the McCray County Maf—"

Hawlings interrupted. "Wait, a second. You're telling me, Mountain Mamie's her mother?"

"That's right," Izzy said.

Hawlings whistled. "Damn. That's all you had to say, man. I get it. I get it." Hawlings pointed to the radio and said, "Wait, so that makes Sawyer Thompson her brother, right?"

"Sure does," Izzy said. "Though she doesn't like to advertise that fact either."

"Jeez. Some family. Oh, hey, here we are. Downtown Mapelton. What's left of it."

They drove through an archway into the commercial district. Izzy was surprised how big the town was. He was expecting a handful of buildings but the heart of McCray was as big as Jasper Creek, and had a similar layout. The centerpiece was an old limestone federal courthouse/post office that loomed like a fortress in the middle of a traffic circle, surrounded by angled streets full of empty storefronts. They passed by an abandoned movie theater with a grand, aging marquis frozen in time, advertising RAMBO – FIRST BLOOD. Hawlings parked in an angled spot outside an old timey diner, called Drewery's Lunch Counter, where a couple of white hairs were being tended to by a soda jerk wearing a bow tie and wedge hat.

The diner was part of a block-long, two-story brick building. Hawlings pointed two doors down at a closed storefront for GRAY'S BARBER SHOP, a little hole-in-the-wall place where, according to Hawlings, people used to come more for the conversation than the cut. The Flash had a reputation for shearing his customers like sheep and giving everybody a set of whitewalls whether they wanted it or not.

"Gray lived in the apartment upstairs," Hawlings said. He reached for the keys to cut the engine and paused to let Sawyer Thompson finish a diatribe about how two hundred years ago, at the beginning of the Industrial Revolution, there were only three hundred million people in the world, less than a twentieth the current population.

We kept pumping out babies to meet industry's need for labor, but now the human worker has become obsolete. We're being put out to pasture. The future is now, friends, and it's full of soup kitchens and breadlines. Unless....

Sawyer paused a long time, filling the car with dead air, then said in a deep, melodramatic voice:

Unless...there's a revolution.

As if on cue, a long line of motorcycles came roaring down the mountain road. Izzy watched the procession grow larger then take a loop around the traffic circle surrounding the courthouse. He got out his phone and tried to call Mary Beth to let her know their biker problem wasn't over, but of course couldn't get a signal.

Probably just as well, he figured. No reason to ruin her evening. He'd let Mary Beth go a little longer thinking she'd successfully dealt with those guys.

13

MARY BETH DIDN'T HAVE much time. She needed to get home, get ready, meet up with her old boyfriend turned U.S. attorney who was trying to indict her, then rendezvous with Izzy in time for the Scarburry Hill Cat Fights. It was going to be a busy evening.

Mary Beth sniffed at her arm pits as she pulled out of Pomfried's office and realized some simple primping wasn't going to do it, she needed a shower. She had hiked up a mountain that morning and stared down a half-senile, trigger-happy sniper, not to mention a horde of armed bikers, and her attorney/legal nemesis, all of which was more than enough to work up a sweat. The clock in her Camarro read 4:00 pm. If she hurried, she'd have roughly thirty to forty minutes at home to make herself presentable, which wouldn't be enough time to wash her hair, but at least she could clean up and change clothes. Which begged the question of what in the hell she should wear? Maybe the lavender blouse with the scoop neck she'd bought in Christiansburg last weekend. With black pants, that would look really cute. No. If she showed up to the station with her going-out-gear on for a mysterious meeting with a man, she'd never hear the end of it.

This isn't a date, she reminded herself. She didn't want to give Patrick the impression she was looking forward to this meeting, because she absolutely wasn't. Not in the least. But at the same time, he was an old boyfriend she hadn't seen in twenty years. She didn't want to roll in there looking like a wildebeest.

Just a nice clean uniform, Mary Beth decided. Nothing fancy. All business. But maybe she would wear that gray, silky push-up bra and leave an extra button of her shirt undone. Oh, and, she'd be sure to get to the station before Patrick did so she could act like she'd forgotten about the meeting. "Why, Patrick," she'd say as she looked up from her desk. "Oh, that's right. Pomfried did mention you might be dropping by. Go ahead and have a seat and I'll be with you in just a few minutes." Then she'd make him wait, while she placed a phone call or two.

Mary Beth was stopped at a traffic light on Bennington Avenue as plans raced through her mind. A powder blue VW Bug was trying to make a left turn in front of her against oncoming traffic and not having much luck. She used the pause to eye herself in the rearview mirror, flaring her nostrils to inspect for any rogue nose hairs. None that she could see. She would need to tweeze her eyebrows a bit, though.

When Mary Beth looked down, the Bug was still idling, so she placed a call to Deputy Goforth who was taking the lead on crowd control at the big football game that night. Her phone was linked to the car speakers via a Bluetooth connection. As it rang there were at least three opportunities that the Bug could have pulled off its turn, but the old fogey driving it wasn't going until there were no oncoming cars in sight.

"Where you been, Sheriff?" Goforth said. "Figured we'd have seen you out at the stadium by now."

"Afraid you're not going to. Me or Chief Deputy Baker, for that matter. We've both got some things to attend to this evening."

"Anything exciting?"

"Nah. Just some loose ends that need tied up." She could hear fans chanting in the background, a call and response where one group would yell "Jasper" and the responders yelled "Creek," then after three rounds, they all yelled "Cougars" in unison.

Goforth said he should be fine without Mary Beth or Izzy. He had everybody else out there, and though the fans were already tailgating, the crowd had thus far been on its best behavior.

Having the rest of the deputies deployed was good, Mary Beth thought. It meant the station would be pretty much empty by 5:00. Less snooping ears and gossipy mouths around.

The light turned red and the Bug hadn't moved, waiting to see if he'd have a more wide-open opportunity to make his turn during the next cycle. Mary Beth lost her patience. She said a quick good-bye to Goforth, flipped on the siren, and hit the gas.

Her house was ten minutes away. Eight minutes later, she pulled into the driveway, screeched to a stop, jumped out of the car and sprinted for the front door of her split-level home. She dashed into the foyer and took a hard right towards her bedroom before she tripped over a duffel bag full of laundry. Her son, Sam, was a student at the local Bible college, living on campus, but still dropped off his dirty clothes so Mom could wash them when she wasn't busy fighting crime.

"Son of a bitch," Mary Beth yelled, realizing she was slandering herself. She rubbed her knee that had come down hard on the dark laminate floor, but there was no time to sulk. Mary Beth got up and hop-walked toward the shower, peeling off clothes as she went, then put on a shower cap and washed as quickly as she could, furiously exfoliating with a coarse loofah. After that, she toweled off and went to work with her various lotions, constantly checking the clock, and dressed as fast as she could, realizing too late she shouldn't have shut the bathroom door because her hot shower had steamed the mirror. Mary Beth turned on the bathroom fan and tried vigorously opening and closing the door to bring in cool air but it wasn't unfogging the mirror fast enough. She put her hair-dryer on the cool setting and blew an oval shaped patch of clear glass big enough to see her reflection.

God, her hair looked a mess. She'd tried straightening it that morning, which was a mistake because her irrepressible curls started springing back into place before she'd had her first cup of coffee. Now her shoulder-length hair was in a wasteland somewhere between straight and her normal reddish-blonde coils, looking like a slinky stretched out of shape. Plus, she had hat-head.

"Shit!"

Mary Beth took a deep breath. She'd just have to keep her hat on during the meeting with Patrick. That's all there was to it. Mary Beth tried several different positions with the Stetson: pushed slightly forward, then slightly back, then a little off-center. She tucked her bangs inside the hatband then wasted nearly ten minutes trying to free one perfect little strand she wanted to fall across her forehead at just the right angle.

Finally, Mary Beth decided it was as good as it was going to get. She dashed outside, hopped in her car, and tore out the driveway with lights flashing and siren blaring, until she got within a mile of the station.

Mary Beth didn't want to admit it, but her heart was doing summersaults the whole way there. She and Patrick Connelly started dating during her sophomore year of high school, not long after she first moved there. He was a year ahead of her in school, and they only broke up when it came time for Patrick to go away to college, having received a full ride to Georgetown. They agreed it would be good to see other people during that year apart, but there was a clear expectation that the separation was temporary. The plan was for Mary Beth to follow Patrick to DC after graduation to attend either George Washington or American University.

Mary Beth dated a few other guys during her senior year, mostly as a lark, but looking back on it, she was somewhat the clichéd, fatherless girl who needed male companionship more than she wished was the case. She eventually ended up going all the way with Bill Cain, who was kind of a big deal at the time, the starting middle linebacker for the Cougars and son of the local sheriff, but really didn't expect it to go anywhere.

Until she got pregnant.

Patrick, despite all his open-mindedness and sensitivity, did not take Mary Beth's *good news* well. Their last conversation was ugly. He called her a whore, and she broke his nose. After that, plans changed. That June, Mary Beth ordered an extra-large graduation gown and wedding dress and celebrated both major milestones, baby bump and all, within two weeks of one another.

And so it was that Mary Beth Thompson became Mary Beth Cain.

Apart from a condolence card after Bill's passing, she and Patrick hadn't communicated since.

Mary Beth pulled into the station's parking lot at 4:55. Already parked there, next to the space reserved for the sheriff, was a shiny black BMW with Maryland tags.

"Fuck!" Mary Beth slapped the dashboard. This was not working out how she'd hoped.

"Okay, okay," she told herself, "I can work with this." She'd just take her time outside, then stroll in ten minutes late and act annoyed that she had to come back to the office for this meeting. That would be just as good.

Mary Beth spent thirty seconds touching up her make-up in the mirror, then checked her watch twice. After that she held for another twenty seconds before deciding she was being ridiculous and went inside.

Her secretary, Vanessa, was packing up for the day. "Somebody from the U.S. Attorney's office is here to see you, Sheriff," she said.

Mary Beth casually panned the waiting area and found it empty.

"He's waiting for you in your office."

Mary Beth felt perspiration bombs explode on the back of her neck as she looked down the hall and spotted Patrick Connelly's profile through her office window.

"You need me to stick around?" Vanessa asked. "The girls and I were hoping to get over to the game before traffic got too bad."

The clerical staff usually worked until five-thirty on Fridays but whenever Jasper Creek and Perry Town played, there was very little work that got done that day. The other ladies already had their coats on.

"Sure, that's fine," Mary Beth said. The fewer people around the better.

She took a deep breath, then two steps toward her office before she saw it.

On the credenza were framed photos of the last three sheriffs, her predecessors. A photo of Bill, her dead husband, staring at her, flanked by portraits of his father and grandfather, Sid and Gus Cain, respectively. Three generations of Cain men, each with their caterpillar mustaches and no-nonsense lawmen eyes, laying judgment.

"Have a good weekend, Sheriff," Vanessa said as she and the other ladies shuffled out and locked the front door behind them.

Jesus. Mary Beth and Patrick were alone. Suddenly, she felt like she was doing something really sleazy. Mary Beth picked up the photo of Bill and kissed it. She swallowed hard then started for the office, cradling the picture of Bill against her chest.

14

IT HAD BEEN WEEKS since Elwood Gray's conflagration but the smoky smell inside his apartment was still strong enough to make Izzy's eyes water. He and Hawlings entered into a living room with a kitchen off to the left, separated by a half wall, and a hallway at the far end that led to the lone bedroom. The springy remains of a scorched easy chair sat atop a soot covered rug, facing an empty TV stand. Otherwise, there was hardly any furniture left in the place.

Izzy looked at impressions in the carpet from a missing couch and un-faded rectangles on the shadow-striped, maize-colored wallpaper where long-hanging pictures had been removed. "You guys didn't secure the scene?"

Hawlings shrugged. "Wasn't a crime scene as far as the boss was concerned. And Gray had all kinds of valuables in here. Sports memorabilia and things from his time in office. So Sheriff Bailey told the family to come get what they could as soon as possible, else it was likely to disappear."

Izzy couldn't believe they'd been so slack. With a suspicious death like that, even if they thought it was accidental, the first thing they should have done was seal off the apartment. Now more than two weeks had gone by and the place was totally picked over.

"Did you at least photograph how everything looked when Gray was discovered?"

Hawlings' expression revealed the answer. "Sheriff Bailey was in charge," he said.

Izzy didn't bother asking whether they dusted for prints. He stooped down and inspected what remained of the easy chair. It was charred like a campfire marshmallow. Izzy photographed it with his smartphone from multiple angles. After that, he took a few shots of the barren living room and worked his way down the hall. In the bedroom, a metal bed frame was pushed against the side wall. Izzy felt a draft of cold air tickling the hairs on the back of his neck and saw that the rear window was shattered.

"Come check this out," he called to Hawlings. When the McCray deputy came in from the living room, Izzy was up on his tippy toes, trying to get a good look at the window that led to a fire escape.

"Now that, I promise you, was not like that when we first found Gray," Hawlings said. "Just thrill seekers, busting in after-the-fact."

Izzy gave him a look.

"Took his family a couple of days to get here. Gray's next of kin was the daughter in Ohio. The window was busted sometime between when we found Gray and she got down here to collect his belongings."

"The place was looted?"

"No, didn't look to me like whoever broke in had taken much. Probably just kids doing it on a dare."

Izzy took some pictures of the window, zooming in for tiny signs of blood, in case the intruder had been cut on the glass but found nothing. The burglar or burglars, had been careful to break out all the glass before making the treacherous climb through. A difficult and dangerous entry for some thrill-seeking kids.

"TV, stereo, all that kind of stuff was still here after the window was smashed out?" Izzy asked.

"Yep. TV for sure. Just about threw my back out helping the family carry it down the steps. Don't remember if he had a stereo. Don't think so."

"What about cash, jewelry, valuables?"

Hawlings scratched his head. "I recall they found a wad of cash underneath his mattress. Some old timers like that don't believe in banks. Oh, and his old rings from the championships back in the 60's. I remember he had them in a glass case on the mantel."

This wasn't making sense to Izzy. Getting through that window from the fire escape would not have been easy. The bottom of the window frame was a good five feet from the ground. Even a tall person would need help, another person or a stepladder to get through it without getting cut.

Meanwhile, the front door was a simple deadbolt in a flimsy looking door frame. If somebody wanted to rob the place, they could have just kicked the front door open and had a much easier time getting in and out. That might have drawn the attention of neighbors down the hall and prompted a call to the police, but it would have been fine for a quick smash and grab. The fact that whoever broke in after Gray's death had chosen the much more treacherous window route, suggested they wanted to get in covertly so they could take their time inside.

"And you're sure nothing was taken after the window was busted?"

"Nothing obvious, anyways. Looked like they'd mostly just rummaged through his papers. Desk used to sit right over there."

Izzy looked in the bare corner Hawlings pointed to.

"You think maybe they were looking for something in particular?" Hawlings asked.

"I don't know why else you'd risk cutting yourself on that window and not take obvious things of value."

"Maybe they did take valuables," Hawlings said, "and we just don't know about it. Shit, for all we know, Gray might have had a stack of gold bars in his desk that they took off with. It's just hard to say."

Maybe that was so. The lack of thorough police work prior to Izzy's arrival left open all kinds of possibilities.

He went back to the living room and considered the easy chair again. Though half the chair back had been reduced to ashes, Izzy could tell it was in its full reclined position.

"Was Gray still in the chair when you found him?"

Hawlings nodded. "Yeah, I'll never forget that sight. Lying right there, all burned to hell. A bunch of people started crowding around, trying to peer in, so the Sheriff told me to get everybody out of here while he checked things out."

"Don't suppose you did an autopsy?"

"His flesh had melted down to the bone. Cause of death seemed kind of obvious."

Izzy was really getting frustrated. Working as a cop in a rural county, he'd encountered plenty of gooberishness and dipshittery before, but these McCray guys were on a whole different level. "Can you at least tell me how he was positioned in the chair?"

"What do you mean?"

"Like, was he turned on his side or lying flat on his back?"

"Flat on his back. Why? What are you thinking?"

"I don't know. I just think if I was on fire, I'd make it out of this chair before I died."

"Not if you were dead drunk when you caught fire," Hawlings argued.

"Can somebody even get that drunk?"

"In McCray County you can."

Fair enough, Izzy thought. He palmed his head, pressing a handprint into his hair. "How were his arms and hands positioned?"

"Kinda like this," Hawlings said, putting up his dukes like he was ready to box.

"Doesn't sound like he was sleeping then, does it?"

"No, that's where you're wrong. I've worked a few burn cases, and old Doc Pruitt in the coroner's office says burn victims always look like that. Even if they were already dead before catching fire. They call it the pugilist's stance. When the tendons burn, see, it causes the elbows to flex and the hands to ball into fists."

Pugilist's stance. Izzy hadn't heard of that before. Maybe the McCray guys were correct, that Gray's death was accidental, but the cursory fashion in which they'd handled it didn't sit right.

"You find any alcohol?"

"Empty bottle of Evan Williams right next to him. The places where it spilled had eaten the varnish off the coffee table, so you can just imagine what that shit does to your insides."

"How about the rest of the house? Any empties in the trash? Somebody's drinking like this, I figure there'd be bottles all over the place."

Hawlings pondered a moment. "That I couldn't tell you. Like I said, Sheriff Bailey took over the investigation and had me working crowd control." He glanced down at his watch like he had somewhere better to be. "Hey man, if you're wanting to go by the Register of Deeds before they close, we're gonna have to move."

"Yeah, okay," Izzy said. "Nothing left to see here, anyway."

As they closed up Gray's apartment, Izzy asked about the keys. "You had those since Gray died?"

"Yep. Landlord said I could hang onto them. He's the one

who let us in, initially. Said he'd change the locks if he's able to re-let the place."

"Anybody else have a set?"

"Other than the landlord? No, not that I know of."

"You given them to anybody else?"

"No. Why?"

Izzy waved a hand. "Nothing," he said. "Just means you probably aren't the one who busted that window out since you could have just opened the door."

Hawlings laughed. "That's good to know. Didn't realize I was a suspect."

They shared an awkward laugh, then Hawlings led them a couple of blocks down the street to where the Register of Deeds office was situated in the basement of Town Hall. It was a dank, sleepy, bureaucratic fiefdom ruled over by "the Registrar," a librarian-looking school marm with grandma glasses and a beehive hairdo. The sign by her neatly-ordered desk, declared she would pull official records for a flat ten-dollar fee and make copies for five cents a page.

Izzy figured they must be her first customer for weeks, but she didn't seem in a hurry to wait on them. He had to clear his throat twice before the Registrar looked up from her copy of *Ellery Queen Mystery Magazine*. But once she realized it was two police officers standing there, her attitude changed.

"How can I help you gentlemen?"

"If it's not too much trouble, ma'am, we need to pull all the deeds recorded over the last six months," Izzy said.

The Registrar started twiddling her pencil. "Shouldn't be a problem. You'll only need to go back about two months. No deeds recorded before then for quite a while."

She excused herself and retreated into the alcoves of green, metal filing cabinets, then returned quickly with the requested documents and copied them free of charge.

"Careful now," she said, handing the papers over.

"Why's that?" Izzy asked, wondering if he was in danger of getting a paper cut.

"I don't want to sound superstitious or nothing, but Commissioner Gray was in here copying those same records not long before his tragic passing."

Well, that's an interesting coincidence, Izzy thought. He shot Hawlings a look.

"Wasn't that just awful?" the Registrar said. "Everybody loved Elwood. For his life to end so...senselessly." She shivered as though chilled by the thought.

"You're saying Elwood Gray came in looking for these same records?" Izzy asked, wanting to be sure he'd heard her right.

"Sure did. Same as you fellas. Wanted to see all the deeds from recent transactions. Said he was curious who it was buying up land in McCray. Said it didn't smell right."

It was starting to smell like a dead body, Izzy thought. Maybe Mary Beth's crazy Uncle Jimmy was right and Gray's death did have something to do with those prospectors. Izzy knew Elwood Gray was a vocal opponent of the efforts to annex McCray County into Jasper. He supposedly had dreams of returning the area to its former glory with some kind of green energy program. If Elwood had learned about some carpetbaggers buying up land, running off what little population was still hanging on out there, he would have made a big stink about it.

"Did Gray say anything else?" Izzy asked.

The Registrar took the pencil she'd been twiddling and plunged it into her beehive hair where it hung like a rusty nail. "No, can't say that he did. Just thanked me was all."

Izzy paged through the stack of deeds and saw that every one was granted to a company called TNT, LLC. "That name mean anything to you?" he asked Hawlings.

Hawlings shook his head. "Nope, never heard of it."

The Registrar hadn't either. Only the person selling the property had to sign the deed, so no one signed for the company acquiring it, which meant Izzy didn't have an individual's name to go on.

"Probably just a real estate holding company," he said. "The question is: who owns it?"

The deeds had all been prepared by a law firm in Charleston, which was at least a three-hour drive from there. That was a little strange. Izzy knew real estate closings were usually handled by a local attorney since it required someone to record the documents at the county office. Whoever set up TNT, LLC wanted to keep their identity a secret from the folks in McCray, Izzy surmised. Maybe Gray found out who that was.

Izzy asked to use the Registrar's computer so he could pull up the Secretary of State's website to do a corporation search. It showed the same Charleston attorney who'd prepared the deed as TNT, LLC's incorporator, but that just meant he was the lawyer who filed the paperwork. There were no documents on file to show who its owner or owners were. No annual reports. The date of incorporation indicated the company had only been in existence for a shade over two months. It all added up to a dead end. At least temporarily.

Izzy and Hawlings thanked the Registrar and were preparing to leave when Izzy thought of another question.

"Did you happen to tell anyone else that Elwood Gray had been in here looking at these deeds?"

The Registrar scratched her forehead. "Well, it's possible. You know after he died, we were all talking about him. I'm sure I've mentioned it."

"I mean *before* he died. Did you tell anyone he was looking into who was buying up the property in McCray?"

The Registrar looked deep in thought. "I'm not sure," she said. "Maybe."

"How about Sheriff....What's his name?" Izzy asked Hawlings.

"Bailey."

"Yeah, Sheriff Bailey."

The Registrar tapped a long fingernail against the desk. "Well, I do see the Sheriff over at Drewery's right regular. Take my lunch there, most days. Suppose I may have. But I'm not one to gossip, now."

Hawlings raised an eyebrow and gave Izzy a look that confirmed what Izzy already suspected. The Registrar was the kind of person who shared all she knew with whoever she happened to speak to. And if Izzy's guess was right, that person was Sheriff Bailey.

15

MARY BETH SEARCHED for a witty remark as she entered the room, but couldn't come up with anything so she settled for, "Sorry to keep you waiting."

Patrick Connelly turned to face her and she immediately felt the electricity—tingles from her fingers down to her toes. He looked exactly the way she remembered him. A fit, runner's build, with perfectly coiffed brown hair, and laser blue eyes that exuded intelligence. Mary Beth had periodically cyber-stalked him over the years, and knew Patrick was divorced and never had kids, which tended to equate to a more youthful appearance amongst her contemporaries.

"I was just admiring this picture of your boy." Patrick pointed to Mary Beth's desk at a framed photo from Sam's high school graduation. "He looks just like you."

"Thanks. Hard to believe he's all grown up."

Patrick smiled. He had that confident look that always made her feel uneasy, like he was making fun of her. But his words sounded sincere. "That's really hard to believe."

They stared at each other for a moment, neither sure what

to say. Mary Beth had forgotten how Patrick was just a smidge taller than her, maybe five foot nine, and not nearly as strapping as Bill had been. Her deceased husband won, hands down, on that score. But there was always something different about Patrick. Something special. In a town where high school football was sacrosanct, the dating pool tended to be big, beefy guys with more brawn than brains, whose pecking order was determined by the biggest bench press or nicest truck. But Patrick played by a different set of rules.

He moved to Jasper Creek not long before Mary Beth did. Transferred from a prep school in Philadelphia when his father took the director job at the local hospital, subjecting Patrick to a culture shock that must have been awful. In Philly he had been a big fish, playing lacrosse, which no one in Jasper Creek had ever heard of, and soccer, which locals viewed as a refuge for wimps too scared to pick up the pigskin. Patrick didn't hunt, didn't fish, and didn't understand why in God's name anyone would sit and watch NASCAR drivers make left turns for hours on end. He was, in some ways, about as useless as a rubber axe, reading poetry and quoting Nietzsche, and needing Mary Beth to change a flat tire for him the time his Cabriolet picked up a nail on Make-out Mountain. But Patrick had talked differently, thought differently, and seen more than anyone else Mary Beth had ever known.

And he always made her feel alive.

Patrick extended his hand. "It's good to see you, Sheriff Cain."

Mary Beth felt a little put off by the formality but tried not to show it. "I'm sorry it has to be under these circumstances," she said, shaking with a firm grip.

"So am I."

Patrick added his left hand to the shake and held it there for a moment before letting go.

"Have a seat." Mary Beth motioned to the low-lying couch

she kept in the office to make sure she always sat higher than the person she was facing. "So, are you here as friend or foe?"

"Friend," Patrick said. "I'm sure your attorney told you I've managed to work out a deal that would wipe your slate clean. But I need you to take it, Mary—I've had to stick my neck way out on this one."

She'd forgotten how he always called her Mary, insisting Mary Beth was a redneck name. "I'm not a redneck," she used to tell him, "I'm a hillbilly." When he would ask her what the difference was, she would say, "We're like rednecks, just more stubborn and distrustful of outsiders." And of course, Patrick had always been one of those outsiders who in return, hated everything about West Virginia, except for her.

"I don't have any wiggle room here," Patrick said. "John Jensen has personally directed this investigation and is serious about tackling small town corruption. This offer is 'take it or leave it.' I need to know your answer by Monday morning. You play games or try to push your decision into next week and you'll miss your chance."

Mary Beth assumed she was supposed to feel grateful, but didn't like the pressure being applied. "To what do I owe this generosity?" she asked.

Patrick stared at her intently. "I've always felt bad about it," he said. "I handled it all so terribly." He rubbed his nose that was still slightly crooked from where she popped him the last time they saw each other face-to-face. "I was just really devastated, you know. Really hurt." Mary Beth couldn't believe what she was hearing. She'd dreamed of this apology about a billion and a half times. "I was really unfair to you," Patrick said. "After all, it was my stupid idea for us to see other people while I was away at school. I just thought—"

Mary Beth ached to hear him finish the sentence but he just let it hang there.

"Thank you," Mary Beth said, finally, just as she realized she was still clutching the photo of Bill she'd carried in from the lobby. Mary Beth gently placed the picture of her dead husband on the desk—face down. "So…what do I have to do?" she asked.

Patrick shot the answer at her like a bullet, fast and deadly. "We need you to arrest your brother."

Boom. Mary Beth felt like a slapstick cartoon character who just had an anvil dropped on her head. "What? Sawyer? Why?"

"Because Sawyer's become an extremely dangerous person, Mary." Patrick reached for his briefcase and worked the combination. "He's been forming what we believe is some kind of militia, and is stockpiling weapons in a mountain compound he's established up at the Old Wengo Mine. We're concerned he's planning to incite some kind of violent revolt against the government."

Mary Beth rolled her eyes. "Please. Sawyer's a jackass. His little wannabe movement up there in the hills is just a bunch of idiots playing weekend warrior. He's not hurting anybody."

Patrick removed a thick dossier from his briefcase. "That's not true. He's got a massive following—nationwide. We've had an informant on the inside with some of the biker gangs and anarchists who are trying to join up with him."

Mary Beth gulped.

"That's right," Patrick said. "I heard how you ran off those bikers. Hate to be the one to break it to you but they didn't go far. Just headed into Kentucky and doubled back into McCray. You know when you were harassing that biker this morning. The old guy you pulled over?"

"How'd you know about that?"

"My informant. He said that while you were wasting your time with him, a group of their leaders had some kind of pow-wow with a few of Sawyer's men. They want them to commit some act of terrorism to prove themselves before they'll officially admit them to their cause. We all need to be on high alert.

And these bikers are just the tip of the iceberg. Guys like that are going to keep coming."

"What for?"

"Let me show you something," Patrick said. "Can I use your computer?"

Mary Beth scooted back her chair so Patrick could access her desktop. He inserted a flash drive and opened a video file of Sawyer preaching about plans to build a utopian, fifties-style community in the forsaken hills of McCray County:

We're going straight up Amish on this bitch. Well… not totally. We'll keep our guns and trucks and electricity and shit… but we're gonna roll back the clock to the 'Leave it to Beaver' days.

Sawyer then made several threats against various government outposts, including Fort Knox, espousing a half-baked plan to incite a global re-ordering of the economy by taking over America's gold reserve.

There ain't nothin' behind them greenbacks folks. We're gonna show the world we don't have near the gold we pretend to. Money's become just a bunch of worthless paper and made-up numbers in a computer somewhere.

"See," Mary Beth said. "This shows you how crazy he is. We haven't been on the gold standard for decades." As she spoke the camera panned from Sawyer to a massive arsenal of assault weapons and explosives stockpiled in the background.

"Being crazy doesn't make him any less dangerous, Mary. And the government can't afford to just brush these guys off as irrelevant anymore. It wasn't that long ago, we had Proud Boys and Oath Keepers and Three Percenters attacking our nation's capital."

"I promise you, Sawyer was at home scratching his ass when that happened. He's all talk."

"Look," Patrick said. "I know you've always had a soft spot for Sawyer—"

"Sisters are funny that way."

"Sure. I get that. And I know you always felt a little guilty that you had to go live with your grandparent after your dad died, while Sawyer stayed back in McCray with your... mother. But if you don't bring Sawyer in peacefully, I'm afraid there's going to be a lot of bloodshed."

"Bring him in on what?" Mary Beth demanded. "I thought the ATF didn't care about guns anymore."

"There's no more assault rifle ban. That's true. But we still draw the line at fully automatic weapons, not to mention, Emulex and C4. We've got good intel your brother's been rounding up explosives. Did you know that in his entire life, Sawyer's never once filed a tax return?"

"He's never had a job."

Patrick laughed. "I hear his family's made a fortune selling drugs. Even sold a lot of them right here in Jasper County, where his sister is the sheriff."

That pissed Mary Beth off. Royally. She suddenly remembered how judgmental and smug Patrick could be. He had no idea the *hercu-fuck-a-lean* lengths she'd gone to, to get all the meth and opioids and hard drugs out of her county.

"Listen," she said, "Maybe, *may-be,* my family has sold some weed in my jurisdiction, but that's it. Period, exclamation point. Anybody deals anything harder than that in Jasper and I come down on them like a fucking piledriver—no matter who they are. And they damn well know it."

Patrick smirked. "Marijuana is a Schedule 1 narcotic."

"That's *federal* law," Mary Beth said, almost spitting the F-word. "You want to do something about it, you and your junior G-men can have at it. Jasper County has more important things to worry about."

Patrick leaned forward, looking serious. "If you won't help

us, that's exactly what we're going to do, Mary. We've got multiple warrants out on Sawyer. But you know he won't come peacefully, and there's a lot of people up there with him who could get hurt. We need your help to avoid all that."

Mary Beth smelled bullshit. Sawyer might be an annoyance to some folks in DC, and she wouldn't doubt there were a few warrants out for him that the federal marshals had wisely been unwilling to serve, but there was no way they'd risk a Waco-style standoff to go squash a bug like Sawyer, who was living in obscurity in the poorest county in the whole goddamn country. She figured they'd love to have Sawyer in custody, but only if she took care of the arresting. If she refused, they'd probably just leave him be. All of which meant the only reason to nab Sawyer would be to save herself.

"What if I won't do it?" she asked.

Patrick gave her a grim look, walked around the desk and sagged back into the couch. "Then we've got you red-handed too, Mary. Conviction will be a slam dunk. The only way I was able to make this deal was by trading Sawyer for you."

Mary Beth crossed her arms. "Bull butter. You haven't got anything on me other than myths and legends."

Patrick pulled another dossier from his briefcase, nearly as thick as Sawyer's, and flipped it on the desk.

"I imagine that's true for some of the stuff in there. Take for instance, the three hundred dead people who voted for you in the last election. I imagine you have your mother to thank for that one. But there are also a lot of complaints of evidence tampering, police brutality, violations of civil rights."

Mary Beth kicked her feet up on the desk to show she wasn't worried. "All completely unfounded."

"Okay," Patrick said. "How about this one? You familiar with something called a U-Visa?"

Oh shit. Mary Beth suddenly remembered Pomfried's

warning not to say anything. Just listen. "You're the lawyer," she said. "You tell me."

"It's a special type of immigration visa given to crime victims if law enforcement certifies they cooperated with authorities. Doesn't matter if the prosecution is successful, or if there's ever an arrest. Don't even need an identifiable suspect. If you can just get someone like say, oh, I don't know, *a sheriff*, to sign off on the form, you can get status for a whole bunch of illegals."

Mary Beth did her best to remain stone-faced, not wanting to give anything away, in case Patrick was bluffing.

"You happen to know a lady by the name of Guadalupe Angeles?" he asked.

"Of course. She was our housekeeper who became Sam's nanny after Bill died. She basically raised my son while I was out protecting the citizens of Jasper County."

"Did you know Guadalupe was here illegally?"

"Not true. She's got a green card now. Soon she'll be a naturalized citizen."

"Thanks to you."

Mary Beth engaged in a staring competition with Patrick, determined not to give anything away.

"You signed a certification, saying she'd been a victim of armed robbery, right?"

"She was."

"No one was ever charged with the crime."

Mary Beth turned up her palms. "Hey, I can't solve them all."

Patrick smiled like he was enjoying this little game of cat and mouse. "Poor Guadalupe's family has had quite a bit of bad luck in the old crime department. According to our records, seventeen of her family members have been victims of violent assaults, all of which were certified by you, and none of which ever resulted in an arrest or even a viable suspect."

Mary Beth clasped her hand to her heart. "I can't tell you how much it pains me that those have gone unsolved. But, unfortunately, immigrants are some of the most vulnerable members of our community. They tend to live in high crime areas. And, I think if you'll look back, a number of them were present during the same break-ins, or robberies, or whatever. It's not like it was seventeen separate crimes. Just maybe, five or six. Or…eight. Ten, tops."

"Well, it's interesting," Patrick said, reading from a sheet of paper. "The last one you certified was for Guadalupe's grand-daughter Vanessa—who's now your secretary, I believe. Appears she actually was the victim of an armed robbery, working as a cashier at the Go Mart down on College Avenue. You made a real, *bona fide* arrest on that one. A tenty-year-old idiot named Parker Howard who pulled the heist as a fraternity prank, using a fake gun, and only took a case of beer."

Mary Beth clapped her hands like she'd just been exonerated. "See. What are you worried about? Totally legitimate."

Patrick wagged his finger. "Ahh, but immigration was on to you by then. They denied Vanessa's petition because they suspected you'd been committing immigration fraud. Even put Vanessa in deportation proceedings."

"Total abuse of discretion."

"Well, as luck would have it, the assailant—the Parker Howard—seems to have fallen in love with and married Vanessa just in time to get her a green card. How's that for a coincidence?"

Mary Beth shrugged. "Love is a mysterious thing."

Patrick fished for another stack of papers and held them close like he wanted to be sure he was reading it correctly. "I don't think there's any mystery at all. We've got an affidavit from Parker saying you threatened to beat him with a rubber hose if he didn't marry Vanessa."

"Men sometimes need a little help to get in touch with their feelings," Mary Beth said.

Patrick stopped smiling. "Play it cute if you want. But we've got more than enough to end your career, Mary. There's one universal truth they teach you in law school, that you need to understand."

"Oh yeah, what's that?"

"The government always wins."

Patrick scooped up his files and returned them to his briefcase. "So, what's it going to be? Either you or Sawyer is going down. You get to decide which one."

He stared at her, waiting for a response. Of course, she had none. Both options were intolerable. Mary Beth had come to a fork in the road, where she couldn't take either route. So she did what she'd always done: Blaze her own path.

Mary Beth stood, shut her office door and locked it.

"What are you doing?" Patrick asked.

Mary Beth began unbuttoning her shirt, as she answered. "Negotiating."

16

IT WAS AFTER FIVE when Izzy and Hawlings left the Registrar's office. They were in Hawlings' Explorer, backing out, and Izzy noticed three prostitutes on the corner, a blonde and two brunettes who were posing for passing cars. "That's something I never thought I'd see around here," he said.

Hawlings frowned. "Yeah, sign of the times."

"You ever bust them?"

"Nah, they're not hurting nobody. Understaffed as we've been, if you ain't killing someone, we ain't real concerned."

And sometimes not even then, Izzy thought.

The hookers looked their way and didn't seem worried about the presence of law enforcement. The brunettes, anyway. One of them even waved. But the blonde woman started backing away towards the alley.

"Let's roll over there," Izzy said.

Hawlings grimaced. "Ah man, if you want a hummer, let's go on up to Mountain Flowers. They've got nice girls up there. These here all got summer teeth."

Izzy watched the hem of the blonde's dress curl around the

corner of a brick building as she slipped into the shadows. "What are summer teeth?" he asked.

"Some are here, some are there."

Izzy didn't laugh.

"You know, meth mouth. Their teeth are all fucked up."

"I'm not looking for a blow job," Izzy said. "I just want to talk to them. Roll on over there."

"What for?"

"Because if they work this corner, they might have seen something the night Elwood Gray died."

Hawlings shrugged and turned toward the alley.

The Fall days were already growing brutally short in McCray's deep valleys, with waning sunlight that filtered weakly through the tree covered mountains and turned the path between brick buildings into a shadowy corridor. Izzy could make out just a flash of the blonde as she glanced back at them before taking off past a dumpster.

"Hit the siren and go around the block," he said. "Flush her back this way."

Izzy jumped out of the vehicle. As soon as his feet hit the ground, he took off toward the alley. Hawlings hit the siren and roared around the corner.

The two stringy-haired brunettes, both drugged-out waifs, started toward Izzy, cooing through sharp, mangled teeth. "What's a matter, baby? Don't you like what you see?" They slowed his progress as they caressed his shoulders with bony fingers. Izzy squeezed between them and saw a dark shape running back towards him as Hawlings' flashing lights appeared at the far end of the alley.

Izzy flattened himself against the brick wall. The blonde-haired woman shot out onto the sidewalk and Izzy grabbed a handful of the faded plaid coat she wore over her paper-thin dress. The woman's momentum carried them both crashing to the ground, Izzy falling on top of her.

"Damn, man. Get the hell off me," she said, trying to wiggle free.

Izzy got to his knees, turned the woman over and held her to the ground.

"Why are you running?"

"Why are you chasing?" The lady spat at him and thrashed about. Izzy heard Hawlings driving back around. When he looked up at the cruiser, the woman sunk her teeth into Izzy's forearm.

"Jesus!"

Izzy grabbed at his arm and the hooker pushed free. She tried to make a run for it, but Hawlings was already out of his vehicle and caught her with a clothesline that would have made Hulk Hogan proud, then pinned her down next to a sewer grate, where she bucked like a bronco until the McCray deputy cuffed her left wrist to the metal bar.

"What the hell, man? You all can't treat me like this. I didn't do nothing!"

"Really?" Hawlings said. "Right now, we got you for resisting arrest and assaulting an officer. You want to go for more?"

"What the fuck? You assaulted me!"

Izzy rolled up his sleeve to examine the bite wound that looked like the bloody outline of a football and hurt like a bastard. "Let's all just calm down," he said. "We just want to ask you some questions."

"I already told you assholes, I ain't gonna say nothing. Just quit hassling me!"

"Whoa, whoa, whoa. Take it easy. What do you mean, you aren't gonna say nothing?" Izzy asked. "Say nothing about what?"

"I done told your man. Go ask him."

"You're talking about another police officer?" Hawlings asked.

The woman shook her matted bangs out of her eyes. "Yes. I gave my statement. And was told not to say nothing else. And that's just what I'm gonna do."

Hawlings pressed, "The guy you talked to, was he wearing a uniform like mine? Real big guy, about six foot, five. Big 'ole belly on him. Got a crew cut and a bushy brown mustache."

The woman gestured locking her mouth and throwing away the key.

"Okay," Hawlings said. He stood up, leaving the woman handcuffed to the sewer grate. "You want us to leave you alone. That's what we'll do. Come on, Izzy, lets go get you a tetanus shot."

"Wait a minute, man! You can't fucking leave me here!"

"Look," Hawlings said, "you don't want to answer questions. You don't want to be bothered. We'll just get out of your hair."

Izzy followed Hawlings toward his vehicle while the woman flopped around like Linda Blair on a bad day.

"I got a baby at home, you can't leave me locked up like this."

Izzy shot Hawlings a troubled look. He knew the McCray deputy wasn't really going to leave her there—at least he hoped he wasn't—but still, he was getting pretty uncomfortable with the way this was going down.

"She's lying," Hawlings whispered, then yelled to the hooker. "What's your address, we'll send social services over there to pick your baby up."

"Fuck you," she yelled. "Just fucking cut me loose."

"You gonna tell us what we need to know?" Hawlings asked.

"Yes, fine. Just uncuff me."

Hawlings winked at Izzy then led the way back and knelt over their captive. "First, you answer our questions," he said. "Then, I'll take off the cuffs." He dangled his keys just out of the lady's reach. "What do you mean you already talked to somebody with the police?" he asked. "Who? What about?"

The woman shook her head like she couldn't believe she was saying anything. "The man you described. Big guy in a gray uniform. Bushy mustache. He was asking me what I saw the night the old man got burned up."

"Elwood Gray?" Izzy asked.

"That's him," she said. "The one they called the Flash. I was out here that night."

"And? What did you see?" Hawlings prodded.

"Look man," she said. "It was really late. Probably close to 2:00 am. I was just about to call it a night. I'm not even sure what I saw."

She lunged for the keys with her free hand but Hawlings pulled them out of reach. "What did you see?" he demanded.

A tear ran down the lady's cheek. "He told me not to say nothing. Held his gun to my head. Told me he'd kill me if I told anybody."

"Sheriff Bailey did that?" Hawlings asked

Her chin trembled as she nodded.

"Well, you don't have to worry about him," Izzy told her. "He's not the law anymore."

The lady rolled her eyes, like that wouldn't be much consolation if he put a gun to her head again and decided to pull the trigger next time.

"Tell you what," Izzy said. "How much do you make for a…date?"

The woman pushed her arms together to perk up her breasts. "Fifty bucks and you can get whatever you want." She said it, emotionlessly. A rote line, repeated a thousand times.

Izzy pulled out his wallet and thumbed through his cash. Friday was payday and although his wife militantly handled their finances, Izzy was permitted two-hundred dollars out of each biweekly paycheck to do whatever he wanted with. He pulled out five twenties and fanned them out. "Here's a hundred bucks," he said. "You can take the night off if you want. Go spend time with your baby."

The woman lunged for the bills.

"Ah, ah, ah…first I get my answers."

The woman scowled like she knew better than to open her trap, but needed the money too bad to keep quiet. "I was just walking past," she said, "and I stopped 'cause I smelled smoke. Then this guy came barreling out the door."

"From Gray's apartment?" Hawlings asked.

"Yeah."

"And?" Izzy said.

"And the guy ran right into me. Knocked me down and fell on top of me. My knee's still skinned up. Look."

She held up her bare leg that was covered with goose pimples in the cool evening air. Sure enough, there was a fading scrape around her knee.

"So, what happened then?" Hawlings asked.

"He just got up and took off down the block. No sorry or nothin'."

"What did he look like?" Izzy asked.

"I don't know. It was dark. Just saw him for a second or two."

"White guy, black guy, what?" Izzy asked.

"White guy."

"What color hair did he have?"

Another shrug. "Dark like, I guess."

"How old?" Izzy asked.

"I don't know. He knocked me down and then he was up and running."

"Okay, what was he wearing?"

The lady rolled her eyes. "What do you want from me? It was dark. Dark clothes, man. I don't know. Everything was just dark."

"How tall was he?" Hawlings asked.

She stopped to think. "Not real tall. I mean, taller than—" she looked at Izzy without finishing the sentence. "He was wide, though. Like built, you know. Like a bodybuilder. Felt like a damn truck ran me over."

Izzy summed up where they were. "So, we got a muscular white guy, with dark hair, wearing dark clothes. That's it?"

The lady shrugged.

"Is there anything else at all that you noticed about him?" he asked. "Anything you may have mentioned to Sheriff Bailey that you haven't told us?"

She squinted, thinking hard. There was something juvenile about the mannerism that made Izzy fully appreciate for the first time just how young this girl was. If she was a day over twenty, he'd be surprised.

"The only thing I noticed was his ear."

"What about it?" Izzy asked.

"When we hit the sidewalk, and I opened my eyes, I was staring right at his ear and I noticed it was all jacked up."

"Jacked up, how?" Hawlings asked.

She struggled to describe it. "It was like, all bubbly. Like it was all full of puss and stuff."

A bubbly ear. Izzy tried to imagine what a police sketch of that might look like. "That sound like anybody you know?" he asked Hawlings.

The McCray Deputy shook his head, no. But something about his expression gave Izzy the feeling he was holding something back.

17

PATRICK WAS ALWAYS amazed by how dramatically his mood could change after climax. One moment, lust was all there was, then the world came crashing back with all its awkward realities and consequences.

It was precisely those consequences Patrick was pondering as Mary Beth rested her head on his chest, leg slung over him, both of them naked on the office floor, and accepted the fact he'd just had sex with the target of a major federal investigation. It could be a career-ending mistake if anyone ever found out, which was a hard truth for a buttoned-up type like Patrick to accept. He so rarely made mistakes. Except when it came to her.

Mary Beth. He still considered losing her the biggest mistake of his life.

They met during a difficult time, Patrick's parents having moved him from Philadelphia to Jasper Creek right in the middle of his junior year. All his traits that had been celebrated in the cushy Philly suburbs—sophistication, intelligence, sensitivity—had made him that "little Yankee, pussy boy," in his new environs, where big beefy guys liked to bump into him in the hallways and people made fun of him for the weirdest things, like the way he pronounced "water" as "wood-er", and called soft drinks "soda" instead of "pop."

At that time, at that age, when everything seemed so important, the whole experience had felt like some kind of *Clockwork Orange* torture session, until Patrick met Mary Beth. She was like an oasis of happiness in a redneck wasteland, the only person in all of West Virginia who saw him for who he really was.

Was that what she was doing now? he wondered. Reading him? Playing him? The moment she started unbuttoning her shirt, Patrick knew she was working him to some degree. But he badly wanted to believe it was more than just an angle to try and save herself and her brother. He hoped she had pined for him over the years, the same way he'd longed for her.

"You know this won't change anything," he said, whispering into her curly hair.

Mary Beth's body tensed. She stood and walked to her desk. He tried to gauge her mood as she fished around inside a drawer before producing a crumpled pack of cigarettes and Bic lighter.

"You still smoke?"

"On occasion," she said. There was a window behind her desk that looked out onto a wooded hillside. Mary Beth cracked it and lit the cigarette. She blew smoke over the threshold as the light from the dying day silhouetted her glorious body.

Patrick prided himself on being a highly-evolved man, but the way Mary Beth's round ass curved into those long pale legs made him want to beat his chest, charge over there, scoop her up in his arms and howl at the moon.

She turned back to him, leaned against her desk, legs spread wide, as naked as the day she was born, exercising her full power.

"It…won't," he managed to say, but could already feel the full course of stirring in his loins. He knew she was still negotiating. *Just leave me and my brother alone and there's more where that came from,* her body was saying.

"Won't what?"

"It won't make a difference. With your brother. Even if I wanted it to."

Mary Beth took another drag of her cigarette and arched her back, staring straight up at the ceiling, her breasts heaving as she blew out a plume of smoke.

She was still offering him the carrot. But what would happen when she decided to use the stick? Would she try to blackmail him? Was Mary Beth capable of that?

The answer to that was, Yes—at least in general. Patrick had read her file and knew she was capable of quite a lot. But was she capable of doing that to *him*? That was the real question.

He would deny it, of course. The word of a decorated Assistant U.S. Attorney versus a small-town sheriff with a sketchy reputation—he would win a credibility contest easily. But this was her office. What if she had recording devices? What if she had cameras?

I'm just being paranoid, Patrick told himself. Mary Beth was a good person. Underneath all her scheming, she had a heart as pure as a mountain spring. Her intentions were almost always good. It was just the means she employed that were question-able—especially when someone she loved was threatened.

Patrick sat up and retrieved his boxer shorts that were hang-ing from a side table lamp.

Mary Beth turned away from the window. She stepped over her crumpled pile of clothes, showed no interest in dressing, and picked up the little gun she'd placed nicely on the corner of the desk. She strapped it to her ankle while holding the cigarette in her lips.

Patrick froze, watching, gaping, as Mary Beth took another pull off her cigarette. "Tell me something," she said.

"Okay."

He thought maybe they were finally going to talk about their relationship, the one they had so long ago, and the one they should have had over the last two decades if fate hadn't been so fucking cruel and they hadn't both been so stubborn.

"What's all the wandering and wondering business about?"

"Huh?" Patrick wasn't expecting that.

"The thing those bikers say whenever you ask them what they're doing here. Wandering and wondering. What the hell's that all about?"

"It's a code," Patrick said. "These guys coming in here are looking to join up with your brother, but they don't know who is and isn't part of his so-called revolution. They've been told it could be anybody. So, they've got a whole elaborate series of questions and responses they use to identify each other."

"Like what?"

"I don't know all of them, but when they're asked what they're doing here, they're supposed to say, 'wandering and wondering.' Then the other person, if they're in with Sawyer, they ask the person if they're from a certain city."

"What city?"

"I think it can be any city. Let's say Charleston. It starts with a C, right? So, the person responding is supposed to say, 'No, I'm from...' a city that starts with the next letter in the alphabet. So, they might say, 'No, I'm from Dallas,' since that starts with D."

Mary Beth nodded. "Or if you ask them if they're from Pittsburgh, they'll say, 'No, I'm from Quebec.'"

"Exactly."

Mary Beth huffed. "That sounds like some stupid shit, Sawyer would come up with."

She took another drag then eyed the half-smoked cigarette like it didn't taste as good as she remembered and dropped it into a coffee cup with a hiss. She crossed the room to him and sat on the arm of the couch, crossing her legs like she was dressed in sequins and lace, elegant and youthful, looking just like she had twenty years ago when they'd talk about their futures, gazing into his eyes with so much longing and hopefulness—asking him to deliver her the world. Patrick knew in that moment that Helen of Troy was more than just a myth. Men would fight a war over a woman. He had certainly moved heaven and earth for this one, leveraging the wheels of the federal government just to try and work his way back into her heart.

"I want you to know how much what you said meant to me," Mary Beth told him. "I'd waited so long to hear you apologize."

"You're welcome."

Patrick wondered if she was now going to apologize for getting knocked up by a redneck simpleton in the first place, and ruining both their lives, but thought it best not to say anything.

"Come here." She leaned close and kissed him long enough to run her fingernails through his hair. He thought they were about to have another go when she pulled back.

"But I need to apologize to you too," she said.

It's about time, Patrick thought.

She pushed him down onto the couch. "I should have understood. You came back from college and found your old girlfriend pregnant. Even though we had agreed to see other people. I probably would have said a lot worse, if things had been reversed. I probably would have killed you."

"It was my stupid idea for us to see other people," he said. "I had no right. It was just...I was heartbroken. And to find out it was a football player of all things—"

Patrick couldn't help the snark in his voice when he referenced Bill Cain. But the truth was, the fact that it had been Big Bill, the epitome of a Jasper Creek oaf, was part of what hurt so much. He always thought Mary Beth saw through all that macho shit as much as he did. For her of all people, the love of his life, to end up like some stereotypical, knocked-up cheerleader, had been absolutely devastating.

Mary Beth pulled away. "Let's not speak ill of the dead," she said.

"I'm sorry." He reached for her and she laid her head back on his chest.

"You know," she said, "I've never told anybody this. But the truth is, I never would have gone all the way with Bill, except I was trying to get back at you for sleeping with Raelynn."

Patrick shot up, propelling Mary Beth off of him. "What the hell? I never slept with Raelynn!"

Mary Beth stared at him quizzically.

Jesus Christ, Patrick thought. Raelynn was cute and all but he had never touched her. Would never. Mary Beth would have cut his balls off if he had.

"It's okay." Mary Beth said. "It was a long time ago. And, we were on a break. I mean…I get it. Raelynn's a hot piece of ass."

"She's a fucking liar—if she told you I slept with her."

Mary Beth reached for him. At first, he thought she was going to take his hand but instead she grabbed his wrist, flipped it over, palms up, and used her thumb to feel his pulse.

"What are you doing?"

"Shh!" Mary Beth stared at him intently and Patrick realized he'd been hooked up to her personal lie detector. He did his best not to blink, hoping his eyes would successfully convey the truth.

"You're serious? You never slept with her?"

"Never."

"Your freshman year of college, when you came home for fall break—"

"What about it?"

"You didn't go to a party out in McCray and hook up with Raelynn?"

"I may have gone to a party out there. Who the hell can remember from twenty years ago. But I swear to God, I have never touched Raelynn." As Patrick said it, a memory triggered from that Fall Break. He remembered Mary Beth had gone out on a date with Bill Cain, something already planned that she couldn't get out of with Bill's family—his grandfather's retirement dinner. Patrick was devastated and went to a party in

McCray to drink his blues away and probably had vented to Raelynn about Mary Beth being out with another guy, but that was it. She must have used that info to make up a story to get back at Mary Beth for God knows what.

"That conniving little—" Patrick didn't finish the thought.

Mary Beth released his wrist. "I am so glad I decked that bitch."

Before Patrick could say anything else, she started kissing him feverishly, clutching the hair on the back of his head. Then stopped suddenly. "Oh, my God!"

"What?"

The next thing Patrick knew, Mary Beth was on her feet, scrambling for her clothes.

"What's wrong?"

She raced around the office like a bomb was about to explode. "I forgot something," she said, hopping on one leg as she pulled her pants on. "I'm supposed to be somewhere."

"Can't it wait?"

Mary Beth dropped to her butt and started pulling up her boots. "No, it can't. Have you seen my shirt?"

Before he could answer, Mary Beth spotted it wedged in the couch. As she lunged for it, Patrick tried ineptly to grab hold of her and kiss her again. "Don't go," he said.

She kissed him hurriedly, two quick pecks as she pulled her arms through her shirt sleeves. "This is important."

"What is?"

"I don't have time to explain. I'll call you." With that, Mary Beth was up off the couch, working the buttons of her shirt as she dashed out of the office and out of sight.

18

WHEN MARY BETH didn't show by 6:30, Hawlings insisted there wasn't time to wait. "It's quite a stretch to Scarburry Hill," he said to Izzy. "We need to roll."

Izzy didn't like the idea of heading off to the Scarbury Hill Catfights without Mary Beth. She knew these people and Izzy hadn't decided if he could totally trust Hawlings. Plus, Mary Beth insisted he meet her at the courthouse. If she got there and he was gone, she'd be super pissed.

"Let's give her five more minutes," he said.

"Don't have time, man. Our best chance to talk to Bailey is to catch him before the fights start. He's got a lot of friends up there. We need to pull him aside and talk to him without making a scene. This is a delicate thing we're doing here. It needs to be handled just right."

Izzy sighed and pulled out his cell phone. He tried calling Mary Beth, but with the near total lack of cell service in McCray County, he'd have had a better chance of communicating by smoke signal. "Shit," he said.

"Come on, Izzy. Your sheriff knows where the fights are at,

right? If she comes along and we're not here she'll know where to find us."

"Yeah, but I told her I'd wait for her here."

Hawlings snickered. "You need your mommy to protect you?"

That pissed Izzy off. He'd been listening to shit like that since high school. "Watch it," he said.

The McCray deputy raised his hands. "I'm just saying, man. You're the chief deputy of Jasper County. Can you handle this situation or not?"

It was a classic manhood dare, and Izzy knew he was being manipulated, but the dare was a classic for a reason. Izzy looked at his phone again. When he saw there was still no service, he said, "Okay, let's go."

The two headed out of downtown in Hawlings' Explorer, driving for what seemed like forever on twisty mountain roads. The sun was setting and a full moon was on the rise. The combination created an orange and silvery glow around the endless trees that was creepy as hell. Izzy felt like he'd stumbled into a slasher movie, a place where you sure as shit didn't want to be the only Black guy.

Up to that point, he hadn't asked many questions about the "event" they were headed to. He assumed the fights would be held at some kind of sporting venue, maybe a local armory or high school gym—a public place where he could feel relatively safe questioning a person who, at this point, was a potential murder suspect. But when Hawlings pulled off-road onto a steep muddy path, Izzy got worried.

"There's an arena of some kind up here?" he asked.

Hawlings grinned. "Something like that."

Izzy tried not to read too much into the cryptic response. "What kind of place is it?"

"Used to be a ballpark, but now they do all kinds of stuff there. Bare Knuckle brawls, demolition derbies, muddin', dog fights, cock fights, you name it."

"Sounds charming."

Izzy tried again to message Mary Beth, but up in those hills, his smartphone was basically a fancy paperweight with Angry Birds. He tried to ease his anxiety with some conversation.

"So, these catfights? Is it like women mud wrestling or something?"

Hawlings laughed. "No, man. I told you it's a cat fight. Real cats."

Izzy was confused. "You mean actual cats? Like, meow?"

"That's right."

Izzy shot Hawlings the same look he gave his wife when she explained how they were saving money buying things they didn't need, just because they were on sale.

Hawlings explained, "You take two cats and tie their tails together, then hang them over a wire, and they start fighting like hell."

"No way."

"I'm telling you, man. It's the most vicious thing you've ever seen. Makes cockfights look as tame as touch football."

"You're serious?"

"Swear to God."

"That's messed up," Izzy said. He had a little Tabby at home named Boots who was really his wife's cat and Izzy didn't even like the thing all that much, but still. Damn. "Man, if I see that, I'm gonna arrest everybody there for animal cruelty," hew said.

"Like hell. You're out of your jurisdiction, pal."

"Then you better arrest them."

"Believe me," Hawlings said, "you don't wanna mess with these folks. Somebody goes up there trying to stop the catfights, they're coming home in a bodybag."

"Great." *What in the hell have I gotten myself into*, Izzy thought. He really should have waited for Mary Beth.

A few minutes later they arrived at an old baseball park surrounded by a sagging chain-link fence. A ring of pickup trucks formed a circle around the diamond, with their headlights illuminating two sawhorses near the pitcher's mound, that were connected by a taut cord. In the backs of the trucks were cages of frisky cats, meowing in a chorus as shrill as fingernails on a chalkboard. A tournament bracket posted near the dugout listed the feline competitors, putting Puma Thurman as the odds-on favorite at ten to one. "She's one mean pussy," Hawlings said. "Might have to put a few dollars down on her, myself."

They parked in the grass, after passing a five spot to a man in overalls and a grease-covered John Deere cap who was directing people where to go. "Seen Sheriff Bailey around?" Hawlings asked the man, as he handed over the bill.

"Sure," he said. "Over by the bar." The man pointed to the a boarded-up concession stand, where a folding table was surrounded by coolers and stacks of Bush thirty-packs. The two officers walked that way, squeezing through a crowd of some of the most hardened looking clodhoppers Izzy had ever seen. The people were mostly headed to the metal bleacher stands by that point, but ex-Sheriff Bailey was still leaned up against a tree by the concession stand, puffing on a cigar, as he talked to a few of his buddies. Hawlings pointed Bailey out as they approached. He was a big ole boy, every bit of six-five, and weighed at least three hundred pounds. He was holding a half-empty, two-liter bottle of Mountain Dew and filling it with Wild Turkey. When he emptied the liquor bottle he tossed it aside and swirled the two-liter concoction into a fizzy tornado. The three men standing with Bailey, weren't as big as the ex-sheriff, but each was good-sized, around six-feet tall.

Hawlings whispered, "We need to get Bailey to take a walk down by the parking area, away from the crowd. Otherwise, if things go south, the masses may come to the rescue and it'll be like trying to fight our way through a stampede."

Izzy was thinking this whole interview was sounding like a

bad idea, when Hawlings announced their presence. "How's it going, Sheriff?"

Bailey blew a big puff of cigar smoke. "You tell me, Hawlings," he said. His hard, flinty eyes fixed on the McCray deputy for a moment then drifted over and down, down, down to Izzy.

"We'd like to ask you a few questions," Izzy said, trying to keep his voice calm and even, not wanting to sound like he was intimidated by the big man or the surroundings.

"About what?"

"Elwood Gray," Izzy said. "We're following up on your ... investigation."

Bailey pointed at Izzy's shoulder patch. "What's Jasper County care about my investigation?"

"Didn't you hear? You're in Jasper County now. Or at least you will be as soon as the annexation goes through. It's become our concern."

Bailey took a hoot of his Turkey Dew and passed the two-liter to the man next to him. Then he butted his stogie against the tree he was leaning on, creating a shower of sparks, and flicked the remains at Izzy's feet.

"Well, you can take your concern and shove it right up your ass, little man."

Izzy maintained eye contact, but could feel his hand shaking as it drifted toward his gun.

Hawlings grabbed him at the elbow. "Easy," he said. "We're all friends here. We just want to talk, Sheriff. That's all."

The roar of the crowd kicked up, hovering just above the shrieks of the first two feline combatants, clawing each other to shreds.

"Okay, talk," Bailey said.

"Why don't we take a walk?" Hawlings said, pointing to the parking area "Somewhere a little quieter."

Bailey looked around. There were a few stragglers there near the makeshift bar but the majority of folks had moved on to the main event. The parking area was deserted. "Tell you what," he said. "Y'all hand over your guns and we'll take a walk with you." Bailey held out his hand, which was twice the size of Izzy's head, with fingers as thick as hotdogs.

"If I pull my gun, it's not gonna be to hand it over," Izzy said. Bailey laughed.

"Easy," Hawlings said again. "Let's not make a scene."

"Fine." Bailey held up his big hand. "Somebody else can hold them. Hey, Trina, come here." Bailey motioned to the lady handing out beers, a teenager who looked stoned out of her gourd, eyes half shut, with black curly bed head hair. "Need you to hang on to something for us," Bailey said.

Izzy tightened his grip on his Colt, but Hawlings was nodding his agreement. "Just talking," he said as he slowly un-holstered his weapon, removed the clip, and handed it over to Trina. Then he looked at Izzy, expecting him to do the same.

Izzy had that feeling he sometimes got, where he knew he was making a mistake but also knew he was going to go through with it anyway. He took a deep breath and drew the long barrel from its holster, spun the chamber to drop the bullets in his palm, and then surrendered his gun.

"Daaaaaaaamn," Trina said, examining Izzy's power-ful weapon.

"Okay," Bailey said. "Lead the way."

Hawlings, lead the way until they stopped in the middle of a long row of vehicles next to a two-tone blue pickup with a bed full of junk. Then Bailey spoke. "I don't know what kind of ideas you boys have got, but you need to understand one thing at the outset," he said.

"What's that?" Hawlings asked.

"I loved Elwood Gray. He was McCray County through and through. And his death hit me as hard as anybody."

Izzy could see the conflict on Bailey's face. It looked to him like Bailey was telling the truth, just not all of it. Like maybe he was covering for someone. Whoever the person with the funky ear was.

"I appreciate you talking to us, Sheriff," Izzy said. He addressed Bailey with the dignity of his former title to try and lower the temperature. See if he could get Bailey to open up. "I think you may have got the wrong impression from us back there. We don't think you did anything wrong. And we aren't trying to play Monday morning quarterback. It's just...."

Bailey looked down at Izzy who paused with the realization of just how big the ex-sheriff was.

"Just what?"

"It's just...my boss," Izzy said. "Sheriff Cain. She insists on us taking a second look at everything. You know how women are?"

Izzy had decided to play the bitch card, a useful tool in inter-departmental issues like these, which sometimes allowed him to tap into the old boys' network that often eluded him. Mary Beth wouldn't mind. They had a long running debate over whether it was harder to be a woman or Black in their job. If it ever got back to Mary Beth, Izzy'd just concede it as a point in his boss's favor, and tell her she just needed to hire a Black female deputy who'd have them both beat.

The gambit seemed to have the desired effect. Bailey's demeanor softened, considerably. "Well, I don't know what to tell you," he said. "Really, wasn't much to it. Cause of death seemed pretty obvious. There were no signs of forced entry. Nothing indicating a robbery. No known enemies. Gray lived alone and we didn't see anything to suggest anyone else had been in the apartment that evening. Just a tragic accident."

"Why'd you shut it down so quick, though?" Hawlings asked. "It was like you didn't want anybody in there."

"Just trying to preserve the man's dignity, is all. It was an embarrassing way to go. Especially for somebody like Gray, who folks thought so highly of."

"So, when you went and checked around, you didn't find

anybody who saw anything?" Hawlings asked. The question sounded innocent, but Hawlings' posture was aggressive and everyone could feel it.

This was the test, Izzy realized. If Bailey lied about intimidating the hooker, then they knew for sure he had something to hide.

"Nope," Bailey said. "Nobody saw nothing. Because there was nothing to see. Like I said, it was just an accident. Just a really dumb, terrible accident."

That was all Izzy needed to hear. No mention at all of the hooker he questioned. Nothing about the man she saw running out of Gray's apartment—the man with the deformed ear. That suggested Bailey was complicit to some degree. But Izzy thought it would be too dangerous to push him on that now, in their current surroundings.

"Okay, then," he said. "Thanks for speaking to us, Sheriff. We'll let you get back to enjoying your evening." Izzy started back toward the bar to get his gun but stopped when he realized no one was following. He looked back at Hawlings and Bailey eyeing each other like two rams about to charge.

Hawlings said, "I know you're full of it, Sheriff, because we found a lady says she saw Scott coming out of Gray's apartment that night."

Izzy didn't know who Scott was but apparently, Bailey did. He looked down at his feet like he was ashamed. Then he swung and cracked Hawlings upside the head with a devastating punch that turned out the deputy's lights.

"Oh shit," Izzy said. He didn't have time to run before Bailey said, "Get him." Izzy backpedaled into the tailgate of a nearby truck as Bailey's men fanned out. There was nowhere to run. He was surrounded.

19

MARY BETH'S SIREN was blaring but the damn cars weren't moving out of the way fast enough, as she weaved through the traffic on Highway 460, headed east toward McCray.

Izzy. She had to get to Izzy.

Mary Beth readjusted in her seat, trying to ignore the mild ache below. The scent of sex lingered, and it smelled like guilt. She felt like she'd cheated on Bill, which was somewhat ironic, because the whole time she'd actually been with Bill, she always kind of felt like she was cheating on Patrick, the man she was supposed to be with. Plus, all the Sawyer talk stirred the guilt she always felt where he was concerned. The little brother she abandoned by moving in with her grandparents after their father's death. She tried telling herself Sawyer was the reason she'd slept with Patrick, to try and wriggle out of the impossible situation she was in: arrest your brother or get prosecuted yourself.

A logging truck was taking its sweet time moving aside, so Mary Beth swerved onto the shoulder, kicking up a cloud of dust, and flipped the driver the bird as she roared past.

"Who am I kidding?" she said aloud. If it had been *anybody* other than Patrick Connelly delivering the government's ultimatum, would she have ended up buck-ass-naked on the cold linoleum floor? Hell no. Of course not. What was she, a fucking hooker? She'd had sex with Patrick because she wanted to. Plain and simple.

And in the process, she'd abandoned Izzy. Just straight up forgot all about her best friend who was headed into a very dangerous situation in a world he really didn't understand.

Abandoning Izzy—that's what she felt most guilty about.

With her son, Sam, in college, only calling or coming by when he needed money or the laundry done, Izzy had become the one consistent presence in Mary Beth's life. And he had long been the only man she could count on. Her daddy and Bill both up and died on her, Sawyer was a worthless piece of shit, and Patrick and Sam had both abandoned her in their own special ways.

Izzy was the only one who was always there. Since that first day they met, sophomore year, in a scene straight out of *Forrest Gump*. Mary Beth the little hillbilly girl from McCray, boarding the school bus with everyone snickering about her dead drug-dealer daddy, all denying her a seat, until she made it to Izzy, who was so short his high top fade was barely visible until she got close enough to see his smiling face. He was the only one to make room. And ever since that day, he was the only one who had cared enough about Mary Beth to suffer through her moods and tell her the truth when she was fucking up.

"Dammit!" Mary Beth slammed her fist against the dashboard. How could she have forgotten?

Izzy. Izzy. Izzy.

She repeated it like a mantra, afraid her thoughts would drift back to the feeling of Patrick on top of her, dripping with sweat. The musky smell of his aftershave, or the way he looked in that crisp Brooks Brother suit, all law-and-order in navy blue with a stark white shirt and power-red tie.

"Oh, Goddammit! Izzy!"

If something happened to him because she was too busy bumping uglies with her old high school crush, Mary Beth would never forgive herself. She cut behind another tractor-trailer, careening into the slow lane right in front of a minivan. Finally, she had a clear path out in front.

Mary Beth mashed the accelerator to the floor.

Ever since he first donned a star, Izzy'd had dreams about bears. Hulking, ferocious 900-pound Grizzlies who'd pop up in the oddest places. He'd be doing something simple like mowing the grass or driving down the road and spot one of the giants off in the distance coming toward him. Or sometimes he'd just be glancing out his front window and there one would be up on its hind legs, snarling and salivating, trying to force its way inside. Dream-Izzy would go searching for his gun to battle the beast but could never find it, or if he did there were no bullets. It took on different variations, but in the end, Izzy would always have to fight the bear weaponless. Feel the awesome force of its swipe, the deep stabbing pain of its claws, the awful breath from its ear-splitting roar through razor sharp teeth.

A year or so ago, Izzy's wife, Princess, convinced him to see a therapist about the dreams. The payoff for six sessions at two hundred dollars a piece was an insulting hypothesis that the bears had something to do with Izzy's "incessant need to over-compensate for small stature." All that flashed through Izzy's mind as Sheriff Bailey closed in on him, his massive arms out wide, ready to scoop Izzy into a crushing embrace and squeeze him like a tube of toothpaste. Bailey's friends were closing in too. Izzy had his head on a swivel, trying to keep track as they flanked his back and sides. He also registered a glimpse of the still unconscious Hawlings splayed out like a scarecrow in the dew-covered grass.

There was no time left to think. Izzy needed to pick a direction and run. If he stood there a moment longer, he'd be swarmed by all four men at once. The guy to his left was a little smaller than the others. Izzy thought maybe he could put a juke on him and squirt past. He started that way but the man moved hard to his right, nearly grasping Izzy's arm. Izzy backed up and tried the same thing on his right, with similar results.

There would be no escaping, he realized. His only hope was to fight his way to freedom. Just pick one guy, and go at him as hard. So Izzy did what he always did in his dream. He darted right at the big old bear, taking the fight to Sheriff Bailey.

That was the part the therapist never got, or at least never believed. In the dreams, no matter how scared Izzy was, no matter how big and nasty the bear, in the end, Izzy always knew he was up to the challenge, because he didn't have "an incessant need to overcompensate for his short stature." He wasn't a small man pretending to be big. Izzy was big. He was a big, badass, son-of-a-bitch, who just happened to be trapped inside of a small body. And he was a third-degree blackbelt in Taekwondo—something Frank Bailey found out when Izzy dropped into a crouch and executed a perfectly timed, spinning leg sweep that cut the big man down like a buzz saw.

Bailey's three hundred plus pounds tumbled forward, landing atop two of his friends who had swooped in just in time to get pancaked. Izzy popped up on the other side of them and got into a middle stance as the fourth man rushed him. The deputy sprung into the air, did a parkour leap off the bumper of a nearby Chevy truck and twirled like a figure skater before smacking his steel-toed boot across the fourth man's face.

Izzy landed with the balance of a cougar and turned toward the mass of humanity on his left. Bailey was in a downward-facing dog, smothering the two men beneath him. There was a bulge near the small of Bailey's back and a glint of steel where his plaid shirt was hiked up. A gun.

Izzy went for it. He seized the grip protruding from Bailey's waistband, pulled it free, then felt like he'd been charged by a rhino as man number four, who'd recovered quicker than expected, plowed into him.

The gun and Izzy flew in different directions. The gun ker-plopped into a mud puddle near where Hawlings was sprawled unconscious, while Izzy stumbled forward and crashed down, jamming his right shoulder against an exposed tree root and sending an electric shock of pain ripping through his arm. Nerve endings exploded from his collarbone all the way down to his fingertips. Izzy cried out. He struggled to his feet and tried to lift his arm but couldn't get it above his waist before it flopped down like an empty sleeve.

His shoulder was separated.

Izzy tried to lunge for the gun with his good arm but the man who had shoved him, seized him from behind, grabbing a hold of his belt. Izzy twisted and fired a left-handed tiger claw into the man's throat, which left him gurgling and wheezing as he collapsed to his knees.

By that time, Bailey had rotated his girth enough for the two men beneath him to squirm free. Izzy tried to dive for the gun before they could get to him but came up way short. He army-crawled the few remaining feet to the revolver as best he could with the use of only one arm, but a sharp elbow plunged into the middle of his back. Followed by a knee and a great weight pressing into Izzy's spine, nearly snapping him in half as powerful hands wrapped around his throat and squeezed.

The world started to kaleidoscope around Izzy until he jammed a thumb into his attacker's eye, skewering it like a marshmallow. Suddenly the death grip was gone. Izzy wheezed as the strangler took off running, half-blind, wailing and bouncing off of parked vehicles.

But there was no time to celebrate. Now the third man loomed over Izzy and his Red Wing boot came crashing down like a pile driver. Izzy rolled to his right just in time to avoid having his face stomped into a crater. The maneuver sent a fresh bite of pain down Izzy's arm, but he pushed through it, driving up onto the damaged shoulder for leverage so he could raise his left leg in a loaded position and unleash a vicious side kick that crumpled this man's knee. He fell, grasped the knee, and writhed in the mud. Izzy rolled onto his back and raised his right leg high in the air, then brought the heel of his boot down like an axe against the man's rib cage. There was a satisfying crack followed by faint gasps for air.

Three down, Izzy told himself. Only Sheriff Bailey remained.

The big man had finally gotten to his feet and lumbered toward Izzy, who braced himself, ready to be trampled. But Bailey rumbled past.

"Shit," Izzy said. The sheriff knew what the real prize was. He was going instead for the gun handle protruding from a murky puddle a few feet away.

Izzy didn't have the energy to move. His whole body hurt. His arm throbbed with every beat of his heart. He craned his neck, expecting to see Bailey turn at any moment, gun in hand, ready to fire. But what he saw instead was like a godsend.

The ex-sheriff dropped to his knees and slowly raised his hands.

"Don't you move, you bastard!" Hawlings was awake, lying flat on his belly in the middle of the muck, arms extended with a two-handed straight thumbs grip on Bailey's gun.

"Just relax," Bailey said. "Take it easy."

"Shut the fuck up!" Hawlings said, getting to his feet.

"You okay?" Izzy asked.

"No, I don't think so. Maybe. I don't know." Hawling looked starry-eyed and pissed. "Get down on the ground," he commanded Bailey. "Hands behind your back."

Bailey began lowering his head and Hawlings helped him out by shoving it down into a mud puddle with a splash like a depth charge. "I'm going to make this as comfortable as possible," Hawlings said before viciously wrenching Bailey's arms behind his back and cuffing his wrists. He raised Bailey up, coughing and spitting dirty water, as his two remaining friends made a run for it, past Izzy who was too exhausted and beat down to try and stop them.

"You got cuffs?" Hawlings asked.

Izzy did, but only one pair. Even if they could catch Bailey's friends they'd only be able to cuff one of them, and there were three of them still out there somewhere. Didn't think it was a good idea to pursue. So far, they'd managed to escape the attention of the spectators, who were so enthralled by the latest kitty deathmatch, they hadn't noticed the human fight.

"Just let them go," Izzy said. "We've got Bailey on assaulting an officer. Let's get out of here."

Hawlings looked back toward the crowd and rubbed the goose egg on the side of his head.

"My arm's messed up pretty bad," Izzy said. "I'm in no condition to chase after those guys. Plus, I've only got the one set of cuffs." Izzy held up the silver rings.

Hawlings frowned, then shoved Bailey a couple of steps in Izzy's direction. Then he pointed his gun at Izzy.

"What the hell are you doing?" Izzy asked.

"I'm sorry," Hawlings said. "But the cuffs are for you."

Mary Beth spun to a stop in the middle of Main Street, lights still flashing, and jumped out.

"Izzy!"

She called several times with no response. The area was deserted other than a couple of prostitutes leaning on a lamppost near the courthouse. Mary Beth called out to them.

"Hey, have you—"

She was interrupted by a deafening sound, a sonic boom that shook the ground, followed by a series of cracks as though a forest of trees snapped simultaneously. Then the six-story lime-stone courthouse shimmied like a square of Jell-O and began to tumble. The prostitutes screamed and tried to run but were quickly enveloped by a mushrooming cloud of gray, a tsunami of debris, that rushed toward Mary Beth.

The sheriff's final thought was a kind of dreamy awareness that she was suddenly off her feet, flying backwards, before the world turned to black.

20

HAWLINGS SHOVED IZZY and Bailey into the back of the Explorer, then slammed the door, locking both men inside the police cruiser. The pain in Izzy's injured shoulder was still raging as Hawlings jumped into the driver's seat and gunned the engine. Tires spun in mud as he raced through the parking area back onto the treacherous mountain road.

"What the hell's going on?" Izzy managed to ask through the pain. "I thought we were on the same side?"

"Quiet!" Hawlings barked.

Izzy's couldn't wrap his brain around the situation. Was Hawlings arresting him? Abducting him? Something worse? Growing up Black in a rural white community, Izzy'd been peppered with apocryphal tales of vigilante police officers who'd drive people out to the middle of nowhere to kick the shit out of them. Was that what was going on? Was Hawlings planning some kind of backwoods *coup de gras* on Bailey, and couldn't afford to leave Izzy as a witness?

"Hey man, I get it," Izzy said. "This guy sucker punched you and you want some payback. Okay. Not what I would do, but this is your jurisdiction. Have at it, Hoss. Why do I have to get mixed up in it, though? I'm like Sergeant Shultz, man, 'I see nothing. I hear nothing.' You know what, I'm sayin'? Just let me out at the next stop."

Hawlings shot Izzy a furtive glance in the rearview mirror and wiped sweat from his brow.

"I don't have to tell you how much trouble you're making for yourself by bringing me along, do I?" Izzy added.

"Quiet," Hawlings said. "I know what I'm doing."

"You sure? Kidnapping a sheriff's deputy?" Izzy whistled. "You're putting yourself in a world of hurt, my friend. This really the way you want to go? 'Cause it's not too late. You could just pull over right there in that little clearing and let me out and I'll forget all about this."

To Izzy's surprise, Hawlings jerked the Explorer to a skidding stop on the side of the road. He scrunched his eyes shut and started rubbing his temples. "How do I know you'll keep quiet?"

That was a good question. Truth was, there was no way in hell Izzy would keep quiet. The second he was free, he'd go gather up a posse and be back to arrest Hawlings straight away.

"I guess you can't know for sure," Izzy said. "But there's one thing you can be absolutely positive of."

"What's that?"

"If I go missing, Sheriff Cain will scour the fucking earth looking for you. Won't rest until she finds you. And then she'll skin your ass alive."

Hawlings leaned back against the headrest and stared up at the dome light for answers.

"I know you know that," Izzy said. "That's why you kept pushing me to leave before we could meet up with her, right? I bet she's not far behind. Could be coming down the road any minute. And she's got a lot of friends and family out here. You know her mama runs the McCray County Mafia. There's not a place you can hide that she can't find you."

"Shit!" Hawlings slapped the dashboard. "Fuck me."

"What's it gonna be?" Izzy asked.

Hawlings bit at his bottom lip. "Screw it," he said, then stepped on the gas, pulling them back onto the road.

Dammit. For a second, Izzy thought he might have talked his way free. He looked over to Bailey who'd thus far remained silent.

"You're awful quiet," Izzy said.

"You're wasting your breath," Bailey told him. "Hawlings, here, doesn't call the shots. He's just following orders."

Hawlings punched the caged divider separating him from his prisoners. "Quiet!"

"I thought you were his boss," Izzy said to Bailey.

"No," he replied. "Not his real boss."

"I said shut the fuck up!" Hawlings yelled, then cranked the stereo, blasting a Jethro Tull song as loud, Izzy had to read Bailey's lips as he mouthed the words, "Sawyer Thompson. The Moonshine Messiah."

Twenty minutes later, Hawlings turned the Explorer onto a gravel road, past a green metal sign for the Old Wengo Mine, and Izzy saw a coal tipple off in the distance, made of faded, rotting wood and rusted metal. The mine looked like a mountain version of a walled-off castle, surrounded by a chain-link fence covered with black nylon screening and topped with curls of razor wire. Hunter platforms, twenty feet high were positioned around the perimeter like guard towers. A spotlight from one of those towers shone down on them, when Hawlings pulled the Blazer up to the gate and was met by a man in combat fatigues, holding an assault rifle.

"Open her up," Hawlings said. "We've got a situation."

The guard pulled his camouflage goiter down beneath his chin as he peered in the back. "Holy shit," he said. "Is that Sheriff Bailey?"

"Ex-sheriff," Hawlings said. "Now he's our prisoner."

"What for?"

"For murdering a Brother of the Cause. Or at least helping to cover it up. I don't have all the details yet, but after a couple days in the hole I figure he'll be willing to tell us all about it."

"You mean—"

"That's right," Hawlings said. "Elwood Gray's death was no accident."

The guard rubbed a hand through sweaty hair. "Jesus Christ," he said. "Does Sawyer know about this?"

"Of course. Sawyer knows everything. He's the one who told me to nab him. Now let me in."

"You talked directly to Sawyer?" The guard said, as though the notion was ridiculous.

"No," Hawlings said. "But I got it from Quiet Clem, and that's just as good, right?"

The guard nodded. "Yeah, guess so." He pointed at Izzy. "What's with the midget?"

"Collateral damage," Hawlings said. "Couldn't leave any witnesses. Now open the gate."

"Yeah," Izzy interjected. "And be sure to tell Sawyer, that its Jasper County Deputy Izzy Baker you fucking dickwads have kidnapped. Who just so happens to be best friends with his sister, Sheriff Mary Beth Cain. Heard of her? Sawyer will probably be super pissed at both of you if you don't cut me loose right now."

The guard stared at Izzy, surprised at first, then smiled wide, and he and Hawlings shared a laugh.

"What's so funny?" Izzy asked.

Hawling said, "Let's just say that Sawyer and his sister aren't exactly on the best of terms."

Izzy felt his heart sink, then something occurred to him. "Wait a second, Hawlings. A few hours ago you didn't even know Sawyer and Mary Beth were related."

"Just playing dumb," Hawlings told him. "Wanted to see what all you knew."

"So, you've been working for Sawyer this whole time?"

"No. I work for Jasper County," Hawlings said. "But Elwood Gray was one of our brothers. And when you raised the possibility that his death was no accident, that made it Sawyer's business. Remember when we stopped at the station so I could make a phone call? Who you think I was calling?"

"Sawyer."

"More or less."

Bailey spoke up. "Good!" he said. "'Cause I'd like to see Sawyer too. I've got some information that will really blow his hair back. You take me to him and I bet we get this whole thing cleared up, right quick. Because you all are barking up the wrong tree, pointing the finger at me."

Everyone looked at the ex-sheriff with surprise.

The guard said, "Last time you was here, Sawyer said he'd blow a hole through your ugly mug if you ever showed up again."

"Things may be different now," Bailey said.

Before anyone could ask what he was talking about, a booming explosion far off in the distance shook the ground and rattled the leaves throughout the surrounding forest. It was followed by resounding cheers from inside the compound and some celebratory bursts of gunfire.

"What the hell was that?" Hawlings asked.

The guard slapped Hawlings' shoulder. "It's starting, my man. You boys are just in time."

Then Sawyer Thompson's unmistakable voice crackled over a PA system:

Whoooooooo Doagies! The revolution will be televised, my friends. Now y'all know what to do. Let's get it on!

The guard, hurriedly unlocked the gate. "Afraid Sawyer's gonna be a little busy right now. This business about Gray is gonna have to wait. Hawlings, you better get your ass on down to the armory and we'll catch you up on what you missed."

"What am I supposed to do with these two?" Hawlings asked.

The guard shrugged. "Like you said. Stick 'em in the hole." Then he called out for somebody named Randy and before Izzy knew what was going on, another man in fatigues was pulling him from the vehicle. Izzy fell to the ground, landing hard on his knees. Someone shoved a grease-tasting rag in his mouth, then a black canvas bag came down over his head.

"Move it!" A gun barrel jabbed Izzy in the back once he was hoisted to his feet. He and Bailey crashed into each other, as the guards marched them forward. Images of hostage videos and jihadi beheadings flashed through Izzy's mind, as he and Bailey were force-walked through the compound. Izzy thought about his wife, Princess, and whether he'd ever see her again.

Meanwhile commotion abounded inside the compound. Even blindfolded, Izzy was aware of people running around, shouting, cheering as though their team just won the Superbowl.

"Hold up!" a guard said.

Izzy heard the shriek of a rusty spring, followed by a clank of metal. Then he was shoved through some kind of doorway. Men smelling of body odor and campfires crammed in close together, filling the tight space. Then another rusty, scraping sound, a rattly engine kicking on, and the floor began to drop.

Izzy's heart jackhammered inside his chest. All he could see through his head-covering was a faint glow that grew dimmer and dimmer. The temperature dropped precipitously, the smell of mud and moisture filled the air, as what appeared to be an elevator rattled on for what seemed like forever. Izzy's mind cycled through every claustrophobic thought he'd ever had. His chest tightened with visions of being buried alive. Then, finally, the winch moaned and the elevator shuttered to a stop.

"Let's go. Your accommodations await," the guard said.

The metal door swung open and Izzy was shoved forward.

"Okay, kneel down."

Izzy did his best to say, "Fuck you," through his gag. His mumbling approximation was sufficient to prompt a rifle butt strike to his chest that wobbled Izzy's knees. "Go to hell," he managed. Then another blow came, this one to his head, and Izzy was down.

21

PATRICK WAS STILL thinking about Mary Beth when he got back to his hotel room. The stunning image of her leaned against her desk, naked other than the pistol strapped to her ankle, would be indelibly seared into hippocampus until the day they put him in the ground. He slipped off his shoes, sat on the bed, and started checking his messages. Two spam calls and one from his ex who showed up on his caller ID as SHE WHO MUST NOT BE NAMED. Patrick deleted the message without listening to it, knowing it was just another sortie in their never-ending post-divorce battle.

Like Mary Beth, Patrick's ex-wife was also a beautiful woman. She and Patrick both graduated at the top of their law school class where they'd been the perfect power couple, collecting each other like trophies. But a fierce competition arose after passing the bar, as the ex became a big firm litigator with a lavish salary, and Patrick took on the role of underpaid government lawyer who touted the nobility of his cause. Resentments stacked upon each other like sandbags until forming a wall neither could traverse.

They toughed it out for a while, cohabitating, while leading separate lives. But when both Patrick's parents died within six months of one another, the insipid hollowness in his marriage became too glaring to ignore. He was determined to find true love, that elusive feeling he had only really known for sure during the brief time he was with Mary Beth back in high school. Fate seemed determined to keep them apart, but just as his divorce was finalized, he learned of the federal investigation Mary Beth was facing, a predicament that he was perfectly positioned to resolve. Either God or destiny or just dumb luck was reaching out to him, saying, this is your chance.

Patrick's phone rang again. He started to dismiss it, expecting it to be the ex, but the display said: QUIGLEY. He was the government's informant inside the biker gangs. Patrick answered quickly and was surprised when the grizzled bikers's normally gravelly voice squawked with excitement.

"They did it, man! They really fucking did it!"

"Did what?" Patrick asked. "Quigley, what are you talking about?"

"The courthouse, man. The big fucking federal courthouse out in McCray. They just blew that shit up."

Patrick didn't have to ask who. Quigley previously told him Sawyer was requiring the bikers to perform some destructive act to prove their worth before he'd admit them to his compound. That was what prompted Patrick's call to Mary Beth's attorney that morning, and his insistence she accept his offer by Monday. He needed her to arrest Sawyer before things got out of hand. But he had no idea the bikers would act so soon.

"You're not serious?"

"Yes, I'm fucking serious, I—"

"Quigley, why didn't you tell me it was going down?"

The gravel in Quigley's voice returned. "Motherfucker, what am I supposed to do when we're all together in the middle of some shit. Say, 'Excuse me guys, I need to go call my handler so I can narc you out?' I could get fucking killed for talking to you."

Patrick palmed his forehead. He immediately saw how this would look when people found out the government had advanced knowledge that wasn't acted upon—like they allowed the bombing to happen as a pretext for moving on Sawyer's compound. *God*, what if they tried to make Patrick the scapegoat? If anyone found out about his past with Mary Beth, not to mention their recent trist, he'd be a convenient sacrifice.

Oh, Jesus, Patrick thought. The only other person who knew about Quigley's intel was John Jensen, the U.S. Attorney out of Charleston. He was the one investigating Mary Beth, the one who Patrick had to persuade to stand down in exchange for Sawyer's arrest, and it had taken some major convincing. Asking a West Virginia prosecutor to target a militia leader was like getting the Pope to disavow Catholics. Patrick pictured the first time he pitched the idea to Jensen, seated on a marble bench under the golden dome of Charleston's capital, the prosecutor munching on a Reuben sandwich with Thousand Island on his chin, saying, "The Moonshine Messiah? Shit, that boy makes a whole lot of sense, you ask me."

Quigley brough Patrick out of his ruminating. "What am I supposed to do?" he asked.

That was a good question. Patrick had no idea. He'd never run an informant before, but Quigley had come to him virtually gift wrapped by the IRS, since the biker had refused to pay taxes for over a decade. Now Quigley's cooperation was the only thing keeping him and his wife out of jail.

"Where are you now?" Patrick asked.

"Gas station near Canebrake. The guys are all headed up to Old Wengo, but a few of them have cold feet. Worried about what's about to happen when the storm troopers show up. I'm thinking it's time for me to bug out of here."

Patrick's mind went to the prosecution. If Mary Beth was able to arrest her brother, did they have enough to convict? Quigley could testify that a delegation of bikers met with Sawyer's right-hand man that morning, a guy they called Quiet Clem, who provided them with the explosives and suggested potential targets. But it was all second hand. Hearsay. With a buffer between the Moonshine Messiah and the guys who planted the bombs.

"I think we still need you on the inside," Patrick said. "We don't have anything direct on Sawyer yet. And if this turns into a standoff, we're going to need information on what's happening within the compound." Patrick had outfitted Quigley with a special satellite phone, so he would be able to communicate with the government no matter how deep into the mountains he got, and could also take pictures and video.

"Man, fuck that," Quigley said. "I'm not gonna be in there when you assholes start sending in tanks and airstrikes and shit."

Patrick was worried about that too. He didn't want Quigley in harm's way, but they needed this case to be airtight, and Quigley was in no position to refuse.

"I'm sorry Quigley. We need more evidence on Sawyer. Quite frankly, you don't have a choice."

The biker growled into the phone. "You're all a bunch of fucking chickenhawks, man. All of you."

"It's going to be okay," Patrick assured him. "This won't get out of hand. I'm working on a way to bring everything to a peaceful conclusion. But we need to slam dunk this conviction, or else it will be my neck on the chopping block."

"Better you than me."

"Quigley, you know what the alternative is. Prison terms and ruinous fines, for you and your wife."

There was a pause, followed by a groan.

"Quigley?"

"Yeah?"

"We have an understanding?"

"I understand you're willing to get me killed so you can make your nice pretty little case."

"That won't happen," Patrick said. He really didn't want Quigley hurt. Didn't want anybody hurt. If not for humanitarian reasons, Patrick knew that if one drop of blood was spilled at Old Wengo, questions would be asked. Like what in the hell was a land use attorney doing mixed up in all of this? One who'd gone to Jasper Creek High School and, oh, by the way, dated Sawyer Thompson's sister, the notorious Sheriff Mary Beth Cain, who was about to score a free pass from federal corruption charges. If the situation turned deadly, conspiracy theories would abound and heads would roll.

"I swear to you, Quigley," Patrick said. "You get in there and get me some direct dirt on Sawyer ordering the bombing or any other acts of violence, and I'll make sure that he is arrested without anybody getting killed."

"Yeah, whatever, man," Quigley said. "I'll do what I gotta do. But you turn my wife into a widow and it's on you, man."

"Trust me."

"Fuck you," Quigley said, and ended the call.

Patrick wiped nervous sweat from his forehead. His stomach was twisted into knots but he didn't have time to brood. He needed to move quickly to try and slow the federal response to the bombing that he knew would be swift. If they moved on the compound before Mary Beth had a chance to work her magic, then this whole thing would be a disaster. So he called the only person with enough clout to slow the government reaction, and a reason to do so.

"Jensen," was the clipped greeting from the U.S. Attorney out of Charleston—a man who was as much a politician as he was a lawyer.

"John, something's happened. We need to talk."

"Hang on just a second," Jensen said to someone near him.

"Need to take this. Give me a minute, okay." Then he was back to Patrick. "What's up? Our girl, gonna take the deal?"

Patrick didn't have a definitive answer on that yet, but, given recent events, felt confident she would. Mary Beth may not have been willing to bring Sawyer in, just to save herself, but arresting him now would be an act of mercy. Maybe the only way to save his life. Not to mention the hundreds of people inside his compound.

"I'm sure she will," Patrick said. "But now we've got a bigger problem. I'm going to need you to buy her the time she'll need."

Jensen was chewing on something and talking with his mouth full. "What are you saying?"

"They've already done it. Those bikers trying to join Sawyer's movement. They just blew up the federal courthouse in McCray."

The chomping stopped.

"Thought you said we'd have at least a week or two."

"I thought we would."

Another pause. Patrick waited as Jensen considered the ramifications of what he'd just been told.

"You realize that if it gets out that we had intel they were looking to blow something up, it's going to look like—"

"Exactly."

"Well, son of a bitch, Connelly! What the—Hold on, let me see if it's on the news yet. Where's the—Oh, fuck, look at that. It looks like goddamn nine-eleven. You watching this? Tune it to channel six."

Patrick looked around his hotel room for the remote. Not seeing it, he got down on all fours to check under the bed.

Jensen said, "Good god, that Princess Baker is a handsome looking woman. If I was ten years younger—"

"John!"

"What?"

"What do you think?"

"Oh, yeah," Jensen said. "We're fucked. Everybody's gonna

know who's behind this. I'd give it twenty-four hours before agents are swarming around that compound like a plague of locusts."

Patrick found the remote and tried to remember how to switch to cable from the hotel's welcome screen. "This can all still have a happy ending," he insisted. "If you can just buy Mary Beth some time, she'll bring her brother in peacefully. Nobody has to die."

"People already have died," Jensen said. "They're reporting casualties. At least six confirmed dead. Cleaning crew inside the building and a few pedestrians. That's all she wrote. People around here may have a soft spot for militias but DC is going to rain down hellfire over this."

Patrick wasn't willing to accept that.

"Jensen, you're the face of the federal government here. *Thee* United States Attorney for the Southern District of West Virginia. Any prosecution of Sawyer or his co-conspirators will have your name on the pleadings. So, if this thing goes Waco, and it looks like the government was just lying in wait for an excuse to take Sawyer out, you're about to become the most hated man in the state's history. And if there's one thing I've learned about West Virginia, it's that these people know how to hold a grudge. Ever heard of the Hatfields and McCoys?"

Jensen started chewing again. "Maybe I can make some calls. But your girl better come through."

"She will," Patrick assured him. He finally managed to switch the TV to cable and found that the national outlets had already picked up the bombing story. Patrick tuned to CNN where he saw a news scrawl that weakened his knees.

JASPER COUNTY SHERIFF AMONG THOSE FEARED DEAD.

Jensen must have seen the same thing on Channel Six, because he said, "Connelly, I hope to hell you've got a Plan B."

22

IZZY JERKED awake but couldn't see a thing. He was surrounded by complete and utter darkness. "Hello!" he called. "Is anybody there? Anybody?" His voice echoed throughout a cavernous abyss, followed by silence, save for the drip of condensation.

"Help!" he yelled, panicking, his heart racing like a hamster on cocaine. "Anybody! Anybody!" But the only response were the reverberations of his own voice, mocking him. "Anybody, buddy, buddy, buddy." Then it dawned on Izzy that the gag was gone, as was the sack they'd put over his head. No need for blindfolds down in the mine.

He also realized his left wrist was handcuffed to something hard and immovable. Izzy struggled fecklessly to get free. He screamed, yelled, bellowed, produced unintelligible, uncontrolled noises, louder and louder, until finally a man's voice boomed in his ear.

"Would you shut the fuck up?"

Izzy jumped, triggering a hot poker of pain in his injured shoulder.

"Jesus, you are a mouthy little thing."

Izzy tried to catch his breath. "Bailey?"

A huff, then, "Yeah, it's Bailey."

"Oh, thank goodness." At least Izzy wasn't down there alone. "What's going on?" he asked.

Bailey let out a sigh like a train releasing steam. "What's going on is we're both handcuffed to a fifty-ton continuous mining machine down in the bottom of the Old Wengo Mine, one of the deepest room and pillar mines ever dug—about fifteen hundred feet below the surface. So, no matter how loud you yell, nobody up top is gonna hear shit. All you're doing is blowing my eardrums out."

Izzy didn't know how Bailey could sound so calm. "But why?" he asked. "Why bring us down here?"

"To break us, obviously," Bailey said. "Didn't take very long with you, did it, Chatty Kathy?"

No it hadn't. Izzy was broken. There were a lot of things he could be tough about, but being buried alive wasn't one of them. Izzy'd sooner have his dear old grandmother, Mum-Mum, working two beds in a house of ill-repute, than spend one more second in that mine.

"Whatever they want from me, they can have it," he said. "I don't know what I'm even doing here."

Bailey's tone softened. "Yeah, I am sorry about that, Deputy. Afraid it's not really you they're trying to break."

"Then just tell them what they want to know. Anything's better than staying down here."

"If I can talk to Sawyer, I will," Bailey said. "But only Sawyer. And he needs to hear it, too, before it's too late."

"Hear what?"

"Uh uh, no way. That info's the only card I've got to play to get us out of here. And, no offense, deputy, but I can't trust you with it. Keeping it close to the vest is the best chance either of us have of ever seeing the sun again."

Oh, the sun. Just the mention of it seized hold of Izzy's heart.

"Hawlings will want to get the truth about why Gray's dead," Bailey explained. "He's nothing if not persistent. And Sawyer won't come to us, personally, I promise you. The Moonshine Messiah's got an ego the size of Kentucky. But eventually Hawlings will gain an audience with his holiness and take us to him."

Izzy prayed Bailey was right, and that it wouldn't take too long, because he was already about to lose his mind. "How long have you known Hawlings was in with Sawyer?" he asked.

There was a scraping noise from Bailey repositioning himself, and the clinking of his cuffs against the mining machine. "Didn't know for sure until I saw him turn the gun on you," Bailey said. "But I had suspicions for months. Ever since some federal marshals came asking for help serving papers on Sawyer, and it seemed like everytime we were going to catch him outside the compound, he got tipped off—like he had somebody on the inside. Finally, I had to risk coming up here to serve him. That's when Sawyer let me know that if I ever showed up again, they'd put a bullet through my brain."

Before Izzy could ask any more questions, they were interrupted by the rumbling of machinery high above. The elevator.

"Just keep quiet when they get here," Bailey said. "Let me do the talking."

The elevator gears cranked and whined for what seemed like ten minutes before the platform finally thudded against the ground. Then there was a loud wrenching sound, the door opening, followed by heavy footsteps and a blinding flashlight beam.

"Got bad news, boys," Hawlings said. "Seems like Sawyer's preoccupied. Fixing to fight a war up there. Could be quite a while before he's in a place to talk. If ever."

"Tell Sawyer, this is important," Bailey said. "Can't wait. It's about to come out and is going to make him look awfully bad if he doesn't address it first."

"Suppose you just go ahead and tell it to me," Hawling said.

"Hell, no. It's for Sawyer's ears only. If you want to know why Gray's dead then you're going to have to take me to the man. I'm not telling your dumbass shit."

The beam of Hawlings' flashlight sliced left then right as he cracked Bailey across the face. Then the light turned on Izzy. "What about you?" Hawlings said. "I imagine you two have been stuck down here long enough to swap stories. You want to tell me what you've learned about Gray?"

Izzy didn't have any intel to divulge. His only play was to trust Bailey's instinct that Hawlings' curiosity was their best bet for escaping the mine.

"Maybe, maybe not," he said, "but I'm not telling your dumb ass shit, either."

Izzy braced himself, expecting to receive his own blow from Hawlings' mag flashlight, but none came.

"Okay," Hawlings said. "Have it your way."

The light turned back toward the elevator. "You boys, be sure to watch out for rats while you're down here. Thousands of them in these mines. Real big, nasty fuckers."

Izzy did his best not to shriek. He hated rats. Now he couldn't help imagining them crawling all around, scurrying over his legs and nipping at his fingers. He remembered the gambit Hawlings used with the prostitute they'd question outside Gray's apartment. How he made her think they'd leave her handcuffed to a sewer grate if she didn't talk. He hoped that was what he was doing now. Just bluffing. Trying to scare them into believing he was willing to leave them down there indefinitely. But unlike the prostitute, Bailey stayed quiet, and eventually, the elevator engine kicked back on. It was all Izzy could do not to shout some pathetic plea as it began to rise. Tears filled his eyes as he watched the glow from Hawlings flashlight climb then fade away.

23

PATRICK CONNELLY WAS NOT an especially religious man, but he paused to say a silent prayer of thanks when he learned Mary Beth was alive. Ironic, he thought, that he should get the best news of his life at the Jasper County Regional Hospital, a place he once hated with a passion, when his father served as its director—the job that pulled their family to West Virginia and so disrupted his teenage years.

The deliverer of the happy tidings seemed odd as well. Deputy Skipwith was a skinny, Ichabod-Crane-looking kid in his twenties, who'd obviously been left in the waiting room while a more senior deputy was allowed back to see the sheriff. Yet Skipwith was preening around the waiting room like a peacock with his bony chest puffed out, saying, "Yep, Sheriff got her bell rung, awful good. Concussion and a bunch of cuts and scrapes and all, but doc says she's gonna be just fine." Skipwith planted a foot on the chair next to where Patrick was seated, leaned over and whispered, "Between you and me, though, we got ourselves a bit of a situation."

That was one hell of an understatement, Patrick thought. As

they sat there, federal agents were already being deployed. Soon, a joint task force of the ATF, FBI and Army National Guard would swoop in and take position outside Sawyer's compound. Getting Mary Beth to her brother, ASAP, was the only way they had of averting a deadly confrontation.

Skipwith blew on a burnt-smelling cup of vending machine coffee, tested it, and, after deciding it was still too hot to drink, said, "Got ourselves a missing deputy. Guess, I can tell you about it, you being a government attorney and all. You know Izzy Baker?"

Yes, Patrick knew Izzy. Back in high school he used to tag along with Mary Beth sometimes when Patrick would take her out. Patrick knew how tight they were and worried Izzy might have been with Mary Beth when the courthouse blew up. But Skipwith said otherwise.

"Izzy was supposed to meet up with the Sheriff at the court-house Friday night but never showed. Was last seen with a McCray deputy, name of Hawlings, who's gone AWOL too. Been nearly forty-eight hours now without a word from either of them. And Izzy's wife's been going nuts, calling down to the station at all hours, all in a panic. That's Princess Baker from Channel Six News, you seen her? Hoowee."

Patrick didn't answer. He decided there wasn't any more time for chitchat. If Izzy was missing, he knew that would quickly become Mary Beth's top priority and that was something he didn't have time for.

"Hey, you can't go back there," Skipwith said as Patrick pushed through the double doors separating the waiting room from the convalescence area.

Fortunately, the sleepy, rural hospital was lax on security. Patrick breezed right past the nurses station, not sure where to go until he heard Mary Beth's unmistakably twangy voice ripping somebody a new asshole.

"Don't give me excuses, Goddamit! I want Izzy found! Now!"

Patrick quickly found Mary Beth's room and hovered outside the door, listening in as one of her deputies timidly explained the efforts they'd thus far made to locate Izzy.

"Forget it," Mary Beth said. "Just leave the keys to your squad car on the table and get the hell out of here so I can get dressed. I'll go find him myself."

"Sheriff?"

"Keys, damnit."

"But—"

"But, nothing, Go forth. My car's still buried under a pile of rubble in the middle of Mapelton Square. So I'm taking yours. Skipwith can give you a ride."

"Sher—"

"Now!"

Something metal slammed down hard. Seconds later, a pot-bellied deputy exited the room and stormed angrily past Patrick. He paused another beat before knocking.

"Just a minute," came the sharp response. A few moments later Mary Beth swung open the door, dressed in full uniform. She had a nasty, purple bruise on her forehead, a gash under her left eye, and a square-shaped bandage over her collarbone, but her expression was sheer determination, in total ass-kicking mode, until she realized who it was standing there.

"Patrick?" Mary Beth's face melted. She looked around quickly to see if anyone was around, then wrapped him in a desperate embrace. Patrick could hear her softly crying, as though she'd bottled up all the emotion from her near-death experience until that moment and was trying to squeeze it out in one hasty blast.

'I'm so glad you're okay," he said. "I was really worried."

"Me, too." Mary Beth dried her eyes and kissed him. Then he sensed her pull away, emotionally, putting the sheriff mask back on. "Thank you for coming," she said. "But I can't talk now. I've got an emergency to deal with."

"I know."

Mary Beth raised an eyebrow. "You heard about Izzy?"

"Yeah," Patrick said. "Deputy Skipwith told me. But that's not the emergency I'm talking about."

"Huh?"

"Your brother?" Patrick said with an obvious note of indignance. "Sawyer? The deal I offered you?" He tapped his wristwatch. "It's been forty-eight hours. Time's running out."

Mary Beth scoffed. "No offense, but I don't care the least little bit about Sawyer or your deal right now. I need to find Izzy."

"No, what you need to do is arrest your brother before we've got a full scale massacre on our hands."

"Quit being so dramatic."

"It's not drama, Mary. It's reality. I know for a fact that there's a federal task force in route, coming to take your brother down. And you know what the odds are of that ending peacefully if you don't get to him first." Patrick couldn't believe he had to explain this to her.

Mary Beth started down the hall. "You G-men can spend your time however you choose. I've got a missing deputy, a militant biker gang, a blown up courthouse, and about a million other things to worry about."

Patrick moved quickly to catch up to her. "Who do you think blew up the courthouse?"

"Those bikers are the first place I plan to look."

She sped up and Patrick did as well, keeping pace at first, then seizing her arm. "Please just stop and listen."

Mary Beth batted his hand away but she did stop. "This is what I've been trying to tell you," Patrick said. "Your brother is the reason those bikers are here. Even if they are the ones who lit the fuse, your brother is the one who gave them the explosive and put them up to it."

"Horse shit. You're telling me that after thirty-six years of never amounting to a thing, Sawyer's suddenly become this criminal mastermind with a whole network of anarchists ready to do his bidding, and then he decides it'd be a good idea to blow up a building in the middle of his own hometown."

"Basically. Yeah."

"Sorry, pal, but that dog don't hunt."

"That dog don't hunt?" Patrick said, mocking her accent.

"Fuck you." Mary Beth flipped him the bird and continued down the hall.

Patrick caught up to her by the nurses' station, where the charge nurse was listening to a clock radio as she typed on her computer.

"Wait!"

Mary Beth stopped. "What now?" You want to accuse my family of the Kennedy assassination?"

"Just listen for a second."

"I've heard enough."

"Not to me. To Sawyer."

Patrick snatched the radio.

"Excuse me," the nurse said.

Patrick ignored her as he searched for 850 AM. When he found it, the signal was filled with static, but he pumped the volume in time to catch Sawyer's booming baritone talking about a "Great blow for freedom against the evil empire" interspersed with clips of the Talking Heads singing "Burning Down the House." Then Sawyer started shouted like a professional wrestler:

Whoooo! There's more where that came from, baby. Move over Oklahoma City. The buildings are gonna fall like dominos. Sunday Bloody Sunday. Payback's a bitch, bitches.

"That's mine," The nurse said, taking back her radio as the broadcast cut to a clip of "Another One Bite's the Dust."

Patrick could tell by the look on Mary Beth's face that she'd heard enough.

"It's not too late," he said. "You know how these things go.

We'll try negotiating for as long as we can. But the sooner we can get you to talk to Sawyer, the better. If his guys start shooting, all hell could break loose."

Patrick expected a sense of urgency but Mary Beth seemed reflective, like her mind's eye was fixed on something far away.

"What day is it?" she asked.

"Sunday. Why?"

"No. The date."

Patrick had to think about it and checked his phone to be sure. "October eighteenth, why?"

Mary Beth's eyes glistened. "That's what I was afraid of."

"What? Why?"

"That's the day our father was killed."

Patrick was dumbstruck. He knew the story of their father's death, knew it well, almost as if he'd been there. Mary Beth told him all about it years ago. About the pivotal moment of her life that divided all other events into before and after. She was fifteen at the time, charged with watching her little brother, and struggled mightily to hold Sawyer still on the front porch as their father, Oliver Thompson, crossed the yard, hands in the air, to surrender to the DEA agents who had surrounded their home. Sawyer was only eleven but already strong. He got loose and charged across the yard. When their father turned to him, a DEA agent thought Oliver Thompson was making a move. A shot rang out. Sawyer got just close enough for his Transformers T-shirt to get splattered with their father's blood when Oliver fell, dead at the boy's feet.

"There won't be any negotiations," Mary Beth said. "Sawyer will make sure the shooting starts today."

Patrick was chilled by the thought. It froze him, but Mary Beth moved into action.

"You listen to me, very carefully, Patrick Connelly. I want you to get on your phone and call every single person you know in the U.S. Attorney's office, the FBI, ATF, DEA, and the A,B, fucking C. I don't care. Get the Goddamn president on the phone if you have to. Do whatever you can to stop them from moving in on Sawyer's compound. Do you understand me?"

"What are—"

"Do you understand, me? Yes or No?"

"Yes." Patrick said. "But what are you going to do?"

"Whatever I have to."

She tried to leave without another word.

"Wait," Patrick said, reaching for her. "I'm coming with you."

"No! You just hold off the feds. What I've gotta do, I can't have an Assistant U.S. Attorney along for the ride."

Patrick's instincts told him to never let Mary Beth out of his sight again, but the rational part of him told him she was probably right. Bringing him along as an extra emissary into Sawyer's compound was a bad idea. He followed Mary Beth out into the parking lot, watching her mash the lock button on her deputy's key fob until the honking horn led her to the cruiser.

Up until that moment, Patrick was so focused on convincing Mary Beth she needed to intervene with her brother, he hadn't sufficiently considered how difficult that might be or the danger it would put her in. But now, those risks were very much on his mind.

"Do you think he'll listen to you?" he asked as Mary Beth climbed into the cruiser.

"To me? I doubt it. Never has before."

"Then what are you going to do?"

Mary Beth flipped on the lights and siren and shouted her answer. "I'm going to see someone he will listen to."

24

MOUNTAIN FLOWERS was the best-known titty bar in Southern West Virginia. Its billboards littered the highways south of Beckley, showing a big busted woman with daisy tassels, proclaiming the club's talent as "West Virginia's second greatest natural resource," with coal as the presumptive first. Mary Beth's stomach turned every time she saw one of those monstrosities, including the one she passed right before pulling into the strip club's parking lot at speed, gravel flying, as she circled around back where a cluster of trailers overlooked a slurry pond. The folks who came for lap dances went in the front of the club, but Mary Beth knew the real money was made in back, where the patrons could get to know the talent more intimately or pick up a bag of Mamie's Mountain Fescue.

She let her siren blare as she exited her vehicle, sending some nervous Johns scrambling for their pickups. They were followed by two armed security guards who were obviously displeased by the interruption. One was older, tall and bald and held a shotgun by his side. The younger one was short but built like a brick wall. He walked with the slow, strained strut of a serious weightlifter, like he was so muscle bound that every step or casual swing of his arms pained him.

Mary Beth remembered seeing that one wrestle a few years ago, a heavyweight for McCray High who still had the cauliflower ear to prove it. She was sorry to see he'd fallen into this kind of work. Seemed like a good kid. Plus, now he was holding a Glock nine millimeter trained at her forehead, holding it sideways the way they did in the movies, arm all twitchy like it was the first time he'd ever pulled on somebody.

Mary Beth walked straight toward the gun like she hadn't noticed it, more worried about the goon shooting her by accident than anything else. Once she was within spitting distance, she turned to the tall bald man, head pink and freckled, and said with the most pleasant of smiles, "Hey, Tommy, why don't you tether your attack dog over here before I rip his nuts off?"

Tommy, who was some manner of cousin, second or third, maybe once or twice removed—Mary Beth was never really sure—nodded to his partner to lower his piece.

"Jesus, Mary. You can't come storming up here like this. It's bad for business."

"Couldn't be helped," Mary Beth said. "I need to see Mom."

Tommy frowned and motioned past the row of trailers to the backdoor of the club. "She's in the office."

He turned to lead the way. The shorter man fell behind, walking with a wide wrestler's stance until Mary Beth hauled off and kicked him square in the nuts, dropping him like a flour sack.

The man balled up on the ground, whimpering and gasping for air. Mary Beth chicken-winged his thick arm behind him and took his gun. "Don't ever point a gun at an officer of the law, dickweed."

"Goddammit, Mary," Tommy said. "You are so much like your mother."

That was just about the worst thing anybody could ever say

to Mary Beth Cain. "Don't mess with me today, Tommy," she said. "I'm not in a pretty mood."

Mary Beth's mother presented herself as the quintessential southern woman. A silver-haired Scarlett O'Hara, with a syrupy sweet voice that masked the moral compass of a sociopath. "Well, as I live and breathe," she said, looking up from the papers on her desk, peering beneath puffy white bangs. "The prodigal princess has returned. To what do I owe this incredible honor?"

"You raised an idiot son, who just blew up a courthouse," Mary Beth said.

Mamie looked legitimately surprised, even scared for a moment. She held her hand to her mouth, flashing three gaudy diamond rings—one for each of her dead husbands. "Well, I certainly don't know what that has to do with me. Sawyer is his own man. He makes his own decisions. A mother doesn't interfere."

"You're gonna have to, Mom. Do you have any idea what's going to happen to him if the feds get to him before I do? You know all those militia idiots are just creaming their shorts for an End Times battle. I need you to intervene."

Mamie fanned herself with her ring-laden hand. "Sweetheart, you overestimate, me. I don't hold any sway over your brother. He doesn't listen to me any more than you do."

Mary Beth rolled her eyes. "We both know that's not true." The truth was, Sawyer had been such a mama's boy growing up, the kids used to call him "hooter," and joked that he'd been breast fed up through middle school.

Mamie stood and stretched her back. On her desk was an old bank teller's lamp with a green glass shade and a ledger of some type. Mary Beth took notice of the book and a map on the wall of McCray County covered with push-pins. Mamie closed the book and pulled the lamp's black chain. "Tell me exactly what it is you think I can do."

"I need you to call him. Or, however it is you keep in touch with him. Tell him we're coming up there. Tell him to tell all his jackass friends not to shoot at us when we do. I'm sure they're all on edge right now and I don't want to get shot before you and I have a chance to sit down with Sawyer and get him to listen to reason."

Mamie sighed and sat back down. She studied her rings as she spoke. "Let's just say I was to do this for you. What's in it for me?"

"You mean other than saving your son's life?"

"Well, you're planning to arrest him, aren't you? A mother can't be expected to just turn her child over. To think, of my son, my baby, wasting away in a prison cell, and you expect me to just—"

"Cut the bullshit, Mom. What do you want?"

Mamie's eyes revealed a flash of the same maniacal glare she used to get while laying into Mary Beth with a switch for one of her many perceived insolents as a child. But Mamie quickly recovered her control and smiled sweetly. "It seems to me, dearest, that circumstances require us to renegotiate our little arrangement—our armistice, as you like to call it."

"What are you talking about?"

"Oh, let's not be coy, Mary Elizabeth. Ever since you became sheriff, I have abided by your rules. Kept my business outside of Jasper County. Made sure no drugs got in there, save for a little old harmless weed here and there. Even provided you with valuable information about the unsavory criminal element in your midst."

"You mean you've used me to take out your competition."

"No, I mean we used each other, dear. It has truly been a beautiful partnership in many respects. And one in which I have paid great deference to your rather impolite insistence upon certain...boundaries. But the times, they are a'changin."

Mary Beth felt her stomach growl—her body clock was telling her it was already well past lunch and she was about to eat a shit sandwich. "Can we just get on with whatever inappropriate request you're about to make?"

Mamie, gaped, hand over heart. "This is none of my doing, sweetheart. But as a result of forces far beyond my control, our longstanding arrangement, which has been so mutually beneficial, will soon be impossible."

"How so?"

"The annexation, of course. Should be finalized any day. And once it is, it won't be possible for me to keep my business interests within the boundaries of McCray County once those boundary lines disappear, and it formally becomes part of your jurisdiction."

Mary Beth groaned. This was a reality she'd been avoiding for weeks. Now here it was, staring at her with a wide toxic smile, despite the stiffness of Mamie's overly-Botoxed face.

Her mother approached, standing close enough that her flowery, old-lady perfume made Mary Beth's eyes water.

"What do you propose?" Mary Beth asked. "That I just turn a blind eye to crime in my own county? Maybe go on your payroll? Become your unofficial enforcer, arresting anyone who crosses you? Actually, become the crooked cop they all think I am?"

"Would it kill you to finally contribute something to the family business?"

"It killed Dad."

Whack! Mamie slapped Mary Beth hard across the face.

"You have always unfairly blamed me for your father's demise," she said. "He was a grown man who made his own choices too."

The sting of Mary Beth's cheek was nothing compared to how the slap instantly transported her back to childhood when she was the headstrong little girl under her mother's dominating thumb. It took her a moment to remind herself she wasn't a kid anymore. She was the Sheriff of Jasper County, by God, and it was high time she showed her mother who was boss.

Mary Beth seized Mamie by the neck, put a boot behind her mother's high-heel and trip-slammed the old woman to the ground.

"Yeah, he made his own choices," Mary Beth said as she squeezed her mother's throat, not hard enough to asphyxiate but plenty hard to make an impression. "Just like you're giving me a choice right now. Just like the way you've always manipulated people into doing what you want them to do. No matter what it does to them. You'd turn your own daughter into a criminal just to make some money."

Mamie spat in Mary Beth's face. A gooey loogie that caught her right between the eyes. Mary Beth recoiled and the crusty bitch came up off the floor with a vicious head butt that busted the sheriff's nose wide open.

"Jesus Christ!" Mary Beth grabbed her nose with both hands and rolled onto her back.

"You little ingrate," Mamie yelled. "Everything I have ever done has been for my family."

The old woman retrieved a soft leather handbag from the corner of the desk and began whipping Mary Beth with it like a flail, until the sheriff kicked her mother's legs out from under her. Mary Beth climbed back on top and each grabbed a wad of the other's hair.

That was when Mary Beth learned her mother wore a wig.

The white tresses came free of Mamie's scalp, revealing a wispy thinning head of limp hair like wilted lettuce. Mamie's insane glare was back as she viciously yanked at Mary Beth's strawberry-blonde curls. Mary Beth screamed, then reared back a balled-fist and was about to put the old girl out of her misery when Cousin Tommy and the wrestler came charging into the room and pulled the women apart.

"You, absolute horror of a human being!" Mary Beth shouted as Tommy restrained her.

"I am not going anywhere with you," Mamie said. "Tommy, get her out of here."

Cousin Tommy dragged Mary Beth toward the door, but she put her arms and legs out like a starfish at the threshold. "Wait!" she said, panting. "Mama, Sawyer is gonna die, along with a lot of other folks if we don't get him to surrender."

Mamie was busy repositioning her wig. "Unlike you," she said, "your brother actually cares about his family. If he's taking a stand against the government that murdered your father, then I'm proud of what he's doing. I won't lift one finger to stop him."

The window of opportunity was closing. Mary Beth could feel it. Then Mamie opened it just a crack.

"But," she said. "I could be persuaded to do one thing for you."

Mary Beth jerked free of Tommy's grip and wiped the blood from her nose. "What?"

"I won't try to turn Sawyer from his course. And I don't think anyone can, mind you. But I do have it within my power to get a message to him. And I can guarantee you safe passage into his compound. So, if you want to talk to him, I will afford you that opportunity."

"Thank you," Mary Beth said. "At least—"

"If—" her mother raised a finger. "You agree to my terms. Free rein in Jasper County."

Mary Beth didn't want to ever see her mother again, much less give her carte blanche, but she was stuck between a rock and a hard place. "Weed and whores," she said. "But that's it. I catch you with anything heavier than that, I bust you. And, if anybody gets seriously roughed up or killed, you're going to personally hand the goons over to me on a silver platter, complete with a signed confession."

"You can't make a living off weed alone," Mamie complained. "It could all be legal any day now. You've got to let me branch out. Meth is doing really well, heroin is coming back in a big way, oxy is—."

"Stop! Just stop." Mary Beth couldn't believe she was having this conversation. "I'll give you oxy."

Mamie smiled.

"But," Mary Beth added. "You're gonna take ten percent of your earnings from it and use it to build an opioid addiction clinic."

"Five percent," Mamie said.

"Done."

"Done," Mamie said, then added as sweetly as a beauty contestant dreaming of world peace, "I'll get them at both ends."

Mary Beth shook her head in disgust. "Just make the call."

25

IZZY HAD BEEN in the dark so long he couldn't tell if he was awake or dreaming when he first heard the sounds of the elevator descending. He was pretty sure it was real, however, when it crashed to the ground and Hawlings came stomping toward them, flashlight swinging, and kicked Bailey in the side.

"This is your last chance, you son of a bitch. I want to know the truth," Hawlings said.

Bailey rolled over from where he'd been resting on his sizable stomach. "I'll tell it to Sawyer," he said.

"Sawyer doesn't give a shit," Hawlings told him. "I just got the word back from the big man, himself. Says he doesn't give a fuck why Gray's dead. That I should just stop bringing food down here and let you die like the rat that you are."

That news got Bailey to sit up.

"Oh, I've got your attention now?" Hawlings sounded different than Izzy had heard him before. Scared. Desperate. "You know I don't want this," Hawlings continued. "But you either tell me what really happened with Gray, or I can't help you, or your son."

The word "son" was the last prod Bailey needed to finally start talking. "You wouldn't."

"Wouldn't what? Tell my brothers in arms that your boy Jason is the one who off'd Gray? You bet your ass I would."

Bailey kicked up a cloud of coal dust as he reached in vane for Hawlings. His right wrist was still cuffed to the continuous miner machine, and though Bailey was clearly a strong man, there was no way he could free himself, short of pulling his hand off. "Goddammit, Hawlings!" he growled. "You know my boy. You know he's a good kid but he's not smart. Anything he did was what he was told to do."

"So you admit it?" Hawlings said.

"Shit, yes, fine, I admit it. But it was an accident. He was just supposed to put a scare into Gray, rough him up a little, and things got out of hand."

"So, what?" Hawlings asked. "He set the fire to cover his tracks?"

Hawlings flashlight centered on Bailey's forehead as it nodded up and down.

"And then he called you to come and clean it up for him, am I right?"

"Something like that," Bailey mumbled.

"So, that just brings us back around to the real question," Hawlings said. "Who's the shotcaller? Who sent your boy in there to do the deed?"

Bailey bowed his back, drawing another line in the sand. "That's the piece Sawyer needs to know. And I'll be more than happy to tell him as soon as you take me to see him."

"I can't!" Hawlings shouted. "Nobody's getting in to see Sawyer. Not with everything going on. We just found out one of the bikers he let in was working with the feds. He had a satellite phone on him and was sending them pictures. Now Sawyer's paranoid as hell. Will only see the top guys. But if you'll just tell me what really went down with Gray, maybe I can help you."

Izzy thought that offer actually made some sense but Bailey refused to say anything else.

Eventually, Hawlings threw up his arms. "Fine," he said, storming off toward the elevator. "At least I tried."

Izzy wanted to call out to him as he left. He wished there was something he could say to make Hawlings stay, or more importantly, to convince him to take them up too, but he had nothing.

"They're going to let us die down here," Izzy said to Bailey as the elevator began its ascent.

"Maybe."

"No, they will. And it's all for nothing too. I know you think you're protecting your son, but Hawlings knows he's the one who killed Gray. Maybe they don't know why, but Hawlings will tell them it was Jason, and they'll eventually get to your boy. You aren't protecting shit."

"That's where you're wrong," Bailey said. "My boy is protected. That's precisely why Sawyer is the only one who can know who sent Jason in there to rough up Gray. If I told anyone else, I'm afraid he might kill me just to shut me up."

"Sounds to me like we're ending up dead no matter what then."

"It is starting to look that way," Bailey admitted.

"Well, do you think maybe you can share it with me, finally? We don't have anything else to do other than wait around for the rats to eat us."

Izzy was about to say that he was pretty certain Hawlings wasn't coming back, but was surprised by a sound above. The elevator was reversing course, growing louder. Minutes later, it crashed to the mine floor and four men with spotlights and machine guns poured out. Before Izzy knew what was happening, he and Bailey were being uncuffed from the continuous minor machine, then handcuffed together and ushered on weary, tingling legs into the elevator.

Both were far too weak to resist their captors with anything more than curses. Bailey's body had gone so limp, he actually leaned against the metal mesh wall of the elevator to support his weight.

"Where are you taking us?" Izzy asked, realizing as soon as he said it, that he almost didn't care. As long as he got to see the sun again, he would be happy, at least momentarily, for whatever this was.

The only response to his questions came from one of the guards who said, "Sawyer's a man of his word."

When they reached the surface, the sunlight burned Izzy's eyes but he was glad for it all the same. Even with tightly closed lids, he could feel its warmth wrapping him in a lustrous hug. Then he and Bailey were yanked from the elevator and marched a short distance. Izzy squinted enough to know they were surrounded by men in fatigues who forced them to their knees next to another prisoner, one of the bikers, in his greasy jeans and leather jacket. That other man was barrel-chested and breathing rapidly, panting like a dog, his white T-shirt covered with blood and sweat stains.

"I tried my best to prevent this, Sheriff," Hawlings said. "But Sawyer is a man of his word. And he said that if you ever showed your face up here again, he'd put a bullet in your brain. This is your last chance. Maybe if you tell them the truth, Quiet Clem here will have mercy on you. Tell them it wasn't you who done it. Tell them it was—"

Bailey, who moments earlier was so weak he couldn't stand, found the strength to charge wildly at his captors. He howled like a mountain cat, dragging Izzy, who was cuffed to him, like a rag doll. But Bailey barely made it a couple of steps before a revolver exploded. Bailey fell forward, twisted, and landed on his back. Izzy came down on top of him, his head sagging into Bailey's midsection. When Izzy pulled up, he opened his eyes long enough to see Bailey's blank stare.

"Christ, Clem!" Hawlings yelled. "I said you didn't have to kill him. We'd have got the truth out of him."

A haunting voice responded, one that was both deep and whispery, like James Earl Jones with laryngitis. "Sawyer's a man of his word."

Izzy gazed up at who he assumed was Quiet Clem, and saw a real life giant, taller even than Bailey had been, probably seven feet, with a blockish head and Caesar-style haircut that looked like it should come with neck bolts.

"Now we'll never know who it was who had Gray killed," Hawlings complained.

"There are more important things. Much to do," the giant said. He handed his gun over to Hawlings. "You take care of the other one."

Izzy assumed they were talking about him but Hawlings stepped past to the third man, the biker, who'd been kneeling with them in the dirt.

"Okay, Quigley," Hawlings said. "Got any last words?"

The biker was breathing so heavily it was hard for him to speak. "Nothing that will make a difference," he managed.

Hawlings said, "Well, you know what they say: Snitches get stitches, but a spy has got to die." His hand jumped from the hard report of the gun as it fired.

Izzy closed his eyes as the man fell on the other side of him. They were dropping like dominoes and Izzy was the only one left.

"Good," Clem said.

"What about the Jasper deputy?" Hawlings asked. "Can't leave any witnesses, right?"

Izzy looked up at the two men discussing his fate, feeling like a goldfish examining the world from the confines of an aquarium. Utterly helpless. Everything surreal and distorted. Then the giant looked down at him and said, "He comes with us. Sawyer has other plans for him."

BY THE TIME Mary Beth left Mountain Flowers, men in ATF and FBI windbreakers were already setting up roadblocks five miles out from Old Wengo and she saw assault vehicles being hauled in on the back of carrier trucks. She could probably have talked her way past the government's barrier, but there was no time to waste on red tape, so she commandeered a four-wheeler from Cousin Tommy and hit the mountain trails.

Ten minutes later she spotted a rifle tower in the distance just as she caught some air of an incline. She crashed down to earth, cut through a stand of pine trees, and maxed out the throttle. Either Mamie had made the call, telling Sawyer's guys not to shoot, or she hadn't. Either way, Mary Beth didn't want to slow down.

She made it all the way to the mine's front gate without a shot fired. Four men with M-16s were there to greet her when she did. The weaponry didn't surprise Mary Beth, but the men's appearance did. She'd expected a bunch of tatted up skinheads with "Born to Lose" written all over their faces. Nothing like these guys who were clean cut, respectable looking, middle-aged dorks turned weekend warriors. She was pretty sure that one of them was the pharmacist at her local Walgreens.

He was the one who said, "Ma'am, we'd better get you inside," then insisted upon relieving Mary Beth of her side arm. She gave it up without a fight, happy that they didn't bother to pat her down and didn't find the backup gun she kept holstered above her left ankle.

"I need to see, Sawyer," she said.

"We know," the pharmacist said. "Follow me."

He directed Mary Beth to park her four-wheeler inside the gate, then had her hop onto the back of a pickup truck where she rode with two of the armed guards through a community preparing for a siege. Everywhere Mary Beth looked, throngs of men and women were busily readying munitions; mostly military grade stuff, rocket launchers and mounted guns behind semicircles of sand bags, along with a plethora of hunting rifles and homemade weapons like long sharpened sticks and stores of Molotov cocktails. They also passed by a haphazardly constructed playground where Mary Beth counted at least thirty children who all appeared under the age of ten. Her eyes fixed on an auburn-haired girl, not yet a teenager, who'd been left in charge and was trying her best to mother the little ones, telling them to "slow down," and "stop that."

Dear God, Mary Beth thought. She really needed to get to Sawyer.

Eventually, they approached a square block building that backed up to the mountainside, atop of which Sawyer's radio tower and satellite dishes were perched.

A burst of automatic gunfire popped off in the distance, followed by shouts about federal scouts in the woods. A series or air raid sirens sounded and women dressed in camo and hunter orange scurried throughout the compound.

"All hell's about to break loose," the pharmacist said as he offered his hand to help Mary Beth down from the truck. He and his friends quickly ushered her into the building and into an ante room filled with more militia men, though these were dressed in black—a sign of status, as Sawyer's special guards. They took possession of Mary Beth from there and whisked her down a narrow hallway to a backroom with a vault-like door.

As the guard worked the multiple locks, Mary Beth wondered what she'd find on the other side. It had been several years since she'd seen her brother. The last time was at a miserable Thanksgiving dinner where Sawyer quoted the Gospel of Luke, about how, "No prophet is accepted in his hometown," in response to Mary Beth declaring just how utterly full of shit he was. And that all happened during the blessing. It only went downhill from there.

Mary Beth never could understand how anybody could follow Sayer. To her, He'd always be that pimple-nosed kid with a stack of Hustlers under his bed. But as the vault door swung open, and she saw him seated at his desk, surrounded by disciples, with a light from a rear window framing him like a halo, Mary Beth had to admit that with his long hair and beard, Sawyer did kind of resemble a blonde-haired, blue-eyed Jesus. If the Messiah had been a raging narcissist degenerate with a bloodlust for guns and chicanery.

Sawyer smiled when he looked up, revealing the front tooth he'd chipped falling off their grandmother's tire swing as a kid. "What in God's name are you doing here?" he asked.

"Trying to save your dumb ass."

"Boys," Sawyer said, "why don't y'all give me and my sister a minute alone?"

The men did as they were told. As they filed out of the room, Mary Beth took note of the bizarre collection of portraits adorning the wall, and tried to figure out what kind of mismatched philosophy a lunatic like Sawyer had woven together, hero-worshipping icons as diverse as Churchill and Che. She also thought about getting the drop on her brother and ending things quickly. She still had her little Beretta holstered to her ankle, but Sawyer was decked out in a bulletproof vest and had a Mac-10 machine gun slung around his shoulder. There was no way she could draw down on him and win, even if she was capable of shooting him. And, as much as the son-of-a-bitch had it coming, Mary Beth was still pretty sure that was a line she couldn't cross.

"So, you're a domestic terrorist now, huh?" she asked once she and her brother were alone. "That'll make a nice addition to the resumé."

"One man's terrorist is another man's freedom fighter," Sawyer said.

"Well, I'm not a man. And you sure as hell aren't a freedom fighter. You're a criminal, is what you are, Sawyer. Blowing up buildings?"

Sawyer waved her off her. "Oh, sure, now that the government's run by a bunch of socialists, and good God-fearing patriots gotta resort to drastic measures, it's something terrible. But back in the sixties when hippies were blowing shit up, or when Antifa goes around looting, then it's just freedom of speech. It all boils down to power, Sis. Who's disenfranchised and dispossessed."

Mary Beth rolled her eyes. "Sawyer, you are a white, heterosexual, Christian male. On what fucking planet, are you disenfranchised and dispossessed?"

"This one," Sawyer said. "This one right here, where that's the one demographic everybody's allowed to shit on."

Mary Beth started bowing an invisible violin. "My God," she said, "that sounds like a Dickens novel."

"Tell me it ain't true, though."

"Listen, little brother. I know you, okay? I used to change your diapers. And I'm telling you, you aren't *disenfranchised*. You're just pissed off. You feel like the world owed you something you never got, and you've wasted your whole sad life searching for somebody to blame for it. "

Sawyer took a step back. "For you of all people to say that to me. Like you don't know what today is."

Mary Beth felt a little of the guilt that normally crept in where Sawyer was concerned, but resolved to push it down. "Of course, I know," she said. "I was standing right there with you when Daddy died. And I've got the same blood running through my veins as you do. But I didn't use what happened as an excuse to be a shithead."

Sawyer scoffed. "We may be blood but we didn't exactly grow up the same, though, did we?"

There it was. Sawyer's trump card. The thing he always held over her head. The fact she got to go live with her paternal grandparents in Jasper Creek after their father died, while Sawyer stayed home, alone, with their mother.

"You know," Sawyer said, "instead of lecturing me, you should be joining me. We're on the right side of history here, Susie Q. We're honoring Daddy's memory."

Mary Beth chuckled, sarcastically. "Daddy wasn't Randy Weaver. And he sure as hell wasn't David Koresh. He was a drug dealer, plain and simple," she said, though it still hurt her to admit it. "I loved him more than anything. But there was nothing noble about the way he lived or died. He was always on the wrong side of the law, and it caught up to him. Just like it's about to catch up to you."

Sawyer spat on the ground. He looked furious, his eyes ablaze. "Daddy was a fucking farmer. He sold his crops just like every man has a right to. Shit, weed's been growing wild in this country since before there was a country. Until some busybodies in Washington, decided it was *ill*-legal and a man, he can't make a living. Then, just like the coal barons, they send their fucking gun thugs down here to shoot him tombstone dead right in front of his goddamn wife and kids. That's the fucking government you work for."

Sawyer moved close, and Mary Beth thought for a moment he was going to hit her. Instead he grabbed her and spun her around to stare at the portraits lining the wall. "You know what all of these people have in common?"

"A lot less than you realize, I suspect."

"That's what you would think. They don't fit into the nice little boxes you like to put people in. But what you don't realize is that all these folks were freedom fighters. They were all trying to repel an imperial force. And that's exactly what I'm doing."

Mary Beth shook her head in disgust.

"I'm serious," Sawyer said. "I bet you expected to see a bunch of crazy skinheads up here, didn't you? And, okay, we got a few. We got some racists. We got some bigots. Just like everybody else. But we're building a broad coalition of people who just want the government to leave them the fuck alone. Quit imposing their misguided *morals* on everybody. We got schoolteachers, dentists, shop owners, little old church ladies who work soup kitchens on the weekends but are sick of seeing their government fund Medicaid abortions. We got pacifists who don't want their tax money paying for foreign wars over oil."

"Are those pacifists the ones up in the gun towers?" Mary Beth asked.

"No. They're the ones who insisted we wait until the courthouse was closed before we staged our little demonstration."

"Demonstration? People died! I almost died!"

"That was unintended," Sawyer insisted. "The building was supposed to be empty so we could show the world how quick your government would be to come up here and try to slaughter all of us, just to avenge a pile of bricks. Everyone up here is willing to die to expose those evil bastards."

Mary Beth was concerned he might have a point. On her way up, she'd glimpsed the firepower the government was amassing.

But she wasn't buying Sawyer's man-of-the-people schtick. She knew how selfish he was. As a kid, she'd twice caught him lifting money from the church offering plate. There was no way he'd set this whole thing up to become a blood sacrifice.

"I just have a tough time buying into your anti-government crusade," Mary Beth said. "Because ten minutes ago, it was about technology. A year ago, it was Muslims. Before that it was gay marriage. Some days it's about the coal companies or nine-eleven being an inside job. The only thing that's consistent about you, Sawyer, is you're crazy and hateful, and you want everyone else to feel as bad as you do."

Sawyer snickered. "Mama always said you were a sanctimonious little shit."

"Yeah, and she said you were so frustrating you could make a preacher cuss."

"Guess she had us both pegged, then."

"This isn't a joke, Sawyer. You do know I came here to arrest you, right?"

"You and what army?"

"How about the army out there that's ready to rush in here and squash you like a bug. If you actually care anything about your people, you'll come with me now. Surrender before anyone gets hurt."

Sawyer rolled his head from side to side. "Listen," he said. I told Ma I'd let you in and hear you out, but that's it. I've got absolutely no plans of going quietly."

"Don't think I can't still kick your ass," Mary Beth said through gritted teeth.

Sawyer laughed. "As much fun as it would be to see you try, I think it's time we get down to business. Don't you want to know why I agreed to let you in here?"

Mary Beth was surprised by the question. "Why?" she asked.

Sawyer grinned devilishly, then stuck two fingers in his mouth and whistled like a horse trainer. "Oh, Clementine," he yelled. A giant man entered the room and dead panned in a raspy voice, "You rang?"

Mary Beth felt a chill of recognition. Quiet Clem had been Sawyer's best friend when they were kids. He lived down the road with his horribly abusive, alcoholic parents, and spent as much time as he could in the Thompsons' home. But Mary Beth hadn't seen Clem since he was a boy and he'd grown at least a foot and a half since then. Her instinct was actually to go and hug him, but he held up a hand.

"Wait."

"Yeah, wait, Sis. Show her what you brought with you, Clemmy."

Quiet Clem had a tablet device that he switched on and turned toward Mary Beth.

If seeing Clem had given Mary Beth a chill, what he showed her next, froze her down to her soul. It was Izzy, on a live feed somewhere inside the compound, handcuffed and blind-folded, as a man in an executioner's hood stood over him wielding a sawed off shotgun.

"The reason I let you in here is that I want you to have to sit and watch as this whole thing goes down, knowing there's not a goddamn thing you can do to stop it," Sawyer said. Then he did a bad impression of Tony Montana, from *Scarface*, warning Mary Beth, "Or else, say goo-bye to your leetle friend."

27

THEY DON'T TEACH you this in law school, Patrick thought as an ATF agent walked him and U.S. Attorney John Jensen up a wooded hillside past a convoy of Bradley Fighting Vehicles to where a command tent had been set up. The special agent in charge was an FBI man named Dennis Lange who, according to Jensen, had a reputation as a flamethrower, a shoot-first-and-ask-questions-later kind of guy. The fact that he'd been assigned to the operation meant the government was not playing games. They wanted a message sent to the booming patriot movements across the country that their nonsense would no longer be tolerated.

When they entered the tent, Lange was seated behind a card table covered with photos, receiving a briefing from other agents and a commander in military fatigues. Lange was a trim man but with a pudgy-face and sagging jowls, like he'd lost an extreme amount of weight recently and the elasticity of his skin had yet to rebound. His attire was a mix of bureaucrat and warrior, a collared shirt and tie beneath body armor. When Lange spoke, he had a real master and commander persona, addressing his team with the clipped efficiency of a field marshal, answering and asking questions with just one word. "Affirmative," "acknowledged," "report," "downside?" "alternatives?"

After standing there long enough to make things awkward, Jensen cleared his throat. Lange looked up at them. "These the lawyers?"

"Yes, sir," said the ATF agent who'd escorted them there.

Jensen extended his hand. "U.S. Attorney John Jensen. Southern District of West Virginia. And this is AUSA Patrick Connelly from DC. It was his informant who sent us photo confirmation of the fully automatic weapons and incendiary devices they have stockpiled in there."

"I saw that in the warrant affidavit," Lange said. He shook Jensen's hand in a way that gave Patrick the distinct feeling he was annoyed by their presence.

Patrick, wanting to prove his relevance, added, "My informant also confirmed that Sawyer's top lieutenant, the man they call Quiet Clem, is the one who ordered the courthouse bombing."

Lange still looked unimpressed. "Thompson's already taken responsibility for the bombing in multiple broadcasts."

"There's more, though," Patrick said. "A local sheriff. Thompson's sister, she's—"

Lange raised a hand to silence him. "I've heard. We'll get to that in a minute, okay? But we're still getting our bearings. You gentlemen caught us in the middle of a briefing. You can listen in if you want, but hang back for a few minutes. Then I want to hear all about this sheriff."

The agent in charge returned to his table, covered with what Patrick could now see were aerial photographs of the Old Wengo Mine.

The army officer pointed to them, and said, "Basic siege warfare. Their defenses are all focused around the fenceline, which they've reinforced with a series of concrete barriers. But they're weak right up the gut. We could neutralize their gun towers from the air, then crash the Bradley's in through the front gate and form a horseshoe perimeter to provide cover for our men who would come in behind. By doing that, we'd have the bulk of their people penned into shooting galleries on either side. Then it would just be a matter of clearing the dozen or so buildings. We hit them one at a time. Tear gas to drive them out, then flash bang hand grenades followed by SWAT teams to clear out the stragglers."

"Good," Lange said. "How many inside, total?"

"Estimate is three hundred."

"Children?"

"Forty. Maybe fifty."

Lange nodded as though that was an acceptable number. "Make sure all our men have their blood types written on their arms or neck to help with emergency transfusions."

Jesus, Patrick thought. This wasn't a police raid they were planning, it was a military assault. "Whoa, whoa, whoa," he said. "Aren't you going to try and negotiate a peaceful surrender."

Lange gave him an annoyed look. "We've already announced our presence and our men have been shot at. I've got an agent wounded."

"But—"

"Hold on," Lange said. "I'm still going to give negotiations a try, of course, but first I want a show of force. We're going to move into position. Let them see the firepower they're facing. And if negotiations prove ineffective or I determine that they're merely being used as a stalling tactic, then we need to be ready to go. The last thing I want is Sawyer Thompson finding a way to escape."

"Is that really worse than killing hundreds of people?" Patrick asked.

Lange turned red-faced. He leaned forward with a response ready to go but caught himself. "Gentlemen," he said, this time referring to his advisers. "Go ahead and get your people in position. I need a moment alone with the lawyers."

The command tent cleared out until it was just Patrick, John Jensen and Lange remaining. "Have a seat," the Special Agent said, seeming calmer now that there was no one left he needed to impress.

Jensen sat in one of the director's chairs arranged around the table.

"I think I'd rather stand," Patrick said. He was appalled by the whole scene. He'd marched up that hill expecting to find Elliot Ness and instead discovered General Patton.

"Please," Lange said. "Have a seat."

Patrick relented and plopped down next to Jensen.

Lange took out a pipe and a box of matches. "You mind?"

Both attorneys responded that they did not. Lange struck the match, sucked in the fire and told them about how he'd cut his teeth working the Oklahoma City bombing and how, in his mind, what had transpired there in McCray County was a hundred times more dangerous. "Back then," he said, "there were maybe fifty, sixty thousand members of militia movements across the country. Now there's twenty times that. And millions more who sympathize. Anti-government sentiment is at an all-time high. Q-anon crazies and every other fucking thing. All disgruntled and disturbed. And this Thompson's becoming their crown prince, like the dark lord of the dark web, tying them altogether. The guy stands for nothing and everything all at once. Trust me, gents. We need to put this fire out now before it burns out of control. Otherwise, we'll be endangering a lot more than three hundred people."

"But surely—"

"Look," Lange said, cutting Patrick off. "I'm not saying we won't try for a peaceful surrender. I told you that. But I don't mind telling you that I'm not overly optimistic." Lange took another puff off his pipe and sat it on the table. "Now, with all that said, tell me about your girl."

"Her name is Sheriff Mary Beth Cain," Patrick said.

"And she's Sawyer Thompson's sister?"

"She is," Jensen answered. "But we've got significant leverage over her. My office was preparing to indict her on a number of public corruption charges, and we've offered to let all of that go if she can bring Thompson in peacefully."

"Okay," Lange said. "So, where is she?"

Patrick and Jensen looked at each other. Patrick said, "We aren't sure."

"You aren't sure?"

Patrick shifted in his chair, wishing he had something more definitive but he'd been unable to reach Mary Beth since they last parted, and none of her deputies had heard from her either. He was worried sick about her, as well as his informant, Quigley, who had also failed to check in.

"Cell service is pretty spotty out here," he said. "But Mary— er, Sheriff Cain, was determined to get to her brother the last time we spoke a few hours ago. She's probably in there already. I've got no doubt she'll come through, if we can just give her some time."

"How much time?"

That was a good question. Patrick looked to Jensen for help but the U.S. attorney was staring at his shoes.

"Listen guys," Lange said, "if we can't get confirmation that she's either in route or already in that compound, then I've got to move. We don't even know for sure that Thompson's still in there. He could be halfway to Mexico by now. Meanwhile, our evidence is getting destroyed while we're sitting out here playing with our dicks."

Patrick said, "If you're worried about ripple effects, the worst thing you could do is storm that complex and make Thompson into a martyr. If this turns into another Waco—"

"It won't," Lange said. "Because the problem with Waco was they farted around for a month before finally doing what they should have done from the beginning. I'm not making that mistake. We're going to mobilize atop this hill, give them one chance to surrender and if they don't, then we're going in. Period."

"But Mary?" Patrick couldn't help the desperate raise in his voice.

Lange picked up on it. "As far as I'm concerned, your Mary is a ghost at this point. Unless you can confirm that she's actually in there talking to her brother."

Patrick grimaced. Over the last hour he'd been debating whether to risk another attempt to contact Quigley, to see if he knew whether Mary Beth made it to Sawyer.

"My informant might be able to confirm it," he said, reluctantly. "But he hasn't made contact in a while. I usually text him a question mark and then he calls back as soon as he can. I don't want to risk calling but—"

Jensen interrupted this time. "At this point it might be worth the risk," he said.

Patrick looked from Jensen to Lange. Both were in silent agreement. Patrick took a deep breath. He knew a direct call to Quigley could get him killed. But, then again, if he couldn't confirm Mary Beth was inside the compound, not calling Quigley might mean hundreds of deaths. He pulled out his satellite phone and dialed the number.

It rang eight times. Patrick counted them and was about to hang up when someone answered.

"Quigley?"

A deep, raspy voice responded, saying, "There is no Quigley."

28

QUIET CLEM HANDED the phone to Sawyer. "There's an Agent Lange, who'd like to speak with you."

A wicked grin spread across Sawyer's face. He snatched the phone and said, "Domino's pizza. Will this be for pickup or delivery? Oh, Sawyer Thompson? I'm sorry, Sawyer's busy right now. He's getting his dick sucked by your mama. You take her easy."

Sawyer flipped the phone on the desk. "Well," he said, "looks like negotiations have failed."

"Sawyer, please," Mary Beth pleaded. "Listen to reason."

Her little brother winked at her, then said to Quiet Clem. "Time to give the Sons of Anarchy their marching orders. Go find that big dumb, bald-headed son-of-a-bitch. What's his name? Nemo or something."

"Nico," Clem said.

"Yeah, right. Finding Nico. Well, find his dumb ass and tell him it's time for them to start their engines. It's about to go down. Any minute now the feds are going to come charging through those gates, gun blazing. When they do, I want that hoard of bikers to zoom around behind and close them in. Shut the door, so to speak. The G-men can come in, but they can't leave. You got me?" Clem nodded. "Good, now get. Oh, and send Hawlings in here. He's been so anxious to talk to me. Now's his chance."

Quiet Clem exited the room as another man, half his size and twice his age entered.

"Uncle Jimmy?" Mary Beth was shocked to see her uncle there, carrying his sniper rifle in one hand and rubbing his face with the other, like he just woke up.

"Nice of you to show," Sawyer said. "You nearly slept through the damn revolution."

"Sorry," Jimmy said. "Raelynn snuck my meds back in on me. Took me a couple days to clear my head."

Mary Beth's head was spinning, too. This was turning into the worst family reunion ever. And considering her kin, that was really saying something.

Deputy Hawlings then entered the room. His eyes immediately fixed on Mary Beth. "Sheriff?"

"Clooney."

Sawyer said, "Well, ain't this sweet—we got the whole band back together. Speaking of which, Hawlings, I believe you owe my uncle an apology."

The deputy removed his hat. "Yeah, Mr. Jimmy. I sure am sorry. If I'd a known you were a Brother of the Cause, we wouldn't have come to your house bothering you the other day. I—"

Jimmy stopped him. "Yeah, if I'd a known you was in with Sawyer, I wouldn't have shot at you."

"No harm done," Hawlings said.

They were interrupted by a blast of static from the walkie clipped to Sawyer's belt, followed by a report that the government convoy was moving up the road and would be at the front gates any minute.

"Alright," Sawyer said. "No time for kumbayas. Uncle Jimmy,

I wanted you and Hawlings to meet because it turns out you were right. Elwood Gray was murdered, just like you said, and Deputy Hawlings here found the proof."

Uncle Jimmy slapped his knee. "By God, I knew it!" Then he jabbed an accusatory finger at Mary Beth. "And you thought I was crazy."

"She was just covering for her boy in blue," Sawyer said. "Get this, Uncle Jimmy. It was Sheriff Bailey who murdered him."

"Son of a bitch," Jimmy said. "I knew the law here was crooked."

Hawlings tried to interject but Sawyer overruled him. "I said, Bailey's the one who off'd him. And that's all there is to it. The sentence has already been passed, Uncle Jimmy. Justice has been served. That fat sheriff's eaten his last happy meal."

Mary Beth could see that Hawlings disagreed but wasn't willing to go against Sawyer.

One of the militia men in black stuck his head in. He was wearing a thick set of headphones, like maybe he was the radio producer. "It's time, sir," he said.

Sawyer gave him a thumb's up. "Be right there. Hawlings, you and Uncle Jimmy keep an eye on Lucy Law-And-Order for me while I go make my final broadcast."

"Sawyer—" Mary Beth moved to try and stop her brother from leaving, but he held up the tablet with the video feed of Izzy held hostage. It stopped Mary Beth in her tracks. Sawyer got on his radio. "Charlie, do me a favor and put your shotgun up to that little deputy's head."

The man in the executioner's mask did as he was told. Izzy, though blindfolded, could obviously feel the double barrels pressed against his temple. There was no audio, but Mary Beth could see Izzy mouth what looked to be The Lord's Prayer.

"Please, no!"

"You gonna behave yourself?" Sawyer asked.

Mary Beth gritted her teeth and mumbled.

"What was that? Didn't quite hear you?"

"Yes," she said.

"Good. Then have a seat."

Mary Beth dropped onto one of the metal folding chairs by Sawyer's desk. Her brother handed a spare walkie to Hawlings. "If she gets ornery with you, tell Charlie to go ahead and kill her friend. Got it?"

"Got it," Hawlings said.

"Good man." Sawyer slapped the McCray deputy on the back and went to leave before turning back to address Mary Beth one last time. "By the way, Sis, in case I don't get a chance to tell you later: it sure was good seeing you again."

A cold October wind whipped through the command tent as Patrick and Jensen watched Special Agent Lange, awaiting his reaction. They'd been sitting close enough to hear how Sawyer Thompson had mocked him and were expecting an immediate outburst, but Lange seemed to be experiencing a slow boil. He looked from the satellite phone to the pipe smoking in his other hand.

"Well," Patrick asked. "What are we going to do?"

Lange gently placed the phone down on the table. "Mr. Thompson thinks this is funny," he said. "We are going to disabuse him of that notion." Then he shouted, "Biggs, get over here!"

Patrick tried to interject something but Jensen shushed him. "Not now," he whispered.

Another agent in an FBI windbreaker charged breathlessly into the command tent. "Yes, sir?"

"Where are we on cutting their power?"

"Should have it off soon, sir, but we understand they have backup generators."

"Shit," Lange growled. "How about communications? The last thing we need is Thompson making a plea to other militias to come to his aid."

"There don't appear to be any hardlines into the compound,"

Biggs said. "And there's no cellular service in the area so their internet must be running off of satellite. Drone images showed a dish up by Thompson's radio tower."

"Can we jam it?"

"Yes, but it will take some time to get aircraft down here with the right equipment. It'd be a lot faster to just take out the dish."

Lange didn't hesitate. "Do it," he said. "And take out the radio tower too while you're at it. I want to shut this guy up."

Patrick couldn't remain quiet any longer. "You don't want to be the one to shoot first," he insisted.

"I can't be," Lange said. "Our men have already been shot at. I told you I've got a man wounded. Thompson drew first blood."

"Yeah, but calling in an airstrike is a hell of a lot more provocative than shooting a trespasser creeping through the woods."

"Trespasser? Is that how you see it?" Lange barked. "Federal officers, who announced their presence, are trespassers?"

"That's how the world will see it."

"Who's fucking side are you on, Connelly?"

Patrick was a little shaken by Lange's tone. Despite being a lawyer, he was generally a pretty non-confrontational guy outside of the world of pleadings and legal briefs. But he knew this was no time to back down. "The side of reason, apparently."

Lange's nostrils flared like a bull and a vein popped up in the middle of his forehead. He obviously didn't like being called out.

"All I'm asking," Patrick said, "is for a little restraint. I've already got an informant in there who's been compromised and may be dead. And Thompson's sister is either in there working on his surrender as we speak, or at the very least is on her way. So, before you light this powder keg, please, Agent Lange, I'm begging you, just ease back for an hour or two, and give Sheriff Cain a chance to resolve this thing peacefully."

Lange scowled. He sat down, looking flustered as he checked various pockets for his matches, then re-lit his pipe.

Patrick held his breath, awaiting Lange's response as he

sucked in the fire and blew out clouds of smoke. He hoped the tobacco would calm him.

After a few more puffs and quiet contemplation, Lange held the pipe to the side and shouted, "Biggs! Wait up!"

Thank God, Patrick thought. Lange was finally listening to reason.

Agent Biggs stuck his head back in the command tent. "Yes sir?"

Lange used the stem end of his pipe to point at Patrick. "Take the lawyers with you on your way to call in that airstrike," he said. "I've had all the advice I can stand."

29

UNCLE JIMMY LICKED his lips as he checked the sights of his rifle. He clearly welcomed the fight. But Hawlings seemed conflicted, worried, as he paced around the room. Mary Beth sensed an opportunity there. A weak spot to probe.

"You didn't agree with what my brother said, did you?" she asked.

Hawlings eyed her suspiciously.

Mary Beth clarified, "About Sheriff Bailey being the one who killed Gray?"

Uncle Jimmy stopped fiddling with his rifle long enough to look up. Hawlings' gaze immediately went to him, like he was nervous about saying anything against Sawyer in Jimmy's presence. "Bailey definitely had a hand in it," Hawlings said. "Confessed as much. There's no question about that."

That seemed to be enough to assuage Uncle Jimmy's curiosity. He returned to doing whatever it was snipers did to prepare.

Mary Beth still had questions though. "Having a hand in it isn't the same as being the one who did it. Last time I talked to Izzy, he said Bailey shut down the investigation, like maybe he was covering for someone, but never said anything about him being the killer."

"Well, we've learned a lot more since then."

"Such as?"

"Such as, right before Gray was killed, Bailey found out he'd been looking into who it was going around buying up all the property in McCray."

That perked Uncle Jimmy's ear. "I knew those prospectors was mixed up in this somehow," he said. "Bailey must have been the one behind them."

"Please," Mary Beth said. "I know how much sheriffs make. There's no way Bailey had that kind of money."

"Could have gone in with somebody," Hawling said.

"Yeah, like who?" Mary Beth wanted to know. "The coal companies have all pulled out of here. There's no more big money left in McCray."

Before Hawlings could offer an alternative theory, Sawyer's radio broadcast boomed out over the PA system:

Good afternoon, K-Mart shoppers. This here is your old friend, Sawyer Thompson, the Moonshine Messiah, coming to you live from McCray County, West—by God—Virginia, where the federal government of the U.S. of A, has invaded our precious neck of the woods. As we speak, they have surrounded our home and are fixing to straight-up murder every last one of us peaceful, law abiding citizens living here at Camp Shangri-La.

While Hawlings' and Uncle Jimmy's attention was focused on Sawyer's broadcast, Mary Beth took note of the satellite phone Sawyer left sitting on his desk. She tried to discreetly inch in that direction, thinking that if she could get a hold of the phone and get a message off to the feds to let them know she was in there, working on Sawyer, it might buy her some time. Meanwhile her brother kept, broadcasting as nonchalantly as a drive-time DJ.

Now you folks at home might be asking yourselves, why? Why would your trusted government want to go and do a mean old thing like slaughter a bunch of innocents? Well, the answer's simple folks. And it's not what they'll tell you. You're not gonna find it on BigBrother.gov, or whatever their website is. No, the reason they're here right now demanding we surrender or die, including all the little children we got living here, has nothing at all to do with law and order. It's about one thing and one thing only—

Sawyer let one of his pregnant pauses hang in the air. Before he could fill it there was a loud whistling noise followed by an explosion that shook the building like a seismic earthquake.

"Jesus Christ!" Hawlings yelled.

Outside, Mary Beth could hear people screaming and yelling. There was a smattering of machine gun fire, then a pelting of something collapsing down onto the roof like a hailstorm. Hawlings got on the walkie, frantically asking what was going on. He kept switching channels, trying to get a response.

Meanwhile Mary Beth took advantage of the confusion. She grabbed the satellite phone and slipped it beneath her coat.

Finally, Hawlings raised a staticy, unintelligible response on the walkie.

"Repeat," he said. "This is Hawlings, please repeat."

The voice came back, more clearly, "It was a fucking drone strike, man. They just took the top off the mountain. Radiotower and satellite dish were blown all to hell."

"Goddammit!" Uncle Jimmy growled. "They're trying to silence us. Don't want the world to know the truth."

"Uncle Jimmy, just—" Mary Beth wanted to say calm down, but she knew that would have been like asking a rooster not to crow at the sunrise. Jimmy tore out of the room, rifle in hand.

Hawlings looked conflicted as to whether he should go too. He tried raising Sawyer on the walkie, without success. Air raid sirens blared throughout the compound. Mary Beth could hear people running and shouting. Hawlings glanced toward the door, the pull of the fight and his comrades seemed to tug at him. But he'd been ordered to watch her.

She hoped he would try to subdue her somehow. Tie her up so he could go join battle. If he attempted such a thing, it would provide an opportunity for her to get the upper hand.

But instead, Hawlings simply said, "wait here." He slipped quickly out of the door and Mary Beth heard a deadbolt click into place.

She was locked in. But she wasn't helpless. Mary Beth pulled the satellite phone out from under her coat, and scrambled to figure out how to find the number of the last call received.

After being escorted from the command tent, Patrick and Jensen were permitted to observe the siege from what they hoped would be a safe distance. They huddled with some other field agents beneath the cover of forest, approximately half a mile away from the Old Wengo Mine.

A long row of Bradley Fighting Vehicles rumbled past them, up the mountain road into a clearing between the agents' wooded position and the compound fencing. There they flared out into an arrowhead formation, with one Abrams tank at the point. It was to be the battering ram that would take down the gate. Once in position, the grinding gears of the heavy machinery came to a halt, and an eerie quiet fell over the mountainside, a calm before the storm, save for the chirping cacophony of cicadas and buzzing locusts, and the occasional call of a whippoorwill.

"You sure this is a safe enough distance?" Jensen whispered.

"Of course," Agent Biggs said. "It'd take one of the best sharpshooters in the world to hit somebody from this range."

Patrick was down on one knee, watching the front gate with a set of field binoculars when his satellite phone rang. The caller ID told him it was a deadman calling.

"Quigley?" he asked hopefully.

The voice on the other end was certainly not Quigley. Instead of the biker's gravel, he heard that sweet, sassy, twangy voice that always set off a tuning fork in his heart, but never as much as it did in that moment.

"Patrick!"

"Mary! Oh, thank God, you're okay. Where are you?"

"I'm in Sawyer's compound."

The momentary joy Patrick felt at the sound of Mary Beth's voice was instantly replaced by dread.

"You have to get out!" he said. "Get out now! They're coming in."

"Patrick, you have to stop them. I just need more time."

Patrick looked to Special Agent Lange who was standing on the back of an uncovered jeep, surrounded by his senior advisers. He held a bullhorn, about to address the militia, and glared back at Patrick like he was taking a call in the middle of a library. "Quiet over there," he scolded.

Patrick waved the phone. "It's Sheriff Cain. She's inside."

Lange scowled, annoyed, but then beckoned for Patrick to bring him the phone. Patrick hurried in that direction. He held out the phone. Lange seized it.

"Sheriff, this Special Agent Lange, FBI...What's your current position?...Well, how do you expect to arrest Thompson if he's got you locked in his office?...Tell me something, Sheriff. do you honestly think there is any scenario under the sun in which your brother will go quietly?...That isn't very reassuring....Well, I was about to give them one last opportunity to surrender and offer safe passage to anyone who wants to exit. If any of them decide to vacate, I suggest you leave with them...In that case, your best bet is to shelter in place. Find somewhere you can hunker down."

Lange started to hand the phone back to Patrick but Mary Beth said something else that Patrick couldn't make out. "What's that?" Lange asked, putting the phone back to his ear. "I highly doubt that...Thompson has a death wish is all...Well, unless they surrender, we're about to oblige them."

Lange handed the phone back to Patrick. Mary Beth was still there, trying to tell him something, but he had trouble hearing her because Lange immediately got on his bullhorn.

"This is Special Agent Dennis Lange, FBI. This compound is currently surrounded by a joint task force of the FBI, ATF and Army National Guard. We have a warrant for the arrest of one Sawyer Thompson and all co-conspirators, John and Jane Doe's, one to one-thousand, on charges of illegal arms possession, conspiracy, destruction of federal property, murder, domestic—"

Lange was interrupted by a whooshing sound, followed by a metallic crunch. He looked down at his hands, which were suddenly empty. Lange appeared confused by the mangled remains of the bullhorn that were now lying at his feet. Then there was another whoosh as a high-caliber bullet ripped a v-shaped trench through the top of his head.

The special agent in charge fell backwards out of the jeep, dead before he hit the ground.

After that, everything seemed to move in slow motion at first as the stunned agents registered what had happened. Then someone yelled "Lange is down! Lange is down!" all hell broke loose.

Machine gun fire roared, raging hot and heavy from both sides. The Army commander who'd been standing next to Lange gave some kind of hand signal to Agent Biggs who got on his radio, yelling, "Take out the towers! Take out the towers!"

Within seconds, three drones screeched overhead. Two launched missile strikes that obliterated the shot towers by the mine's front gate. But the third one was taken out by an anti-aircraft rocket fired from inside the compound. That last drone swirled and crashed into the woods like a burning lawn dart, setting the dried grass and pine straw ablaze. Jensen turned and ran for deeper cover, while units of hunched-over agents in body armor rushed into position behind the armored vehicles, ready for the siege.

The whole thing was a surrealistic nightmare. Patrick was frozen in place, his head spinning like a pop bottle at a teenage smooch party. Meanwhile Mary Beth yelled at him over the phone. "Make them stop! Do something! Do something! Do something!"

30

SAWYER BURST into the room like a kid on Christmas morning, so delighted by the chaos he was causing, he skipped right past Mary Beth without noticing or caring that she was holding the satellite phone. She quickly switched it off and tucked it under her coat.

"Please, Sawyer," she begged, "you've got to stop this!"

Instead of responding, Sawyer got down into a three-point stance, and squared up to the large floor safe in the corner of the room. He launched at it like a tackling dummy.

Sawyer was a big man. Big enough that he could have played football for McCray High if he'd ever been able to pass a drug test. But despite his considerable size it took some real effort for him to wrestle the safe from its spot. When he finally did, it revealed a trap door.

"What is that?" Mary Beth asked.

"Think of this as kind of like Hitler's bunker," Sawyer said. "The place you go just before the enemies move in. Only this one connects to an old mining tunnel that will take us all the way into Virginia."

Mary Beth wanted to spit, she was so disgusted. "You piece of shit," she said. "I should have known you were too big of a pussy to ever be a martyr."

"Hey, don't get your panties all in a bunch. I promised Ma I'd get you out of here safely. And just to show you what a nice guy I am, Clem is even gonna swing by and get your boy, Izzy. As soon as they get here, the four of us will all head down."

"And what about all of your other people?"

Sawyer shrugged. "Every great general has had to sacrifice soldiers. And it won't be in vain. Trust me. People will be so outraged by the slaughter here, it will spark a revolution. And I'll need to be around to lead it. Plus," Sawyer said, smiling like a Cheshire cat, "if we were to die out there with them, I wouldn't get a chance to bask in the glory of my delightful surprise."

"Surprise?"

"This little baby right here." Sawyer held up some kind of remote. "Soon as the feds breach the walls, and we're all safe down in the tunnel, this trigger is hooked up to enough Emulex to blow this place to Kingdom come."

Sawyer laughed maniacally. Mary Beth was too horrified to speak. She kept her eyes on the remote. Her first impulse was to rush Sawyer, to try to wrestle it away from him. But he was armed with a mini-machine gun and, despite what she'd said earlier, the days when Mary Beth could kick his ass were long gone.

"Sawyer, you can't just—"

"Wait," he said.

"What?"

Sawyer looked concerned. "Listen." He cupped his ear. "The shooting. It stopped."

They both stood there expecting the rat-a-tat-tat of the automatic weapon fire to resume any second but it didn't. Sawyer got on his radio to find out what was going on.

"Yo, Clem, what the—?...He's what?...You're not serious?"

"What?" Mary Beth asked.

Sawyer shook his head. "There's some jackass out there in a Brooks Brothers suit, standing in front of the tanks like its fucking Tieneman square."

Oh my God, Mary Beth thought. Patrick.

"Clemmy, do me a favor. Have somebody shoot that stupid son-of-a-bitch and let's get it on."

It was at that moment that Mary Beth finally accepted that her brother would never again be that little boy she'd tried to shield from their parents' criminal lifestyle. She saw him for the man he'd become, a psychopath, completely indifferent to the carnage he was about to cause. Like a once beloved dog who'd gone mean. And once that happened, there was only one thing you could do: Put him down.

Mary Beth reached into her boot and pulled her backup gun, the subcompact Beretta she called her hummingbird. It was smaller than her hand but could drop a man Sawyer's size with no problem.

"Put down that trigger. Get on your radio. And tell your people to surrender," Mary Beth commanded.

Sawyer's mini machine gun was on a strap, still slung around his shoulder. There was no way he could swing it around in time before Mary Beth got off a shot. He managed to say, "I don't think—" before a bullet tore through his foot and the Moonshine Messiah tumbled like a tower of blocks.

"Jiminy, God!" he screamed, rolling around in pain. "Motherfucker!"

Mary Beth seized hold of the remote, then kicked Sawyer in the ribs with the toe of her boot. He rolled to his left, and she yanked the machine gun free.

"Oh, you bitch," Sawyer wailed. "You fucking bitch."

A faint plume of smoke wafted up from the barrel of her hummingbird as Mary Beth pointed it down at her brother. "Next one goes in your shin," she said. "I'll work my way up from there."

31

WITHIN MINUTES of Sawyer's announcement, the peaceful surrender of his followers was well underway. Mary Beth called Patrick to let him know they would be marching from the compound in an orderly fashion, unarmed, with their hands on their heads.

"You sure you're okay?" Patrick asked.

"I'm fine," Mary Beth said. "How about you? I heard you were staring down the barrel of a tank out there."

"Yeah, I still can't believe I did it. Something just took over, you know."

"I do," Mary Beth said. "You saved us."

"No, you saved us. You saved all these people."

Mary Beth smiled. "Well, can't argue with you there."

Patrick laughed. "Modesty never was one of your strong suits."

"Counselor, that's the first thing you've charged me with that I'm actually guilty of."

Patrick laughed again. "Would you hurry and come out here? I'm dying to see you."

"I'll be along soon," Mary Beth said. "Just one other thing I need to take care of first."

She got off the phone with Patrick and forced Sawyer to radio his man Charlie, Mr. Executioner Mask, who then escorted Izzy to Sawyer's office.

Not since the birth of her son, had Mary Beth been so happy to see someone. She hugged Izzy tight, not realizing how badly he'd injured his shoulder.

"Ouch, damn, take it easy," Izzy said.

He was smiling, but there was an awful haggardness behind Izzy's eyes. Looked like he'd been through hell. He quickly recounted to Mary Beth about his time in captivity. Sawyer was still cowering on the floor and Mary Beth kicked him twice more when she heard about Izzy's time in the mine. Then she turned back to her friend. "The next time I tell you to wait on me, do you think you could listen?"

Izzy looked up at her with a weary smile. "MB, that's one thing you don't have to worry about."

She took the cuffs Izzy had been shackled with and placed them upon his captor, Charlie. Then she handed Charlie's shotgun to Izzy. "You think you can handle escorting this prisoner outside? I know you've only got one good arm."

"Sure," Izzy said. "But what about you?"

Mary Beth looked at her brother, who was balled up in a fetal position, really acting like a little bitch, whining about his wounded tootsie. "I'm taking Sawyer in."

"Okay," Izzy said. "Let's go. He can throw an arm over his man here for support and we'll walk them out together."

Mary Beth shook her head. "No, we aren't going out that way." She pointed to the trap door.

"What? Why would you—"

"Because I don't want the feds snaking my collar. I arrested Sawyer and—" Mary Beth paused turned to her brother. "You're under arrest, by the way. You have the right to remain silent but we both know there's no chance of that happening. You also have the right to—oh whatever, you know the rest." She turned back to Izzy. "Like I said. I arrested him, and Sawyer's head is going on my wall."

Izzy gave her the look he got when she was about to do something stupid. "Fine," he said. "It's your bust. The lawyers will have to decide who gets first crack at the prosecution, regardless. But if you go sneaking out the back door it's gonna look like…."

Izzy trailed off as Sawyer cut in. "What her highness isn't telling you, is she's worried some government sharpshooter out there might get an itchy trigger finger and pop a cap in my sweet ass."

Mary Beth kicked at her brother once more. "Shut up," she said, "before I shoot you again."

"Is that it?" Izzy asked. "You really think—"

"I'm doing what I'm doing," Mary Beth said. "You don't have to worry about it. Unless, of course, you want to go down in the mine with me."

"Hell, no," Izzy said. "I plan on sleeping with the light on for the rest of my life."

Mary Beth squeezed his shoulder. She really hated all that he had been through.

"So, what am I supposed to tell the feds?" Izzy asked.

"Tell them that Sawyer is *my* prisoner, and if they want him, they're gonna have to get in line."

32

PATRICK WAS WITH John Jensen when Izzy exited the compound. Everyone was waiting to see the hero sheriff and her bounty, the notorious Moonshine Messiah. Then when Izzy explained that they wouldn't be making an appearance, they all went into panic mode.

Jensen, and even Patrick, feared Mary Beth was helping her brother escape. Some federal agents went down into the mine after them, but eventually gave up trying to navigate its labyrinthine tunnels and corridors. Others were sent to scour the woods for exit points. Meanwhile extended roadblocks were set up, on every thoroughfare in and out of the county.

Once that was all underway, Jensen pulled Patrick aside for a proper ass chewing.

"Goddamn it, Connelly, she fucked us! I told you this would happen. I knew it. I fucking knew it. The bitch is more corrupt than Tony Soprano. She snuck her brother out the back door and fucked us right up the ass."

Patrick held his head by the temples. He wanted to tell Jensen he was wrong, that he was way off base. But he knew that everything the U.S. Attorney was saying could very well be true. Misguided loyalty to her no-good family had always been Mary Beth's Achilles heel. Patrick couldn't put it past her to do something like letting Sawyer go free. But he also wasn't totally convinced that was what she was doing.

"You've got to understand her history," he said. "Her father was killed while trying to surrender to the DEA. I can see her being concerned that the same thing might happen to her brother. Just because she snuck him out of here doesn't mean she's going to turn her brother loose."

"She better the hell not. Because if she does, you and I are absolutely fucked, my friend. Agent Lange is dead. The FBI is super fucking pissed. You can bet your ass there's going to be one hell of an investigation into all of this."

"Just don't freak out yet," Patrick said. "Give Mary Beth a chance to come through."

Jensen tried loosening his tie, then got frustrated and yanked it from his neck like a whip. "I'm not waiting around for any-body," he said. "If she doesn't come out of that mine with her brother in handcuffs and deliver him to the closest jail then I'm not going to get caught with my pants down."

"What do you mean?"

"I mean it's CYA time. Cover. Your. Ass."

Patrick was all for a little ass covering but didn't know how that was possible. Most of the things that could point a suspi-cious finger his way, may not have been public knowledge, but it was all technically a matter of public record. They weren't the kinds of things that could just disappear. Not legally.

"What do you propose?" he asked.

Jensen looked around to make sure no one could overhear. He leaned close and suggested exactly what Patrick had thought impossible. "I mean, it's time for any record of the McCray proj-ect to vanish."

Patrick backed up a step. "But they're government records, how are you—"

"Trust me," Jensen said. "You don't get to my position without learning how to defuse a timebomb."

It was slow going through Sawyer's tunnel. He was really hobbling, milking his bullet wound for all it was worth, and Mary Beth had to periodically kick him in the ass, both literally and figuratively, to move things along. Thankfully, they eventually came across an old coal cart and Mary Beth took pity on her little brother, letting him climb in while she pushed.

"I still can't believe you were just going to let everyone die," she said. "Even Uncle Jimmy?"

Sawyer waved her off. "That old bastard would have loved nothing more than to go down in a blaze of glory. It's putting him out of his misery, if anything."

"You are a monster. A complete and total narcissist."

"Hey," Sawyer said, "narcissists are people too. If you prick us, do we not brag?"

"This isn't a joke, Sawyer. All these years I just thought you were a fucking idiot, a little retarded maybe, but actually you're just plain evil."

Sawyer laughed. "You just keep telling yourself that you're any different, Mamie Mini-Me."

That got Mary Beth fuming. She jacked up the coal cart and dumped Sawyer on the ground.

"You're walking from here," she said.

Sawyer got up on one foot, and Mary Beth pulled her gun to subdue him, if necessary, as he hopped around to face her.

"Struck a nerve, huh?"

"You know what?" she said. "I shouldn't even be doing this. I should have just marched you out that front gate and let you suffer whatever fate you've brought upon yourself. In fact, as soon as we get out the other side of this tunnel, I'm going to use this satellite phone to call the feds and tell them they can come do whatever they want with you."

"Hey," Sawyer said. "Do what you gotta do. Whatever will help you sleep at night."

After another hour of hiking and bickering, the siblings finally exited the mine tunnel into a wooded area near a stream where the water ran fast over smooth round rocks big enough to stand on. It was nearly nightfall, but a full moon was on the rise and there was some ambient light from passing cars up on Highway 52 off in the distance.

Mary Beth was savoring a deep breath of fresh air and the smell of honeysuckle, relieved to be back in the world, when she heard someone racking a load.

Her cousin Tommy stepped out of the shadows and pointed his shotgun at her. "That's as far as you go, Mary Elizabeth. Put that gun down and turn Sawyer loose."

Mary Beth gave Sawyer a shove, to keep him moving. "Piss off, Tommy," she said. "You aren't gonna shoot me."

Tommy lowered his weapon. "No," he said. "But he will." Tommy nodded toward a thicket of mulberry bushes where a squat, powerfully built man was crouching low. It was the wrestler Mary Beth kicked in the nuts back at Mountain Flowers. He still looked a little bow-legged as he stood, pointing his pistol right at Mary Beth's head.

"Come on now, Mary," Tommy said. "Nobody wants anybody to get hurt."

Mary Beth thought about whether she could wheel around and shoot the wrestler before he killed her. The only way would be if he hesitated. He had a dead aim and he looked like he was holding a grudge over their prior tussle. Mary Beth thought about her son, Sam, who was probably about the same age as the guy pointing the gun. He had already lost one parent in the line of duty. She dropped her gun.

"That's a good girl," Tommy said.

Mary Beth gave Sawyer one last good kick in the ass that made him stumble as he hopped toward Tommy who helped him stand.

"So, what is this?" she asked. "You're all working together?"

Tommy shook his head. "Mamie said she'd get you into Sawyer's compound so the two of you could talk. She never said she'd let you arrest her boy."

Sawyer gave Mary Beth a cocky smile, showing that chipped front tooth. It was the look he used to give her as a kid when something happened to reveal he was their mother's favorite.

"So what happens now?" she asked.

Tommy said, "Now, we're going to handcuff you to a tree. Then once we're a safe distance away, we'll call your deputies and let them know where they can come find you."

The wrestler seized Mary Beth's arm and wrenched it behind her back so violently it lifted her off the ground. She screamed, in spite of herself. The wrestler took her hard to the ground. His weight pressed down on her, matched by the strength of his body odor. Then he dragged her face first across the forest floor, over pine cones and tree roots, scraping her flesh raw. Within seconds he had her in a seated position, arms behind her, shackled to the base of a sturdy tree.

Mary Beth struggled to catch her breath as the men readied to leave. "Wherever you go, Sawyer," she panted, "they'll find you."

Sawyer winked at her. "Maybe," he said. "But not if I find them first." He put one arm over Cousin Tommy and the other over the wrestler. They walked that way, like a three-legged race, up the hillside and out of sight.

33

WHEN MARY BETH heard the voices and saw the flashlights in the distance, her first thought was that they got there too soon. Cousin Tommy would want to get at least an hour down the road, before placing a call to her deputies, but they'd only been gone maybe fifteen, twenty minutes.

"Over here," she yelled. "Hurry! They're getting away!"

The flashlight beams turned in her direction. She was hoping to see some of her deputies emerge from the darkness, but instead it was six FBI agents who side-stepped their way down the grassy hillside from the highway into the meadow where Mary Beth was handcuffed. They had their guns drawn.

"Where's Thompson?"

"He's in the wind," Mary Beth said. "I got ambushed as soon as we exited the mine. Two men were lying in wait for us. They just left. If we hurry, we can catch them." Mary Beth shifted her weight, scraping the cuffs against the dried bark of the tree she was shackled to. "The keys to the cuffs are on the rock over there to my right." Mary Beth pointed her boot at the large anvil-shaped stone where Tommy left the handcuff keys.

"They leave by vehicle or on foot?" the lead agent asked.

"They went up the hillside on foot. Sawyer's wounded. I shot him in the lower extremity to subdue him back at the mine. The other two men had to help him walk. But I'm sure they had a vehicle parked up near the highway somewhere. Like I said, if we hurry, we—"

"Which direction did they go?"

"I don't know for certain. But I would expect they're headed south. No reason to go back into West Virginia where he knows we'll be looking for him."

The agent asking the questions bent down to where Mary Beth could get a closer look at him. He was a light skinned Black man, who wore a black FBI jacket and tight fitting jeans, with guns strapped to each leg. He nodded to one of the other agents and told him to "Call it in." He turned back to Mary Beth and said, "I'm Agent Biggs."

"Sheriff Cain. I'd love to shake your hand if you could..." Mary Beth raked her cuffs against the tree.

Biggs ignored the suggestion. "Can you describe Thompson's appearance? What he was wearing?"

"Sure," Mary Beth said, "but can you get these cuffs off first? I'm starting to lose circulation."

Biggs stared at her without blinking. "Description please. We'll need it for the APB."

Mary Beth squirmed, futilely trying to get comfortable. "Let's see," she said, "Sawyer's about six, two. Probably weighs two hundred twenty pounds. He's thirty-six years old, going on six. Has shoulder length blonde hair, a little lighter than mine. Blue eyes. A full beard, that kind of comes to a point beneath his chin. Sort of devilish looking, which is appropriate. Last I saw him, he was wearing green camouflage pants, a black turtleneck, and a tan-colored bulletproof vest." Mary Beth paused to think, if there was anything else. "Oh, he's got a pretty noticeable chip in his front tooth, a barbed wire tattoo on his left bicep, and a tattoo of kissy lips on his right butt cheek, so he's perpetually telling the world to kiss his ass. May have more tattoos I don't know about. We haven't kept in touch much the last few years."

Biggs wrote all of this down on a notepad. When he finished, he tore off the sheet and handed it to the agent who was reporting everything to someone by phone.

That's when Mary Beth made the connection. The satellite phone. These guys weren't there because her cousin Tommy called to disclose her location. They must have been able to track her by the satellite phone she was still carrying. As soon as she exited the mine, they would have been able to get a fix on her position.

"So, you are some relation to Sawyer Thompson?" Biggs asked.

Mary Beth was surprised by the question. She couldn't tell if it was an honest inquiry, or an accusation.

"Uh, yeah. I'm his sister, *Sheriff* Mary Beth Cain. You know, the one who arrested him, and averted a full-scale war back there, saving hundreds of lives. You're aware of all that, right?"

Biggs put down his pen. "I'm aware, ma'am. I was there. In fact, I was standing right next to the special agent in charge when one of Thompson's men blew his head off. That man's name was Dennis Lange. During the time you and your brother were traipsing through the mine, I had the pleasure of calling his wife to let her know he was dead."

Biggs had a quiet demeanor. He'd kept his voice nice and even, though the emotion behind his words was clear. Mary Beth felt anger radiating off of him.

"I'm sorry to hear about Agent Lange. Thank God there weren't more people killed," she said.

"Oh, there were. Multiple casualties on each side."

This guy was determined not to give her any credit at all.

"Well, thank God for me, or there would have been a hell of a lot more."

Biggs's lips stretched into a thin smile. He leaned in close.

"Ma'am, I'm only going to ask you this just one time. Where is your brother going?"

Mary Beth wanted to be pissed off by the question, but instead she felt her sphincter tighten at the insinuation she and Sawyer were in cahoots.

"Listen, if you think—"

"I don't *think* anything, ma'am. What I *know* is—"

"Call me sheriff, please," Mary Beth said, reclaiming some of her usual swagger.

"Excuse me?"

"You keep calling me ma'am, like I'm some damsel in distress. I'm a sheriff. I bust heads and arrest motherfuckers for a living. Call me sheriff."

Biggs nodded. "Okay, Sheriff. What I was saying is, I don't *think* anything. What I *know*, is that you allowed your brother to evade custody by surreptitiously shuttling him through an underground tunnel across state lines. We have a term for that. It's called aiding and abetting a fugitive, and it makes you an accessory after the fact."

"Bullshit," Mary Beth said. "He was in my custody the entire time. Police custody. And I had full authority to transport him by any means I deemed necessary. Given the high emotions of the situation, I was concerned that if I were to bring him out the front, someone might take a shot at him. And as my prisoner, I had a duty to protect him. If I hadn't been ambushed by—"

"Riiiiight," Bigg said. "The *two men*. The ones who were nice enough to leave the handcuff keys behind."

Mary Beth shrugged, realizing how it sounded. "What do you want?" she asked. "Sawyer is my brother. He was just trying to escape, not leave me for dead. In fact, any minute now, I expect they'll place a phone call to my deputies letting them know my position. If we could stop wasting time here, we could try to set up a trace for when they do."

Biggs pointed to the agent with the cell phone. "Let's go

ahead and get on that," he said, then to Mary Beth. "These two men who ambushed you. Can you describe them?"

Mary Beth paused, which was a mistake since Biggs was obviously skeptical as to whether these guys even existed. But Mary Beth realized she had another problem. She was obviously capable of describing the men who helped Sawyer. One was a distant cousin and the other was a guy she was pretty sure used to wrestle for McCray High. With a few minutes in front of a computer she could probably serve up their social security numbers. But implicating them would also implicate their employer—her mother—and Mary Beth wasn't sure she wanted to go there.

Mamie obviously had some fore knowledge of Sawyer's plans, in order to have two of her guys waiting outside the mine, so the feds would probably assume she'd been in on the whole thing and charge her with the truckload, conspiracy and murder. Mamie might deserve a lot but she didn't deserve that. Not over this. Mary Beth was fairly certain Mamie was in the dark about Sawyer's planned massacre. Not that Mamie was a humanitarian, but Sawyer's plan would be bad for her business. Bring way too much heat. The old lady probably didn't have any details beyond Sawyer's escape plan, and, as mad as Mary Beth was at Sawyer, she couldn't really blame Mamie for wanting to save her son.

"Sheriff?"

"Yeah, sorry," Mary Beth said. "I was just trying to think."

"Think? Of what they looked like?"

"Yes," she said, trying not to sound guilty. "It all happened kind of fast," she said, hating the way it sounded. "It was already getting dark, you know. And those militia guys pretty much look the same in their fatigues. Plus they had face coverings," Mary Beth said, trying to think up on the spot an explanation for why a trained law enforcement officer would be unable to provide a detailed description. "Gaiters, I think you call them.

Pulled up over their noses. And hats. So, I couldn't really see their faces. Two white guys, about Sawyer's size. That's all I can really tell you."

Biggs maintained his tight-lipped expression, but Mary Beth could tell he wasn't buying it. "Anything else?"

"No, I don't think so."

"Okay, then." Biggs gestured to one of the other agents. He retrieved the keys and uncuffed Mary Beth's left wrist.

"About time," she said.

But as soon as she stood free of the tree, the same agent seized her other wrist and re-cuffed both hands behind her back.

"What the—"

"Sheriff Cain," Biggs said. "You are under arrest as an Accessory After the Fact. You have the right to remain silent. Anything you say—"

"I know my rights, asshole. What I don't know is what in the hell you think you're doing."

Biggs continued undeterred. "Anything you say can and will be used against you in a court of law. You have the right to an attorney. If you cannot afford an attorney, one will be provided for you. Sheriff Cain, do you understand these rights as I have read them to you?"

"I understand you're making the biggest fucking mistake of your life. I demand to talk to Patrick Connelly."

"Connelly?"

"Yeah, dickhead. Patrick Connelly. He's the AUSA involved with this whole operation."

"I know who he is," Biggs said.

"Good. Then take me to him."

Biggs didn't move. His thin-lipped smile grew wider. "I was about to say that Connelly is the one who said that if we found you without your brother, we should arrest you."

Mary Beth felt a pang in her heart at that news, but then

Biggs shook his head. "That's not right, though. It was the other one. Jensen. He's the one who said to make the arrest."

Mary Beth breathed a small sigh of relief. If Patrick had turned on her, she'd really be up shit's creek. With him still on her side, though, she was confident she'd be able to sort this mess out.

"Connelly is who I want to talk to."

Biggs repeated the name. "Connelly, right." He snapped his fingers and pointed at Mary Beth. "Connelly's the one who told us that if we found you without Sawyer Thompson, then we shouldn't believe a single word you say."

34

THEY PASSED UP several perfectly good state-run jails to take
Mary Beth to FPC Alderson, the nation's first federal wom-
en's prison and former home to the likes of Martha Stewart,
Billie Holiday, Tokyo Rose, and the Manson Family's Lynette
"Squeaky" Fromm. It was minimum security, but it was federal, and far enough from Mary Beth's orbit to cut down on the
chance she'd run into a prison guard who owed her a favor. The
place was called "Camp Cupcake" because it looked more like
a college campus than a detention center. No barbed wire and
plenty of greenery around postcard worthy brick buildings with
columned porticos.

A far cry from Moundsville, Mary Beth thought. West
Virginia's most notorious prison had looked like a gothic torture castle and was a virutal hell on earth before it closed back
in the nineties. That was the first one Mary Beth had ever seen.
Six years old, visiting her mother's Uncle Ot, who had regaled
her with stories of shankings and showerroom rapes, despite
her tender age. Then of course there was the McCray County
Correctional Center where Mary Beth's father twice did time.

A six month fall shortly after she was born, and a two-year stint while she was in middle school. Mary Beth would never forget the Christmas they spent there during extended visiting hours, how hard it was to put on a happy face and pretend to be excited about the crude angel her father had fashioned for her from a bar of soap.

Given all that, Mary Beth supposed she should be pleased with her temporary assignment, but that didn't keep her from crying the following morning when she got her first visitor.

"Sam?"

Mary Beth's son looked like a twenty-one year old, male version of his mother. Slender and blonde with Mary Beth's pale skin that concealed emotions about as well as a pair of chaps could cover your ass. She could tell he was devastated by the sight of his mother in her khaki prison clothes.

"You're allowed one embrace," the guard who'd led Mary Beth in, said. "Not to exceed ten seconds. Otherwise, there's to be no physical contact besides hand holding."

Mary Beth seized hold of Sam and squeezed.

"I'm sorry, Sam. I wish you didn't have to see me like this." She'd tried so hard to give him a different life. Now here Sam was, visiting his parent in prison, just like she'd had to do.

"It's okay, Mom. We're going to get you out of here."

He actually sounded confident about it. Sam might look like his mother but their personalities were polar opposites. She was used to him being timid and shy.

"You've reached your initial embrace time limit," the guard said.

Mary Beth and Sam separated and took a seat at a round table with fixed picnic-style benches.

"Where's Izzy," she asked. That was who Mary Beth used her one phone call to contact and who she'd been expecting to see.

"Princess isn't letting him out of her sight," Sam said. "She took him to the hospital and they had to reset his shoulder. He didn't tell you?"

"No. We didn't have a lot of time to talk."

"Why didn't you call me?" The hurt in Sam's voice was palpable, tethered to their long running conflict: Mary Beth's desire to protect her son, and his constant complaint that she infantilized him.

"I just didn't want you to have to get involved in this."

"You mean you didn't think I could handle it."

Mary Beth struggled to respond. "Sam, I—"

"Forget it, Mom. It's okay."

Poor kid, Mary Beth thought. He'd lived his life squeezed between her suffocating protection and the considerable shadow of an idolized father. The late, great, Big Bill Cain, had been a high school football hero and celebrated county sheriff, a man's man, whereas Sam was bookish and awkward, and his idea of exercise was playing video games until his thumbs were worn down to nubs.

"It's just that time is of the essence," Mary Beth said. "Sawyer's on the run and tomorrow they're taking me up to Charleston for my first appearance. I need a lawyer to spring me right away."

Sam, tapped nervously on the tabletop. "Izzy's tried, Mom. So have I. We've called every lawyer in town, but they've all declined. They've got this crazy idea that if they were to represent you it might create some kind of conflict that would prevent them from ever defending another case in Jasper County."

"Shit." Mary Beth palmed her forehead. "It's Pomfried. He's poisoned the well with the local defense bar." *Fuck*, her chickens were really coming home to roost.

"Is it true what they are saying on T.V.?" Sam asked. "Did you really shoot Uncle Sawyer?"

Mary Beth had done her best to keep Sam far from her family, but they'd run into each other at the occasional obligatory family gathering, and Sam, the fatherless boy, would inevitably gravitate to his Uncle Sawyer, who was at about the same level of emotional maturity and probably seemed like a real righteous dude to a teenager.

"Only in the foot," Mary Beth said, not sure how Sam would react.

"Then how can they think you helped him escape?"

Mary Beth smiled. "Maybe I should hire you to defend me."

"I wish I could."

Sam actually was pre-law, and at the top of his class. No doubt he would make a good attorney someday, but not soon enough to help Mary Beth with her current situation. She squeezed her son's hand. "Me, too, sweety. Me too." This was the most attention Mary Beth had received from her son in years. She was almost enjoying it, despite the circumstances. To keep the conversation going, she asked, "What else are they reporting in the news?"

"At first they were all calling you a hero, saying how you saved hundreds of people. But then the coverage really turned, making it sound like you helped Uncle Sawyer escape."

"That's what I was afraid of." Mary Beth stopped to think. "Listen," she said. "I need you to get back in touch with Izzy. See if Princess can get us some positive press coverage. I'm probably not her favorite person right now, but if she could get my version of events out there, maybe come here and do an interview, it could really help."

"Shouldn't you consult a lawyer about that first? They probably wouldn't want you talking to the press."

"Trust me on this, Sam. I may not be an attorney but I've been around the block enough times to know that what's said in the media is just as important as what's said in the courtroom."

Sam nodded. "Okay, I'll see what I can do."

"Good. Now tell me what else they're reporting. What have they said about casualties?"

Same paused to think. "There were three or four federal

agents killed. More wounded. A couple of army national guard soldiers too. I think they said a total of six people from inside the compound were killed before the shooting stopped."

"Any word about Uncle Jimmy?"

Sam hung his head. "He's listed as presumed dead. The paper said he was in one of the gun towers that the government drones took out. They haven't found any remains, but it's unlikely he could have survived."

Mary Beth kissed her index finger and pointed skyward. "Godspeed, Uncle Jimmy. At least you didn't live long enough to find out what a charlatan, piece of shit Sawyer is."

Sam tried to pat her arm but the guard intervened. "Physical contact is limited to hand holding."

"I'm sorry," Sam said. Then to his mother: "I'm sorry about your Uncle Jimmy. He's the one who fought in Vietnam, right?"

"That's right. He was a neat old guy. Used to stand on his head at family reunions. Then when he'd get good and drunk would start skeet shooting with full cans of Budweiser. The kids would throw them into the air as high as we could, and Uncle Jimmy would blow them out of the sky. He always put on quite a show."

"I'm sorry I never got to know that side of the family very well."

"No, you're not, Sam. Trust me." Just then Mary Beth thought about Quiet Clem, the only other person she really knew up in the compound. "Hey, did they say anything about a Clement Stenson? Do you remember seeing that name?"

Sam shook his head. "No, I don't think so. The only other one I really remember was they said a McCray Deputy was killed?"

"Hawlings?"

"Yeah, that's it. Apparently, he was trying to use some kind of improvised explosive device and it backfired on him."

"Kind of fitting," Mary Beth said. She didn't mourn Hawlings' passing at all. He'd been a fellow brother in blue, but was a traitor in her book, responsible for Izzy's harsh captivity.

"So what are we going to do about getting you a lawyer? There's not enough time between now and tomorrow for anyone who doesn't already know the case to get up to speed."

Mary Beth shrugged. "I guess I'll just have to represent myself. I've seen these things enough time in state court to know how to say "Not Guilty" and then swear to the judge that I'm not a flight risk."

"You can't be serious," Sam said. "Ever heard the saying that 'A person who represents themself has a fool for a client?'"

"I've been called worse."

"This isn't funny, Mom. Besides, federal court is a lot different from state court. Different procedures. And there's likely to be press and everything there tomorrow. You shouldn't be making any statements at all. You need a lawyer."

Sam rose from his seat, looming larger than she'd ever seen him. Mary Beth realized how grown up he is now; she was kind of proud of the forceful way he'd addressed her.

"There's got to be somebody," he said.

Mary Beth sighed. She leaned back and closed her eyes.

"Mom?"

"Yes," she said, "there is *somebody*."

"Great. Who?"

Mary Beth felt bile building up in the back of her throat thinking of all the crow she was about to eat, and all the "Sugars" she'd have to wash it down with.

"Sammy," she said, "I need you to call Alexander Pomfried."

35

"WELL, HOWDY, SUGAR."

Alexander Pomfried wore his trademark seersucker suit and bow tie, and was smiling like he just won the lottery, looking down at Mary Beth. She was cuffed to a wooden bench in the courthouse's holding cell, essentially a closet with a steel door.

"I can take it from here," Pomfried said to the marshal who closed the door, leaving lawyer and prisoner alone. The rotund attorney sat down next to Mary Beth, smelling like English Leather aftershave, his egg-shaped body reminding her of Humpty Dumpty as he teetered back and forth.

"Let's not bother with the pleasantries," she said. "We both know we don't enjoy each other's company. But, what can I say? I'm in a tough spot."

"You can say that again."

"How bad is it?" she asked.

Pomfried made a face like he'd just bit into a lemon. "I expect there's more charges to be filed, but right now they're coming at you for a violation of 18 U.S.C. section 3, Accessory After the

Fact. Carries a sentence of up to fifteen years." Pomfried recited the statute from memory:

Whoever, knowing that an offense against the United States has been committed, receives, relieves, comforts or assists the offender in order to hinder or prevent his apprehension, trial or punishment, is an accessory after the fact.

"I wasn't helping him escape!" Mary Beth shouted.

"So you say."

"Listen!" Mary Beth yanked her cuffs against the metal bar bolted to the wooden bench. "When they catch Sawyer, and I pray to God they do, they'll find a bullet hole in his foot that I put there."

"Sugar, that may not matter. They've already got you admitting to a Special Agent Biggs that you took your brother on an hours long sojourn through underground tunnels for the express purpose of evading his apprehension."

"Yes, but I was taking him to jail."

"Then why not take him out the front?"

"Because I was afraid he might have an unfortunate accident if I turned him over to the feds."

Pomfried grimaced. "That sounds an awful lot like hindering or preventing apprehension."

"But he was already apprehended. By me."

Pomfried rolled that over. "It's a tough sell," he said. "Especially with your family connections and reputation. Presumption of innocence be damned, you're not gonna get the benefit of the doubt here, Sugar."

Mary Beth banged her head against the plaster wall, then said, "Well, I guess you'll just have to get me out of here and I'll go catch Sawyer myself. That would pretty much make the prosecution moot, wouldn't it."

"It would," Pomfried agreed. "They'd be sure to drop the

charges in that instance. But getting bail in a case like this is no easy lift. You're already charged with a crime of evasion, and this whole mess has received a ton of publicity. Given the government a hell of a black eye. They need a scalp, quick, and you should expect them to come at you, guns blazing—both barrels. I hear John Jensen's planning on handling this thing himself. No question they'll oppose bail."

"What would you say my chances are?"

"What? Of walking out of here today?"

"Yeah."

Pomfried pondered. "In the hands of most lawyers, I'd say not too damn good. But with someone of exceptional ability, like yours truly…" Pomfried fanned his elbows like a chickadee trying to take flight. "I'd say you'd probably be looking at fifty-fifty."

A coin flip for freedom. Mary Beth was hoping for better odds but she'd take it. What choice did she have? "Well, I guess it's a good thing I've got you then," she said.

Pomfried smiled so wide he nearly split his face. Clearly a moment he'd been waiting for. "Woah, woah, woah, Sugar. Slow down, now. You seem to be under the impression I'm agreeing to represent you."

"Why else would you drive all this way?"

Pomfried raised his bushy eyebrows, wrinkling his liver-spotted forehead. "Sugar, I drove all this way just for the delightful pleasure of telling you to kiss my big, fat, hairy, white ass."

Mary Beth felt her stomach drop, which was made worse by the heavy knock on the steel door. A federal marshal stuck his head to let them know the hearing was about to start.

Mary Beth thought that was it, she'd have to go it alone, but Pomfried told the marshal to, "Hang on a sec."

"There something else you want me to kiss?" she asked.

"No, there's something else I wanted to say," Pomfried told her. "I didn't get to finish. My reason for coming down here, initially, was to tell you to kiss my ass. But…" Pomfried raised a finger. "As I was pulling up to the courthouse this morning I couldn't help notice all the news vans out there. This sucker's really blowing up. Representing you has gone from a matter of local interest to national news. A hot damn story. And I'm thinking it could use a leading man," Pomfried said, raising his pudgy chin and stroking his trim white Hemmingway beard. "So, I've decided that under the circumstances, I'm willing to help you out of this jam, provided, of course, you sign this."

He pulled a yellow pad from a worn brown leather satchel.

"What's this?" Mary Beth asked, looking at what appeared to be a legal document handwritten in all caps.

"This is probably the broadest waiver possible of any and all past, present, or future conflicts of interests. It will absolutely bar you from ever seeking to disqualify me from any other case, on account of my representation of you. Now, if you'll just put your sweet little Janie Hancock on the dotted line there, we can get down to business."

Mary Beth groaned. She'd been so proud of her little ploy to conflict Pomfried out of representing criminals in her county, the idea was hard to let go of. But Pomfried had her over a barrel. He pulled out his gold pocket watch and started twirling it around his index finger to emphasize the time pressure.

"Give me a pen," Mary Beth said.

"Got a special one, right here." Promfried handed her a gold fountain pen, monogrammed with his initials.

She used her free hand to scribble her signature, then dropped the pen atop the pad. "There. Fine. Now what's the plan?"

"Don't worry," Pomfried told her. "I've got a few little tricks up my sleeve."

The confidence in Pomfried's voice gave Mary Beth felt the first real twinge of hope she'd felt since the moment the feds first put the cuffs on her. She knew how infuriatingly effective Pomfried could be and was actually glad that for once they'd be on the same side. The thing he said about tricks bothered her, though. "I thought you couldn't get away with surprises in federal court, the way you can in state court."

"Generally, that's true," Pomfried said. "But today the cameras are rolling. And remember, I'm just a poor old, country lawyer who don't know no better, up against these city slickers and the big bad, old gov'mint. The judge is just gonna have to cut me a break."

Mary Beth had seen Pomfried pull this aw-sucks routine before, to great effect. It often allowed him to get away with things other lawyers wouldn't dare try. She just hoped it would work in this kind of high-profile setting.

The hefty attorney covered his heart like he was pledging the flag. "Jensen may have the law on his side, Sugar, but today I'm going in there to talk about *justice*."

36

THE COURTROOM HAD a stuffy, bureaucratic feel. Sleepy, powder blue carpet and walls made of cherry wood interspersed with pale, yellow padded panels that muffled the swirl of whispers from the sizable crowd—all of which stopped the instant Mary Beth entered the room. She had perp-walked tons of criminals in her career, but had never before appreciated how immense the shame could be. Overwhelming. Mary Beth, the sheriff, in her beige prison garb, shuffling in with hands and feet shackled like a zoo animal. She hung close to Pomfried, trying to use his rotundness to shield her from the gawkers.

The marshal uncuffed her once she got to her seat. Then Mary Beth heard the sweet voice that simultaneously warmed and wounded her heart.

"Mom?"

Sam wrapped his arms around his mother's neck, but, quick as a frog's tongue, the marshal lashed out and got in between. "No touching the prisoner," he barked.

Sam backed up, startled. "She's my mom."

"Doesn't matter, son. You want to stay in this courtroom, you'll need to go take your seat."

"It's okay, Sammy," Mary Beth said. "Everything's gonna be okay."

Sam bit at his bottom lip like he was about to break up, but held it together. "I'll be sitting right over there, Mom." He pointed three rows back to an open seat next to Izzy and Princess. Izzy's right arm was in a sling. He smiled at Mary Beth and held up a fist with his left. Next to him, Princess was stunning as usual, a head taller than those around, and two heads taller than Izzy. Her long dark hair was highlighted with caramel streaks, straightened today, and parted in the middle. She stared coldly at Mary Beth. The two women had never particularly warmed to each other, separated by something like jealousy or competition for Izzy's loyalty, and Mary Beth wasn't sure whether her presence was a sign of support, or just an attempt to keep her husband on a short leash.

Mary Beth did her best to smile. She waved to them just before the judge entered the room and they were all commanded to rise.

"Oyez, Oyez, Oyez, this United States District Court for the Southern District of West Virginia is now in session, the Honorable Judge Jim Parsons, presiding. God save the United States and this honorable court. You may be seated."

Judge Parsons was straight from central casting. A white-haired man, who kept a pair of half lens reading glasses perched at the end of his nose with an air of indignity, like the presence of the litigants already annoyed him. He called the case and Mary Beth realized just how much she was up against. "The United States of America versus Mary Beth Cain." She'd taken on a lot of tough adversaries in her time but never an entire nation before.

John Jensen identified himself as the country's attorney. He wore a navy blue suit with a striped politician's tie and was flanked by two junior attorneys on either side. Sitting behind him was Patrick, who stared down at his lap, avoiding eye contact.

"Will counsel for the defense please identify yourself for the record?" the judge said.

Pomfried wiggled to free his girth from the arms of his chair. "Alexander Tyrell Pomfried," he said, once he'd managed to stand. "From the Jasper County Bar, your honor, representing the *wrongfully* accused, *Sheriff* Mary Beth Cain, hero of the Old Wengo Mine Fiasco, and rescuer of more than three hundred West Virginia residents not to mention numerous fed—"

"Objection." Jensen was on his feet, red faced, looking from the judge to all the media filling the gallery.

"Sustained," the judge said. "That will do, Mr. Pomfried."

Mary Beth's lawyer raised a chubby hand of apology. "Can't help it if it's true, your honor."

The judge peered over the top of his reading glasses like he was about to dish out a rebuke but then decided to just get on with it. "Mr. Pomfried, your client has been charged with a violation of 18 U.S. Code section 3, Accessory After the Fact, for aiding in the escape and/or otherwise hindering the arrest of one Sawyer Thompson, who is in turn charged with multiple counts including, eighteen counts of murder, over six hundred counts of attempted murder, domestic terrorism, sedition, destruction of public property, reckless endangerment, kidnapping, wrongful imprisonment, thirty-six counts of endangering a minor, battery, assault, multiple violations of the RICO statute, weapons violations..."

Mary Beth zoned out somewhere in the middle of the list. She could feel all the stares, stinging her like bees, as the judge rattled off the offenses, painting her with Sawyer's brush. When he finally finished, the judge said, "Does your client wish to enter a plea?"

"Yes, sir," Pomfried said, triumphantly. "My client, the hero of the Old Wengo Mine Fiasco, is most decidedly not guilty."

Mary Beth got the feeling that every time Pomfried referred to her, he planned to call her the Hero of the Old Wengo Mine Fiasco. Jensen must have had the same inkling because he objected to that very thing.

"Sustained," the judge said. "Mr. Pomfried, you will refer to your client as the Defendant or Sheriff Cain. Is that understood?"

"Understood your, honor. And I do hope your honor will forgive me." Pomfried waddled around to wave to all the press in the audience as if apologizing to them, too. He had an intentional, bumbling way about him that, combined with his weight, evoked a level of sympathy, as well as amusement. He wiped his forehead with a pocket kerchief even though the air conditioning was pumping, and said, "It's just that I have so rarely had the opportunity to represent someone of such heroism, such valor. When I stop to think of the hundreds of souls she saved, and that she was willing to shoot her own brother to do it, I just—"

"Your honor!" Jensen looked like he was about to lose it.

The judge turned up his palms. Jensen was right, of course, even Mary Beth knew that Pomfried's little asides and grandstanding was improper. But the judge motioned for the U.S. Attorney to sit down.

"There's no jury here, Mr. Jensen," he said, meaning there was no one there to be unfairly prejudiced by such comments. But that's where the judge was wrong. Pomfried knew it, and Mary Beth did, too. The jury of public opinion was in that courtroom, represented by the gaggle of reporters and three television cameras, who Pomfried was really performing for.

"Let's just move on, shall we?" the judge said. "Mr. Jensen, what is the government's position on bail?"

"We oppose bail. Given the nature of the charge, evading capture, combined with the sheer gravity of the situation, we believe the Defendant presents a significant flight risk in a case of immense public importance. As you know, Judge, the Defendant is charged with aiding in the escape of or at least hindering the arrest of Sawyer Thompson, her brother, a man who as of today is number one on the FBI's Most Wanted List. Right at the very top. In addition, your honor, there are multiple media reports dating back to the summer that...."

Jensen paused and motioned for one of his flunky attorneys to distribute copies of newspaper articles to the Judge and Pomfried. "This is a recent exposé about Sheriff Cain, titled *Rough Justice*. As you can see, your Honor, they document not only a pattern of corruption on the part of Sheriff Cain—a certain systematic disdain for procedure—but also her family ties to a local drug enterprise, the so-called McCray County Mafia, allegedly controlled by the defendant's mother. This connection, your honor, not only gives the Defendant access to significant funds but also the underworld contacts who could very easily shepherd her out of the country. Given all of that, we do not feel that bail is warranted in this case."

As if that wasn't good enough to seal Mary Beth's fate, Jensen then put a cherry on top. "Finally, judge, because it has a significant bearing upon the Defendant's motivation to abscond, I will go ahead and inform the court that my office has been conducting an investigation into Sheriff Cain over the last couple of months and is preparing an indictment right now for various public corruption charges related to some of the very issues described in these articles."

Mary Beth glanced behind her and immediately regretted it. The press was eating it all up. Typing away. She could see the headlines now. *Criminal Sheriff Denied Bail. A Criminal Family Affair. Like Mother, Like Daughter.*

Mary Beth tugged on Pomfried's suit jacket. "Do something," she whispered. "I've got to get out of here." She was becoming more and more convinced that catching Sawyer was her only way out of this mess.

Pomfried stood even before the judge addressed him. "Your Honor, let me begin by saying we object to the mention of any phantom charges that have yet to be brought. The only thing we can fairly respond to at this point is the charge at hand. And, Judge, our response to that is: bring it on. My client cannot wait to get her day in court. Would never dream of running." He picked up his copy of the newspaper clippings and fanned himself with it. "I've read these articles, Judge, and while there's a lot in there we vehemently disagree with, one thing they do make clear is that this young lady ain't afraid of a thing. Shoot, you could drop her in a nest of vipers, and she wouldn't flinch. Just days ago, Judge, she stood between two armies loaded to bear and brought them both to heel like she was Moses parting the Red Sea. She sure as anything, ain't afraid of Mr. Jensen."

"Objection."

"Overruled," the judge said.

Pomfried looked surprised to have won that one but wasted no time in continuing. "Your Honor, the thing we typically look at with pretrial release is ties to the community, right? Well, this lady has got those in spades. Has lived her *entire* life in Southern West Virginia. All her family's here. And she's an elected official, Judge. Spent her career protecting Jasper County. Now, I can't imagine how someone could have deeper ties to a community than Sheriff Cain has to hers." Pomfried made a grand gesture to the reporters behind him and said, "Not to mention the fact she's now so recognizable, it would be awfully hard for her to go anywhere without being noticed."

When Pomfried finished, the judge said. "Is there anything else you'd like to add, Mr. Pomfried?" Mary Beth didn't like the way that sounded, like he was about to rule against her, but was giving Pomfried one last chance to persuade him otherwise.

Pomfried held up a finger. "Yes sir, your honor, yes sir, there is more I, uh…" Pomfried paused. Mary Beth couldn't tell if he was searching for something to say or trying to decide whether to unleash a final card he'd kept in his back pocket up until that point.

"Mr. Pomfried?"

"Yes, your honor." He gave Mary Beth a furtive glance then cleared his throat. "In addition, your Honor, we are so anxious for trial, that my client is willing to consent to have it heard by a magistrate and hereby demands a speedy trial, pursuant to 18 U.S. Code section 3161, which, by statute, cannot be held later than seventy days from today's date. But that will put us immediately into trial prep mode your honor, and my client will need to be granted pretrial release so that we can get ready."

Jensen was on his feet objecting that they'd been given no prior notice of a speedy trial request. Meanwhile, Mary Beth was lodging her own objection, whispering to Pomfried. "Seventy days? Sawyer could be in Timbuktu by now. How in the hell am I supposed to track him down in seventy days?"

Pomfried leaned down. "Listen, do you want out or not?"

Mary Beth groaned. Of course, she did, but she was thinking she'd have something more like a year of pretrial release to hunt for her brother.

"Well, do you?"

"Yes," Mary Beth said through gritted teeth.

"Then, you're gonna have to trust me."

The judge finished explaining to Jensen that the defendant had an absolute right to a speedy trial, regardless of whether there'd been prior notice, then announced his ruling on the bail issue.

"The Court finds that the defendant has no prior criminal record, that she is a duly elected sheriff of Jasper County with deep ties to her community, and that she has exhibited her resolve to fight the charges against her by requesting a speedy trial. Based upon those findings, I am ruling that the defendant be granted pretrial release."

Mary Beth pumped her fist.

Jensen tried to object. "Your Honor, I—"

"Just a minute, Mr. Jensen," the judge said. "I'm not finished.

As a condition of this release, however, given the nature of the charge, and the gravity of this matter, including its importance to the public, I am ruling that the Defendant be fitted with an electronic monitoring device and is instructed not to leave the state. Any violation of that condition will result in an immediate revocation of this order. Is that understood?"

"Understood, You Honor," Pomfried said, looking satisfied with himself.

After that, the judge declared the court in recess and dropped his gavel like he was hammering the final nail into Mary Beth's coffin. She now had only seventy days to catch her brother and couldn't even leave the state to do it.

What in the hell was she going to do?

Mary Beth buried her head in her hands. When she looked up, Pomfried was staring at her, bristling. "Hey," he said. "A thank you might be nice."

37

MARY BETH HAD to hang around the courthouse while pre-release paperwork was completed and the marshals calibrated the monitoring bracelet—the anchor that would confine her to the mountain state until her quickly approaching trial. The crowd cleared out. The press scurrying off to post their stories or take position by the exits where they could molest Mary Beth with microphones and questions as she tried to leave. But the trio of Sam, Izzy, and Princess had stayed behind. Mary Beth saw Princess mouth to her husband, "I'm going to go talk to her." Izzy stood to stop his wife but she gave him a look that put the deputy back in his seat.

Princess straightened her long skirt before cat-walking down the aisle. "Congratulations, Sheriff. Glad to hear you'll be getting out," she said. Her words were stilted, drained of any warmth.

"Thank you," Mary Beth said. "I appreciate your support."

"Oh, I'm not here to support you."

"No? Why are you here then?"

Mary Beth was seated. Princess bent over her, clasping a hand to her chest to keep her blouse from drooping, and spoke directly into Mary Beth's ear. "I'm here to make sure you know that my husband is on medical leave. So, he won't be joining you on any more adventures for a while, understand?"

The two women stared at each other like rival lionesses circling on the Serengeti. Mary Beth was the first to back down, because she really couldn't blame Princess for her concern.

"I understand," she said.

"Good."

Princess had made her point and turned to leave but Mary Beth called to her.

"Hey, Princess?"

"Yes?" she said, swiveling around.

"I really am sorry about all that Izzy went through. I can't tell you how much."

Princess looked her up and down. "Uh-huh."

"What do you say I make it up to you?"

"And just how do you propose to do that?"

Mary Beth smiled, trying to muster some of her usual swagger despite the humbled position she found herself in. "What would you say to an exclusive interview?"

To Princess' credit, she didn't jump at the opportunity right away. She maintained the stern look of the protective wife. But eventually, she nodded and said, "Call me tomorrow."

"You got it."

As Princess retook her seat, John Jensen reentered the courtroom, surrounded by his phalanx of assistants. Lagging behind was Patrick, whose body language suggested he'd rather be anywhere else in the world.

Jensen beckoned to Pomfried and pointed to the jury room.

"Come on, Sugar," Pomfried said. "The government's about to make us an offer."

Mary Beth and her attorney followed Jensen's cavalcade into the jury room where they all took a seat around a long conference table—everyone but Patrick, who stood in the corner behind Jensen, trying to be a fly on the wall.

"You dropping the charges?" Pomfried asked.

Jensen tried to laugh, but it wasn't natural on him. "You wish," he said. "The reason I asked you in here is to offer a plea."

"Figured as much," Pomfried responded. "Let's hear it."

Jensen cleared his throat. He looked especially stiff, like he had the long arm of the law shoved up his ass. "Given the severity of the charges, the gravity of the situation, and the strength of the evidence, we are prepared to recommend a reduced sentence of six years if the Defendant pleads guilty. That's less than half the maximum."

"No." Pomfried said it quickly, without emotion, then sat there silently, hands on the table.

"That's it?" Jensen asked. "You don't even want to discuss it with your client?"

"No, need. The answer's no. Isn't it, Sugar?" Pomfried said, looking at Mary Beth.

"Not only 'No,' but 'Hell No,'" she said.

"See," Pomfried said. "I told you."

Jensen looked truly shocked. "You realize we've got her dead to rights."

"That's what you think," Pomfried said. "Tomorrow morning, I'm planning to file a motion to suppress any statements made to Agent Biggs, along with a motion to dismiss."

Jensen huffed. "Dismiss on what basis?"

"Your probable cause comes from the statement to Biggs, and those were made before she'd been read her rights. Now I may just be a poor old country lawyer, but even I know that violates the Fourth Amendment. We gonna have to throw that out."

"She wasn't in custody at the time," Jensen argued.

"Not in custody? She was handcuffed to a damn tree."

"Not by us," Jensen said. "According to your client, it was her brother's men who cuffed her there. So, at the time those statements were made she was still a cooperating officer in a manhunt."

"Not true," Pomfried said. "Biggs even admitted that he'd been instructed—by you—to arrest her if she was discovered without her brother."

Globs of spittle formed at the corners of Jensen's mouth. "But she didn't know that," he said. "The issue is whether a reasonable person in the defendant's position would consider themselves to be in custody at the time the statement was made."

"And you don't think being handcuffed to a tree, while a team of six armed FBI agents grill you, qualifies?"

One of Jensen's lackeys whispered something to him. "Right," he said. "Good point." He stared Pomfried down. "You know what, who cares if you get the statement tossed? She obviously took her brother through the mine."

"Did she?" Pomfried asked. "I don't know that. For all I know, she could have been Sawyer's prisoner. Dainty little lady like this with the FBI's most wanted man. Who knows what he made her do?"

"But she told her deputy she was taking Thompson out through the tunnel. He told us that as soon as he exited the compound."

Pomfried swatted that assertion away like a fly. "Izzy was delirious. Had spent days in captivity. Didn't know what he was saying. Besides, with all he's been through, I wouldn't be surprised at all if Deputy Baker's not well enough to testify—if you know what I'm saying." Pomfried winked, like he had already secured such a commitment from Izzy not to show up at trial.

"There was also the man from the compound." Jensen consulted his notes. "Charlie Radford. The man who'd held Deputy Baker captive. He also heard the sheriff say she was taking Thompson through the tunnel to evade the federal officers outside the gates."

"You mean the same Charlie Radford who is currently in

federal custody, charged with aggravated kidnapping, amongst other crimes. That's your star witness? The jury will just assume he's saying what you told him to, in order to get himself a deal."

Jensen's mouth fell open for a millisecond before locking his jaw in a grind of determination. He quickly huddled with his minions. Even Patrick joined in and, from Mary Beth's vantage point, soon looked like he was taking over as quarterback and started calling the plays.

When they broke, Jensen said, "I can't believe I'm doing this but, on the advice and recommendation of my co-counsel from DC, we'll agree to a suspended sentence, provided we get Sheriff Cain's full cooperation in apprehending her brother. As long as she cooperates in good faith, she won't spend another day in jail."

"Who decides whether it's good faith?" Pomfried asked.

"We do. But we won't require success. She doesn't have to guarantee that Sawyer will be apprehended, just that she will comply with all requests for information and assistance to the best of her ability."

Pomfried turned to Mary Beth, beaming like he should get a World's Greatest Attorney trophy.

"But I'd still have to plead guilty?" she said.

"That's right," Jensen said.

"Then I won't do it."

Pomfried tried to hold Mary Beth back from where she'd leaned over the table. "Hold on now, Sug—"

"Don't Sugar me," she said, swatting her attorney's hand away. "If I plead guilty, the County Commissioners would start up a recall tomorrow. I'm not giving up my office. I'll go catch Sawyer myself and put an end to this nonsense."

Jensen leaned forward too. "We aren't waiting around anymore. We'd much rather put all of our collective focus on pursuing your brother. So, if you want to do this, then you need to make the deal. We'll draw up the paperwork and have it ready by ten o'clock tomorrow morning. You can have until then to decide."

"You can have my decision, now," Mary Beth said, shoving her middle finger in Jensen's face.

Pomfried looked like he was about to have a stroke as he pushed her arm down. "Sugar, please, we need to discuss this."

Jensen and his minions stood to leave. Patrick whispered something to him. Jensen frowned then said, "AUSA Connelly requests permission to speak with the defendant alone."

"Absolutely not," Pomfried shouted. "We already tried that once and look where it got us."

But Mary Beth put her hand on her attorney's shoulder. "It's okay," she said. "I want to hear what he has to say."

38

PATRICK SAT OPPOSITE Mary Beth but kept his gaze on the table.

"So," she said, "the silent partner finally speaks."

Patrick whispered his response, "Just take the deal, Mary."

"No way."

He looked up at her with red eyes, like he hadn't slept in days. "Please, just take the deal and leave this place. Come away with me," Patrick said, reaching for her hand. "Leave this whole mess behind you. Your mother, your brother, everything. Just—"

"Just what?" Mary Beth snapped, pulling her hand away. "Go bake cookies in DC? Wear a little black dress, and hang on your arm at cocktail parties with politicos? I don't think so."

"You could do whatever you want, but we would finally be together. Like we always should have been. Just cooperate and we can put everything behind us."

"Us?" Mary Beth was offended by the suggestion. She was the one in hot water, and Patrick helped put her there.

"Yes, *us*. You've put me in a really terrible position, too."

"Oh, really?" Mary Beth tugged at her prison clothes.

"I'm serious, Mary. I could lose my job. Maybe even get prosecuted myself."

"For what?"

"I put the deal together. I'm the one who sent you into that compound. And then you...." Patrick stopped short of saying she'd helped Sawyer escape, but that was obviously what he was thinking. "I should have known you'd choose your family over doing what was right."

Whack! Mary Beth slapped the table hard. "I didn't help Sawyer, goddammit! I'm the one who stopped him from blowing the top off that mountain and killing every living soul up there."

"No one disputes that. It's what happened after."

"After? Patrick, you of all people should know why I didn't march him out of that front gate. I agreed to arrest him, not serve him up to the firing squad."

"That wouldn't have hap—"

"How do you know? Agents were dead. You're really telling me there's no chance somebody would find an excuse to take a shot at him."

Patrick leaned back in his chair. "Would that have been so bad?" he said.

Mary Beth couldn't believe her ears. "Fuck you!" she said. "Are you serious?"

"Yes, I'm serious. I was right there when Agent Lange was killed. I saw the bullets flying like it was the Battle of the Bulge or something. And Sawyer's men murdered my informant, a man named Quigley. A man with a family, who I put in harm's way. And, if it weren't for you, Sawyer would have murdered everyone up there. Everyone. Hundreds of people. Not to mention the people already killed in the courthouse bombing. If he isn't caught soon, I'm sure he'll try to pull off something even bigger next time. So yeah, forgive me, Mary, but I don't think it would have been such a bad thing if someone shot him."

It took Mary Beth a moment to absorb that blow. "He's still my brother," she said.

Patrick rolled his eyes and adopted a kind of sad, wistful expression that really bugged the shit out of her. "Have you ever heard of Stalin's chicken?" he asked.

"That come with marinara sauce?"

"No," Patrick said, unamused. "It's a legend about Joseph Stalin. That one time he brought a live chicken before the polit bureau and ripped all its feathers out. Then while the chicken was cowering in the corner, bald and bleeding, he started dropping little scraps of bread and the chicken followed him around. The point was that no matter how badly they treated the peasants, they would still follow the hand that fed them."

Mary Beth didn't see the relevance. "Patrick—"

"I used to think about that a lot," he said, not letting her interrupt. "When I used to live here, in this backwards fucking state. It's been raped and pillaged by coal barons for over a century, but if anybody ever says anything against coal, they get viciously attacked because everyone is so desperate for the crumbs the coal companies throw at them."

"Are you working your way up to a point?"

"My point is: that's you, Mary. You act like you're this big badass, but you're really just like that chicken when it comes to your family. Whether you let Sawyer go on purpose or he just got the drop on you after you took him through that tunnel, really doesn't matter. You never should have been there in the first place. Jesus, Mary, you never should have come under federal investigation at all, but there's always a cloud over you because you won't cut ties with your mother. You're so desperate for whatever little crumbs of love or family, or whatever in the hell it is you think you get from them, that you've let it ruin your life. And mine too."

"Your life? What are you talking about?"

Patrick shook his head.

"Hey, don't start holding back now. Is there anything else from my childhood we need to discuss?"

Patrick swallowed hard like he was working up the nerve to say something important, then let her have it. "I think you got pregnant on purpose."

"What...in...the...hell, are you talking about?" Mary Beth said.

"In high school. I think you got pregnant on purpose so you'd have an excuse not to leave."

Mary Beth started to fire back an insult, a witty retort to let Patrick know how unbelievably stupid that was, but for some reason her mouth wouldn't work. A sudden swirl of emotion seized hold of her, shock and sadness, and a reluctant recognition that pressed down on her chest like a heavy stone.

"Going away with me made too much sense," Patrick said. "Just like it does now. No rational reason not to. But you couldn't leave your mother and brother. Couldn't pass up those little crumbs. So, whether it was subconscious or whatever, I think you were looking for an excuse not to go."

Mary Beth wanted desperately to deny it, to tell Patrick what he could go do with his little opinions, but couldn't bring herself to do either.

"I guess I'm guilty of the same thing," Patrick said. "God knows I've let my inability to let go of you jeopardize my career. Taken insane risks. Even stared down a fucking tank. And, if I'm being honest, it probably had something to do with the failure of my marriage. Like, I was always holding something back. Saving it for you. But that's over now, Mary. I can't keep sabotaging myself. So this is the last time I'll ask you to come with me. If you don't take this deal, I promise, you'll never see me again."

Patrick stood, and held out his hand like he was trying to pluck Mary Beth from a raging sea. "Take the deal," he said.

Mary Beth stared longingly at his smooth, uncalloused hand. Then crossed her arms and turned away.

"Yeah, that's what I thought," he said, sadly. "Goodbye, Mary."

Patrick sounded like he meant it. The last time he spoke those words, in that same tone, it had been nearly twenty years before they'd seen each other again.

"Patrick, wait."

He looked back to her from the door. "What?"

Mary Beth felt a breathless pounding in her chest, thumps echoing a notion that had haunted her for years. Something she'd never been willing to fully articulate, not even inside her own mind, but the moment it coalesced into words, there was no doubt that they were true.

"He's your son."

39

MARY BETH WAS expecting some response, but Patrick just stared at her. Eventually, she filled the silence with explanation.

"We'd parted with such harsh words. I never wanted to see you again. And then Bill proposed the instant he found out I was pregnant. The next thing I knew, I was married. It just seemed obvious that Bill was the father. You and I had only been together over your Fall Break. I—" Mary Beth paused. "And when Sam was born, he looked just like me." She smiled wistfully, thinking back to those early days of motherhood. "But there'd be these little gestures, you know. Little mannerisms that would remind me of you."

She gazed up at Patrick who looked like he'd just watched an alien spacecraft land right in front of him.

"Well, say something."

Patrick's face went through phases. First shocked, then puzzled, but eventually settled on something like disgust.

"You're really unbelievable."

Not the response Mary Beth was hoping for. "I'm sorry I didn't tell you sooner," she said. "But I couldn't. Honestly, I never really admitted it to myself until just right now. It would have killed Bill if he'd known. It would kill Sam." Mary Beth covered her mouth thinking about what this revelation could do to her boy. "To this day, he has no idea. Sam idolized Bill."

Patrick wasn't buying it. He shook his head, like a habitual mark realizing he'd been suckered yet again. "You know, I always thought there was some line between you and your mother. Some barrier you wouldn't cross. But you are every bit as shameless. To make up some story about your own son. What kind of soulless—"

"It's not made up. I swear," Mary Beth pleaded. But she could see it was no use. Patrick was in full denial mode. He turned the doorknob.

"You should have just taken your clothes off again," he said. "I still would have known you were manipulating me, but at least it would have been fun."

With that parting shot, he left Mary Beth alone. She put her head down on the conference room table and allowed herself to sob for several minutes, feeling all the guilt and hurt and frustration.

Eventually, there was a gentle knock on the door.

Izzy peeked his head in. "How we doing?" he asked.

Mary Beth ran to her friend and hugged his neck, careful not to catch his injured arm this time.

"You okay?" he asked, pulling back to look at her.

Mary Beth dried her eyes. "Yeah." She stumbled for something else to say, then told Izzy she had a big decision to make. "The government's extended what Pomfried thinks is a good offer: Suspended sentence, no jail time, as long as I cooperate with the search for Sawyer, which of course I'd do anyway."

They each took a seat.

"That's a good offer," Izzy said. "Considering everything. But you'd still have to plead guilty, though, right?"

"Yeah. Which means I could pretty much kiss my office

goodbye." Mary Beth rubbed at the base of her skull, feeling a headache coming on. "Oh God, Izzy, I don't know. What do you think I should do?"

Izzy spent a moment considering the question. Mary Beth assumed her more cautious friend would suggest she take the deal but instead he surprised her by telling her exactly what she needed to hear.

"I think that with this McCray County annexation happening, all the baggage it brings, Jasper County would be in a whole mess of trouble if it didn't have you to protect them."

Mary Beth smiled for what felt like the first time in days. *Hell fucking yes*, she thought. Mary Beth grabbed Izzy and kissed him on the forehead.

"Okay, okay," he said. "Don't go all soft on me, now."

There was another knock at the door. It was Alexander Pomfried, letting her know that the marshals had the paperwork and tracking device ready, and he was to escort her down to the third floor to finalize things. Mary Beth said that was fine, but first insisted that they send Sam home. "I don't want him to see me getting fitted with that thing," she said, but the truth was, she wasn't sure she could face her son after what she'd just admitted about his parentage.

Sam really had worshipped Bill. She could still see them playing in the backyard. Bill flinging little Sam so high into the air, it had to feel like flying. The two always shared a bond that went well past the usual affinities of gender. So much so, it had often left Mary Beth feeling like the odd man out in her own home. Bill was the fun one. The big, strong hero who got to come home at the end of the day, after all the chores and homework nagging were done, and wrestled around with Sam on the living room floor. Mary Beth was the angry, frustrated lady who yelled a lot and made Sam eat his vegetables. If Sam were to ever find out that Bill Cain was not his father, she feared it would just be far too great a mindfuck for her fragile boy to handle.

Izzy volunteered to talk to Sam and walk him to his car. They were close, too. Since Bill's death, thirteen years earlier, Izzy had probably been the most consistent male presence in Sam's life.

Once they were gone, Mary Beth followed Pomfried down to the third floor. She filled out paperwork and put on the clothes Sam had brought for her. The only thing she wanted to wear. A clean, nicely pressed uniform, and her floppy brimmed Stetson.

As the marshal secured the monitoring bracelet, he explained how it worked. "This is one of the new ones we're trying out. Most of them communicate with a satellite, kind of like GPS, but those don't work so well down in your neck of the woods where coverage is so spotty. We use one of those, and every ten minutes the signal goes out, and we get a message to come arrest you. So, we are going to try this one. It doesn't have active monitoring. More like the blackbox inside your car. So, when you get home each night, you're going to have to hook it into this device," the marshal said, pointing to what looked like some kind of modem/router combo. "Do it every night by ten pm. Takes about five minutes. It will alert us if you have been out of the state. If we get that report that you have, or you fail to jack in on time, we're going to come and take you back to jail. Understand?"

"What if something goes wrong?" Mary Beth asked. "Like my power goes out or something and I can't connect?"

The marshal handed her a business card. "If you have technical difficulties, call this number. And you better have a damn good story when you do."

Mary Beth looked down at the square black box strapped above her ankle. "Well, I was never much for skirts anyway," she said.

The marshal told her she was now free to go. "Good luck to you, Sheriff."

Mary Beth gave the marshal a two-fingered salute. Pomfried said his goodbyes, too, after securing Mary Beth's promise to seriously consider the government's offer and meet him back at the courthouse the following morning. Meanwhile, Princess was impatiently waiting, hand on hip. After walking Sam to his car, Izzy had met them on the third floor and offered to give Mary Beth a ride back to Jasper Creek.

"So, what now, boss?" he asked her.

"I don't know." Mary Beth pointed to the bracelet. "I can't leave the state to go hunting after Sawyer, and now I've got a ten pm curfew to boot."

"Well, I've got an idea," Izzy said.

"Okay, shoot."

Izzy stroked his chin. "I can't stop thinking about Sheriff Bailey. How he said there was more to Gray's death. We pretty much know it was his son who did the deed but he was working for someone. Someone other than Bailey, I think."

"Whoever was buying up the land in McCray," Mary Beth said.

"Right. And I think we both agree it's unlikely Bailey had that kind of money, so there's at least another player."

Mary Beth sighed. "Yeah, there's definitely a lot of things to follow up on there. But right now I need to focus on how to find Sawyer."

"True. But you're not gonna find him tonight, right?"

"Not unless he's at home waiting for me."

"So," Izzy said, "I understand Bailey left a widow. What do you say we ride out and talk to her?"

"*Ex-cuse* me," Princess said. "You must be joking."

Izzy looked up at his wife. "Baby, it's just a house call. Nothing dangerous."

"If it's just a house call then why do you need to do it?" Princess asked. "You the only deputy on the force?"

"No," Izzy said. "But I've got history with Bailey. I was hand-cuffed next to the man for days. And I was there when they killed him. I owe it to his wife to go see her. She's got to have a million questions. If things were reversed, wouldn't you have wanted Bailey to come tell you what had happened to me?"

Princess had a hard time arguing with that but didn't let it go without a warning.

"Okay," she said, pointing a long, slender finger. "You and your friend run off and do what you want. But if you get hurt, don't bother coming home, you understand I'm not spending days waiting by the phone again, not knowing whether you're alive or dead."

"Of course, baby. This is nothing to worry about." Izzy stood on his tippy toes and puckered his lips like a little kid asking for a kiss. Princess brushed him off and pointed at Mary Beth. "And you. I want your word that you're not going to pull any of your typical cowboy shit."

Mary Beth raised her hands in surrender. "Princess," she said. "You have nothing to worry about."

40

MARY BETH AND the Bakers made the long drive home from Charleston, traveling down curving highways through West Virginia's rolling hills, beautiful scenery, but Mary Beth's attention stayed trained on the dark blue Lincoln Continental that tailed them from the moment they left the courthouse. Feds.

"Should we try to lose them?" Izzy asked.

Which was a dumb question because Princess was driving. They were in her burgundy-colored Acura and she wasn't having it. "I know you don't think I'm gonna engage in a high-speed chase with the FBI."

"Baby, they're not traffic cops. It's not like they're gonna give us a ticket."

"Isaiah Baker. Have you lost your damn mind?"

"No, I'm just saying—"

"Saying what? And you better choose your words carefully, 'cause you're on strike two as it is."

Mary Beth interrupted before things got any more heated between husband and wife. "Don't sweat it, Princess," she said. "Let the FBI follow. I've got a better idea."

They eventually made it to Izzy and Princess's home, a brick colonial on the south side of town, where Izzy's monster-truck-sized Blazer, Beulah, was parked in the driveway. Princess parked along the street, knowing by that point that Mary Beth and Izzy were planning to take Izzy's vehicle. The Lincoln circled the block then came back around and stopped three houses down. It was a surveillance move that might have worked in a more urban setting, but in Izzy's quiet neighborhood, a place aptly named Idle Acres, the feds were about as subtle as a streaker at a funeral.

Mary Beth gave the G-men a little wave as she climbed into Izzy's truck. Princess kissed her husband and chastised both officers one last time to be on their best behavior. After that, Izzy fired up the Blazer, and he and Mary Beth reversed quickly out of the driveway. He roared down the block and stopped right by the feds so Mary Beth could roll down her window and yell at the two square-headed men in mirrored sunglasses who were trying to look anywhere other than at their subject.

"We're headed into McCray," she shouted. "You guys go ahead and turn around. We'll wait."

Izzy gunned the Blazer a short spurt, down to the end of the block. He had a custom built, methanol-injected engine that sounded like an F-16. Every time he gassed it, the Blazer's rear shocks coiled and crouched like a bullfrog before leaping forward.

The feds made a hasty three-point turn, tires and brakes squealing, and pulled into pursuit behind them.

Izzy and Mary Beth had fun taunting them all the way into McCray. Izzy stopping and starting, alternating between fast and slow, while Mary Beth blew the feds kisses and beckoned for them to keep up. They crested the Old River Mountain and were taking the slow winding turns down toward Honeysuckle Pass when Mary Beth let Izzy in on the rest of her plan. "You know how it opens up down here, the straightaway with the steep dip where your stomach drops out?"

"How could I forget?" Izzy said. "I think you hit it at about eighty the last time we came through."

"Think you can do the same?"

Izzy shrugged. "I guess so. But why? I'm not gonna outrun that Lincoln with this gas guzzler."

"True," Mary Beth said. "But right before the road levels out down there, there's a kind of half-assed runaway truck ramp, off to the right. We used to call it Skidders Row."

"What?"

"Yeah," Mary Beth said. "Like a lot of things in West Virginia, it was a good idea that never came to fruition. They started building a runaway truck ramp years ago, but ran out of money and never got around to putting in the gravel or sand, so it's basically just a super steep dirt path, with a bunch of jumps."

Izzy gave her his look of disapproval. "You're not serious."

"Sure, I've done it on a four-wheeler plenty of times."

"This truck weighs about twenty times more than a four-wheeler."

Mary Beth punched Izzy on the shoulder. "Come on," she said. "Let's see what this baby can do. What's the point of having a monster truck if you can't run over some shit now and then?"

They were just coming out of the last big curve, and Izzy was starting to pick up speed, with the feds close behind.

"If you can make it all the way to the top, there's a service road that leads back down into the west side of Mapleton," Mary Beth said. "No way those guys can follow us...if you can make it."

Izzy gave her one more side-eyed look. "Goddamn you, MB," he said as he mashed the accelerator. The engine growled, and they picked up a real head of steam, the immense weight of the monster truck plunging down the mountain.

The feds kept pace, just a few car lengths behind. Then at the last possible second before the road leveled out, Izzy jerked the vehicle onto the dirt road so sharply he momentarily went up on two wheels.

"Holy shit!" Mary Beth shouted. For a second, she thought they were about to roll, but the Blazer righted itself, crashed back down on all fours, and caught traction as they carved a thirty-degree incline back up the south side of the mountain.

The FBI tried the same move, pulling behind, into the Blazer's wake of dust and dirt.

The ramps on Skidder's Row were spaced twenty yards apart. The Blazer caught air off of each one, hopping like a ten-thousand-pound jackrabbit up the mountainside. But the feds nose-dived after the first jump. The Lincoln crashed down into the mud, smashing up their front end, then rolled to a stop halfway up the second ramp, with smoke pouring out the sides of its badly warped hood.

Meanwhile Izzy's Blazer continued to roar, climbing and leaping until finally coming to rest at the top of the mountain.

"Whoo!" Mary Beth grabbed Izzy by his non-injured shoulder and shook him. "Now that's some driving!"

Izzy looked more relieved than excited. He got out to assess any damage. Beulah was covered with mud and grime and had suffered a couple of dings, but it was nothing that a good detailing couldn't take care of.

Mary Beth walked around the truck, still catching her breath, and took a moment to appreciate the valley. The sun was setting on the Fall colors of the tree-covered mountains and glistened off the stream that snaked through the valley past the old saw mill. It reminded Mary Beth of the cool creek bed mud she used to wiggle her toes in it as a kid during hot summer days spent catching crawdads and skipping stones. Upstream was the steam from Jacob's Bread Factory, whose buttery rolls Mary Beth could taste in her mind. Not far past there, were the remaining tents of what would be McCray's final county fair, with its apple bobbing and cotton candy, deep fryers full of funnel cakes, and excited squeals from the tilt-a-whirl.

Mary Beth allowed herself a moment to see and taste and hear it all.

Then she thought again about Patrick. The whole ride back from Charleston, she kept wondering if he was right. Was she that pathetic little chicken, just clinging to her family and this place because it was all she'd ever known?

Maybe.

Maybe she had stayed simply because she was afraid to strike out somewhere else or try something new. That was the classic wrap on Appalachian people. Stubborn. Stoic. Scared. Yesterday's people, never spreading their wings beyond the penumbra of their parents' shadow, in a place where "moving out" often meant just pulling another trailer into the yard.

She was sure that was how Patrick saw her. And it had really bothered her at the time. But at that moment, standing atop the world, basking in the majesty of the mountains' autumn glow, she found that she didn't so much give a shit. She was who she was.

Mary Beth walked to the edge of Skidders Row and strained to spot the FBI agents down at the bottom. She couldn't quite make them out but knew they were there somewhere, trying to figure out what in the hell to do next, with a wrecked car, out in the middle of nowhere, in a place where their cell phones wouldn't do them any good.

She made a megaphone with her hands and shouted. "Welcome to West By-God Virginia!"

41

SHERIFF BAILEY HAD LIVED in a superintendent's home that dated back to when Mapelton was a company town. It was modest, though large, with white wood siding, a foundation of brown river rock, and a multi-tiered black slate roof. Sat on a hill above an abandoned company store that still had hitch posts outside and bullet holes from shootouts between the union and coal company gun thugs.

Mary Beth and Izzy parked down by that old store, and walked up an uneven set of stone steps to a wooden porch that creaked loud enough to announce their presence. Before they cold knock, Bailey's widow was at the door greet them. She was a small woman, maybe an inch or two taller than Izzy, and sleight of build, with dyed brown hair that was teased out and form-fitted to her head. She took one look at the star on Mary Beth's chest and said, "About time. Was wondering if anybody was gonna come tell me my husband was dead."

Mary Beth removed her hat. "I'm very sorry for your loss, Ma'am."

Mrs. Bailey had big steely eyes like battleship rivets. An

outsider might have confused her demeanor as indifference over her husband's passing, but Mary Beth recognized the hundred yard-stare endemic to McCray's hardened inhabitants, especially the old-timers. It was the same Appalachian sternness she'd seen on numerous women growing up—the ones who'd lost husbands to mining accidents but had to keep it together for the kids.

"Well, you've done your duty, then." Mrs. Bailey tried to close the door but Izzy stopped her.

"I was with him when he died."

Mrs. Bailey looked down as though just noticing Izzy.

"If you don't mind, there's some things we'd like to ask you about," he said.

Mrs. Bailey thought for a second, then pushed the screen door open. "Come on, then."

She led them to a wood-paneled living room with taxidermied animal heads on the wall. The two officers took a seat on a tweed couch next to a credenza covered with framed family photos.

"I just made some coffee," Mrs. Bailey said. "You want some?"

"No thanks," Izzy said. "Too late in the day for me. I'll be up all night."

"I'll take a cup," Mary Beth said. "I can drink it all day long."

"Me too," Mrs. Bailey said. "Thirty years married to a cop, you spend a lot of nights waiting up, worrying."

Mary Beth smiled at her. "I remember. My husband Bill was sheriff of Jasper County before I put on the uniform. I used to stay up drinking coffee, too. In fact, it was about thirteen years ago when I had some officers come pay me a visit like this, telling me he'd been killed."

Mrs. Bailey nodded. "Not a club I wanted to join."

"No, I'm sure it isn't. Again, my condolences, Mrs. Bailey."

"Nora. Call me Nora." Mary Beth and Izzy offered their first names as well. Nora, said, "Well, I guess I better fetch that coffee. Afraid I don't have any cream or sugar. Black okay?"

"Perfect," Mary Beth said.

While she left for the kitchen the officers inspected the photos on the credenza. Izzy pointed out a picture of who they both assumed was Nora's son, Jason Bailey, a hulking, smiling, dark-haired young man in a wrestler's leotard, with a big gold medal hanging around his neck.

"Checkout the ear," Izzy said. There was a bulbous deformity, cauliflower ear, a common condition for serious wrestlers, where blood collects from frequent strikes to the head.

Mary Beth couldn't believe she hadn't made the connection sooner. "Jesus," she said. "Maybe I really do have blinders when it comes to my family."

"What do you mean? "Izzy asked.

"This guy works for my mom. I saw him up at Mountain Flowers just the other day. Might of have kicked him in the balls while I was there."

Izzy's mouth fell open. "That makes sense," he said.

"It did. He totally deserved it. Pointed a—"

"No, I mean it makes sense with what Sheriff Bailey said when we were down in the mine. The carrot he kept dangling to try and get us out of there was something important he said he needed to tell Sawyer about why Gray was killed. And he wasn't willing to tell anyone else. Said it was something Sawyer needed to know before it came out some other way. But he was also worried Sawyer might kill him when he found out."

"So, what are you saying, exactly?"

"I'm not entirely sure," Izzy said. "But if this guy worked for your mom, and he killed Gray after Bailey found out Gray was looking into who was behind the prospectors…well, it sounds to me like your mother and Bailey—"

Izzy stopped talking when Nora Bailey reappeared in the hallway carrying two cups of coffee.

Mary Beth held up the photo of her son. "This your boy?"

"Yeah, that's my Jason."

"I saw him wrestle when he was in high school," Mary Beth said. "He was a real wrecking ball. What's he up to now?"

Nora frowned. "Knocking around. Works as a bouncer."

"Where at?"

"Oh, I don't know. Some club."

Mary Beth knew Nora was being evasive but didn't read too much into it. If her son was working at a strip club, she wouldn't go around telling people either.

"You actually just missed him," Nora said. "Left just a few minutes before you got here."

Mary Beth did her best to hide her surprise. "Jason? Your son?"

"Yeah, why?"

Mary Beth assumed Jason Bailey would be on the lam somewhere as far from McCray County as a person could get. "Oh, no reason," she said. It bothered her that Mamie was so confident Mary Beth wouldn't "rat" on her family that she didn't even bother sending Jason and Tommy into hiding.

Nora sipped her coffee. "I know you said you have questions about my husband, but would you mind if I start out asking you some?"

"Of course," Mary Beth said.

"Okay, where to start? I guess, can you tell me what in the hell he was doing up on that mountain? The paper made it sound like he was part of that militia up there, but I just can't believe that."

"He wasn't," Izzy said. "Sheriff Bailey was their prisoner. We both were. It was the militia who killed your husband."

"Why?"

Mary Beth jumped in, afraid that if Izzy gave Nora too much of the truth, it might shut her down.

"We aren't sure," she said. "We think he was investigating something."

"He was retired."

"Old habits are hard to break," Mary Beth said. "Do you have any idea what he may have been working on?"

Nora shook her head.

"We're not looking to sully your husband's name," Mary Beth told her. "But McCray County is about to become our jurisdiction."

Izzy added, "I really want to honor his memory. I saw those militia guys shoot him, and I'm pretty sure they did it because he'd found out something they didn't want exposed."

Nora looked from one to the other, without anything to offer.

"Is there anything at all you could tell us," Mary Beth asked. "Anything about what he may have been involved in?"

Bailey's widow finally said, "There is something I should probably show you." She excused herself again briefly and returned with a red folder. "I got a call from the bank yesterday, saying that since my husband had passed, I needed to come down and empty out the contents of his safety deposit box. So, I said, 'What safety deposit box?' And they said, 'the one he opened up earlier this year and listed me as the beneficiary or whatever, should something happen to him.' So I go down and find this." She opened the folder up onto the coffee table. Inside was a copy of a lawsuit.

IN THE UNITED STATE DISTRICT COURT FOR THE

THE UNITED STATES	)	*COMPLAINT IN*
OF AMERICA,	)	*CONDEMNATION*
Plaintiff;	)	
v.	)	
THE OLD WENGO	)	
REALTY TRUST,	)	
Defendant.	)	

SOUTHERN DISTRICT OF WEST VIRGINIA

NOW COMES, The United States of America, by and through the Attorney General of the United States and hereby alleges and pleads as follows:

This is a civil action for the taking of real property under the power of eminent domain and for the ascertainment and award of just compensation to the rightful owners in interest, THE OLD WENGO REALTY TRUST, a Delaware corporation with a principal place of business in Allegheny County, Pittsburgh, Pennsylvania.

The property to be taken is that certain real estate generally known as The Old Wengo Mine, in McCray County, West Virginia, more particularly identified in the metes and bounds description attached hereto as Exhibit A (hereinafter referred to as "the Property.")

The public use for which the Property is to be taken is the McCray Hydroelectric Lake Project, the plans for which are subject to change but generally available by request from the Land Use Division of the United States Attorney General's Office.

Mary Beth stopped reading and looked up at Izzy. "What in the hell is the McCray Hydroelectric Lake Project?"

"I don't know," Izzy said. "But I think I know who to ask." He pointed to the bottom of the complaint, which Mary Beth read aloud.

This the 18th day of March, 2021.
By: Patrick Connelly
Patrick Connelly
Asst. U.S. Attorney
Bar # 32751

"Son of a bitch," Mary Beth said. She felt like an idiot for not seeing it sooner. "Why else would a land use attorney be mixed up in a criminal prosecution against Sawyer?"

Izzy said, "Sheriff Bailey told me some federal marshals had come to him a few months ago, asking him to serve some papers on Sawyer. This lawsuit must be what he was talking about."

"Right," Mary Beth said. "Once this condemnation was filed, Sawyer's militia was squatting on federal land. I bet the marshals got an order of eviction from a local magistrate and put the onus on the local sheriff's office to try and eject them from the property."

"That makes sense," Izzy said. "Bailey told me he kept trying to catch Sawyer outside of the compound but eventually had to go up there. And that's when Sawyer told him that if he ever saw him again, he'd put a bullet through his brain."

Nora Bailey winced.

"Sorry, ma'am," Izzy said.

"I'm surprised he got out of there alive the first time," Mary Beth said. "Or that he managed to meet with Sawyer directly. The only way I was able to pull it off was—"

Mary Beth stopped short, realizing that the only way she, Sawyer's own sister, had been able to arrange a meeting with the Moonshine Messiah, was by going through their mother. Tingles of revelation pulsed through Mary Beth's body.

"There's something else," Nora said. She flipped to the back of the folder and pulled out a piece of thick bond paper with an elaborate light green border. "I was hoping maybe you could tell me what this is."

SHARE CERTIFICATE

This is to certify that
Raymond John Bailey
   of McCray County, West Virginia, is the registered owner
of a five percent (5%) share of TNT, LLC, a West Virginia
Limited Liability Company.

"TNT," Mary Beth repeated. "Is that—"

"Yes," Izzy said.

"What is it?" Nora asked.

Mary Beth and Izzy looked at each other, wondering how much they should tell her. TNT, LLC was the entity that had been going around acquiring property in McCray County. Mary Beth now had a strong suspicion that its property was about to become valuable coastline once the McCray Hydroelectric Lake Project was completed. That's when it hit her: the map, the one she'd seen in her mother's office with red push pins in an arc like a banana.

"Fucking bitch," she said.

"Excuse me?" Nora said.

"No, no, I'm sorry," Mary Beth said. "Not you." She pointed to the share certificate. "TNT."

"Like dynamite," Izzy said.

"No," Mary Beth told him. "Turner, Newton, Thompson. Those are Mamie's three married names."

"Mamie?" Nora asked. "Not Mountain Mamie?"

"I'm afraid so," Mary Beth said. "I'd hold onto that share certificate. It may be worth a lot of money."

Nora held it up to the light, inspecting it like it might be counterfeit.

"Mrs. Bailey," Mary Beth said, "would you mind if we take this complaint with us?"

Nora looked at it and then the share certificate again. "No," she said, "I'm sorry, Sheriff. I think I better hang on to it, too."

"We'd promise to bring it back," Izzy said.

Nora closed the folder and held it to her chest.

"It's okay, Izzy," Mary Beth said. "We don't need to take her copy. After all, it's a public record."

42

AS SOON AS THEY left the Baileys' home, Mary Beth and Izzy sat in his vehicle and compared notes.

"So here's what I'm seeing," Izzy began. "The feds come to Bailey to get his help evicting Sawyer's militia so they can build their lake. Bailey can't get to Sawyer without getting his head blown off, so he goes to see your mother."

"Exactly," Mary Beth said. "And knowing mom, her first question would be, 'What's in it for me?'"

"Right. So, Bailey tells her there's a public works project coming down the pike that she could take advantage of."

"Only he wants a piece of the action," Mary Beth said.

"Exactly. Then Mamie sets up a company—this TNT, LLC. She gets Bailey the go-ahead to safely serve his papers on Sawyer, while also getting her lawyers to go around buying up valuable future coastline property for dirt cheap, until...."

Mary Beth finished the sentence. "Until, Elwood Gray started looking into it. Gray was all about trying to preserve McCray County. If he found out about the lake project, he would have railed against it and either got it squelched or at the very least, driven real estate prices way up once the public learned about it."

Izzy nodded. "So, Bailey learns that Gray is snooping around. He tells Mamie, who sends her guy to rough him up."

"Her guy who just so happens to be Sheriff Bailey's son," Mary Beth said. "That way, she knows there'll be no blowback. Bailey's not going to arrest his own son. But Jason gets carried away. Gray dies. Then he calls Daddy to help him cover it up."

Izzy snapped his fingers. "That was Bailey's trump card. The piece of info he was holding onto that he thought could get us out of the mine. He was going to tell Sawyer that his mother was behind Gray's death, not to mention mixed up with a plan to literally sink half of McCray County."

"That info wouldn't have made Sawyer too popular with the other militia guys," Mary Beth agreed.

Izzy was nodding but then got a concerned look.

"What?"

"I wonder if that's why they were so quick to kill Bailey," he said. "Like maybe Sawyer already knew and wanted to shut him up."

Mary Beth didn't like thinking about that, but it did make sense. "They pulled you guys out of the mine and executed Bailey right about the time I went to see my mom. Maybe when she called Sawyer about getting me into the compound, he said, 'We already got one sheriff here,' and then she went and told him the rest of the story. So, Sawyer realized he needed to off Bailey before the information got out."

"Or," Izzy said, "Maybe Sawyer and your mom were working together the whole time. Maybe the whole showdown with the feds had something to do with this land grab scheme."

Mary Beth rolled that over. "No," she said. "Sawyer was standing in the way of the project. If he was in cahoots on the land grab, he'd have moved his militia somewhere else. Plus, my mom never would have gone for the kind of high-profile blood thirsty crap, Sawyer had planned. Not her style. That revenge plot was all Sawyer."

Izzy shrugged. "I guess that's probably true. So how do you think Patrick fits into all this?"

"Simple," Mary Beth said. "He's in the land use division. The DOJ has a public works project in McCray and they assign it to Patrick since he went to high school in Jasper and knows the area. Only Sawyer is gumming up the works. They've got a militia on the land they need to condemn and no one's willing to go in there and risk bloodshed to drive them out. At the same time, he and everybody in creation know about the scrutiny I'm under from John Jensen, and Patrick puts a deal together to solve both problems."

Mary Beth told Izzy about her recent visit with Patrick, minus the sex, and how the feds had offered to wipe her slate clean if she arrested her brother.

Izzy slapped the dashboard. "That's why the feds are coming so hard at you now, MB. They know that if this all comes out about the lake project it's going to look like they were up there ready to kill all those people so they could take their land."

Mary Beth saw it, too. "I think you're right, Izzy. That's why Patrick's got such a stick up his ass."

"Maybe we could use that somehow to get you out of the jam you're in."

Mary Beth smiled. "I like the way you think, my friend. First things first, though."

"What's that?"

"Since we're out this way, let's run on up to Mountain Flowers. I think I owe my mom a visit."

Izzy pointed to the clock. "Sure we'll have time? You've got a ten o'clock curfew, remember?"

Mary Beth scoffed. It was barely even dark. Plenty of time for another detour. "Sure," she said. "We can swing it."

"Okay," Izzy said. "But if I catch any shit from Princess over going to a strip club, this was your idea."

43

MOUNTAIN FLOWERS' WALLS were painted black and lined with mirrors that reflected fluorescent purple lights, giving the whole place a kind of pornographic funhouse feel. Mary Beth was in uniform, which exempted them from having to pay a cover charge, but garnered plenty of stares from the Tuesday-night clientele—mostly trucker types, a lot of mesh caps and greasy hair. Up on the main stage, a platinum blonde with robust silicone enhancements, and zero clothes besides a g-string and high-heels, was spreading her knees like butterfly wings and gyrating her posterior to Trace Adkins' "Honkytonk Badonkadonk."

"Very classy," Izzy said.

Mary Beth was disgusted by the whole scene. She scanned the crowd. "Check out your three o'clock," she said.

Izzy looked to his right where two white men were seated, both in flannel shirts and overalls. "Yeah? What about it?"

"Their clothes look awfully new. Not a stain or tear in sight."

"You think they're undercovers?"

"Yeah," Mary Beth said. "Bad ones. Looks like they just

stopped off at Walmart and bought the kind of clothes they think we wear. I mean, how many people do you know who actually wear overalls?"

"Well," Izzy said. "In the feds' defense, they didn't have much time to put it together. It was just a few days ago that Sawyer skipped town. Before that there was no reason to think they'd need to be staking out his mother's strip club."

"Anyway, why don't you grab a seat and keep an eye on them while I go say hi to Mom."

"You just want me to wait here?"

"Sure," Mary Beth said. "Enjoy the show."

Izzy shrugged and took a seat at a nearby table while Mary Beth walked over to a black metal door near the bar. She gave it a hard pound. It swung open and there was Cousin Tommy and his partner, the wrestler who Mary Beth now knew was Jason Bailey. The latter's eyes went wide, and he started to reach for his gun.

"Easy there, Odd Job," Mary Beth said. "I come in peace. I just want to see my mom."

Tommy stepped in front of Jason. "It's not a good time, Mary. Maybe give her a call tomorrow. Set something up."

"You mean have my people call her people? Schedule a lunch? I don't think so. Just go tell her I'm here to make an investment in TNT, LLC."

The name obviously registered with both men. "Just a second," Tommy said. "Let me go talk to her."

"Fine, but take Kujo with you," Mary Beth said, pointing at Jason. "We don't get along so well."

Both men went down the dark hallway to Mamie's office. A minute or two later, Tommy was back out, waving for Mary Beth.

She entered the office and immediately noticed the map of McCray County was gone, though a ripped corner of it was still thumbtacked in place, like someone had just torn it from the wall. Mary Beth pointed to it. "Redecorating?"

"I don't know what you mean, dear," Mamie said. She was dressed oddly casual, in a fuzzy, peach colored tracksuit that looked like they could have been pajamas. Tommy stood behind her but Jason Bailey was nowhere to be seen. Probably out back stuffing the McCray map into a trash bin.

"What's this talk about you wanting to make some kind of an investment?" Mamie asked.

Mary Beth smiled. "Oh, just getting your attention is all. I know I'd have a better chance of sweating a confession out of a road apple than getting you to tell me anything about your little land grab. Besides, I think I already know everything I need to."

If Mamie was worried about that, she didn't show it. "Sounds like there's nothing for us to discuss, then."

"Sure, there is," Mary Beth said. "But let's take a walk, okay."

Mary Beth tapped her ear, then pointed at the walls.

"There are no bugs in here, I assure you."

Mary Beth wasn't so sure. With a few days of lead time it was possible the feds had already obtained a warrant and planted a listening device somewhere in Mamie's office, and she didn't want to take a chance on saying something that could come back to bite her.

"Come on, Mama, the night air will do you good."

There was a black fur coat draped around the back of Mamie's chair that Mary Beth seized and wrapped around her mother's shoulders.

"Oh, fine. Very well." Mamie stood with a little difficulty. Mary Beth pushed the panic bar for the fire door and the two women exited into the gravel lot. Tommy came too and leaned up against the wall where he lit up a cigarette, giving the women enough space to speak privately. They walked to the end of the lot that looked down on the murky sludge of a slurry pond a hundred feet below.

"I'm a little surprised you've got Tommy and Jason back up

here so soon, after they helped Sawyer skin out," Mary Beth said. "Figured they'd both be vacationing down in Mexico."

Mamie gave her a look of surprise that could have won an Oscar. "Sawyer? Why, whatever do you mean? Those boys don't have nothing to do with Sawyer."

"Sure, Mama." Mary Beth kicked a stone down the mountainside. "You know, I've been thinking, after your boys handcuffed me to that tree, the feds showed up awfully quick. Within minutes. Turned out they were already tracking me by a satellite phone I was carrying. I figure that's something you and Sawyer wouldn't have been counting on. The plan was for them to have a couple hours head start."

Mamie remained stone-faced. "Again, dear. You're just not making any sense. All I know about your brother is what I read in the papers. They even suggest you had something to do with his escaping."

"Anyway," Mary Beth said, "I'm wondering if maybe the feds were able to get their roadblocks up before the boys could get out of Dodge."

"Dodge, dear? Are we talking about trucks now?"

"No, Mama, we're talking about Sawyer. You remember him, right? Remember when he was young, how much he liked roughing it out in the woods, going on his little 'walkabouts" he called them. He'd be gone some times a week at a time. Probably knows every cave and hiding spot in this county. An outsider would have a hell of a time trying to track him down. Especially if he had help. Somebody to bring some food and supplies every now and then, until the heat dies down."

"Sweetheart, I have no idea where your brother is. That's the truth."

Mary Beth watched her mother's eyes. She prided herself on her ability to tell when people were lying. But when it came to her mother, she always had to remind herself that Mamie's lack of conscience meant she was not plagued by the typical tells of the nervous liar: rapid speech, flushed skin, sweaty brow, or a subtle pulsing of the carotid artery. A sociopath like Mamie, might as well have been made of steel.

"Well, that's too bad," Mary Beth said.

Mamie sighed like she was tiring of the conversation. "You feel free to scour the woods if you want to. I'll wish you good luck."

Mary Beth glanced down at her watch. She still had over an hour until check-in, but wasn't inclined to push her luck on her first night out of the clink. "Afraid I don't have time for that," she said. "I'm gonna need you to go look for me."

Mamie laughed. "And just why would I do that?"

"Because you want to stay in business."

Mamie's eyes flashed with rage. "Hold on, now," she said, "we had an arrangement."

"I'm not your problem," told her. "It's the feds. Like those two tenderfoot undercovers they've got in there right now. I'm sure you noticed them. Guys like that will be watching your every move from now until the second coming, just on the off-chance Sawyer might try and contact you some day. And anything they get on you along the way, they'll use it, Mama. Will bust you for the tiniest infraction to get your cooperation."

"I've been under surveillance before," Mamie said. "It'll pass."

"Not like this, Mama. You've never dealt with anything remotely close to this. Federal agents were killed. The government's embarrassed, and pissed. Never again will you be able to go anywhere without a tail, or make a call without a tap. From now until the day you die, every time you turn around there'll be some man in an overcoat and fedora pretending to read the paper. You'll be seeing G-men in your sleep. Good luck running a business under that kind of scrutiny."

Mamie turned pensive, looking up at the stars. "It'll pass," she repeated.

"Will it? The FBI still hasn't given up searching for Jimmy Hoffa. They're a tenacious bunch."

"Let's not resort to threats, Mary Elizabeth."

"It's not a threat, Mama. None of this is coming from me. I'll have absolutely nothing to do with it. Or anyway to protect you from it. For all I know you could be telling the truth. Maybe you don't know where Sawyer is. All I'm saying is, if you do know, or have the ability to find out, then you're gonna have to make a decision."

"Which is?"

"Are you going to protect your child or your business?"

Mamie huffed and turned away.

Mary Beth placed a hand on her mother's shoulder, then scraped her boot across the gravel, drawing a very deliberate line between them. "Just make the same choice you always did," she said. "Only this time, it'll be the right one."

44

WHEN MARY BETH and Pomfried showed up at the courthouse the next morning, they had a new member of their legal team. Princess Baker, stunning as usual, wearing a killer, royal blue jumpsuit with a sassy red belt and matching hoop earrings. All eyes turned to the former runway model as she strutted into the conference room, Jensen and his minions seated on the far side of the long table, spread out like the last supper, and Patrick leaned up against the wall.

"You hire a new associate, Pomfried?" Jensen asked.

"In a manner of speaking," Pomfried said. "Y'all know Princess Baker, don't you? Six O'Clock News."

Princess took it from there. She had a small handheld recorder that she clicked on and slid to the middle of the table. "U.S. Attorney Jensen, would you care to comment on what role the McCray Hydroelectric Lake Project played in the government's decision to raid the Old Wengo Mine, putting hundreds of lives at risk?"

Jensen had a litigator's poker face. Mary Beth knew he was probably shitting himself, but you'd never have known it from looking at him. Patrick, the desk lawyer, was less adroit. His eyes bulged like someone had screamed.

"The what, now?" Jensen asked, putting just a little too much good ole boy in his response.

"The McCray Hydroelectric Lake Project," Princess repeated. "Sources tell us there is a major federal works project designed to flood a large portion of McCray County, and that, as part of this project, the Old Wengo Mine was condemned by the government. Only Sawyer Thompson's militia was unwilling to vacate after months of peaceful attempts by law enforcement to evict them. So, my question is, what role did that state of affairs play in the government's decision to send armed troops and assault vehicles up to the militia's compound this past weekend?"

Jensen's minions squirmed, looking to their boss like everything Princess was saying was news to them. But Jensen stayed cool. "Ma'am," he said, "I'm a prosecutor. I'm not in a position to comment on any government operations outside the workings of my office."

Princess looked to Patrick. "How about you, Mr. Connelly? Can you tell us the details of what the McCray Lake Project is supposed to entail? I'm sure residents would be very curious to know since it's received absolutely no publicity that I am aware of."

"Mr. Connelly has no comment," Jensen said. He switched off the tape recorder and then his whole demeanor changed. "I don't know what the fuck you are trying to pull, Pomfried, but we came here to discuss a deal. Now let's cut all this other bullshit."

"Fine by me," Pomfried said. He wiggled his mass to sit upright in the tight confines of his armed chair. "The deal is this: you drop all charges against my client and issue a statement clearing her name. In exchange, we bury the story about the lake project."

"No way," Jensen said. "I don't give into blackmail. And I

truly have no idea what you people are talking about. This lake nonsense all sounds fabricated, to me."

Pomfried leaned forward, his stomach pressing against the table. "Do you have any idea what is about to happen to you, John, if that story comes out? Everyone is gonna think you all went up there to murder those people and steal their land. Around here, you'll be about as popular as Bernie Madoff and Benedict Arnold rolled into one."

Jensen reached for a blue file folder he spun around and slid in front of Pomfried. "All your threats aside, this is the only deal we are prepared to discuss."

Pomfried opened it. Mary Beth saw a two-hole-punched plea agreement. The one they described the day before. An admission of guilt in exchange for a suspended sentence, contingent upon her full cooperation in the search for her brother.

"If we walk out of here without a deal," Pomfried said, "this story airs tonight."

"What story?" Jensen said. "There is no lake project as far as I know. Doesn't even exist. You say different or try to smear me in any way, and I'll sue the news station and everyone involved for defamation."

Princess and Pomfried both looked unsettled by Jensen's bravado. They turned to Mary Beth.

"I saw the lawsuit," she said. "U.S. vs. the Old Wengo Realty Trust, signed by him." She pointed at Patrick who was staring out the window, resting his head on his chin like a Rodin statue.

"Show me," Jensen said.

But, of course, Mary Beth didn't have a copy. She elbowed Pomfried. "Pull it up on PACER," she said, referring to the federal court's electronic filing system.

The night before, while pitching this whole set up to Princess, Mary Beth had searched the case and knew PACER had a listing for it. But because she was not an attorney with an active account, she hadn't been able to download any documents.

Pomfried, however, should be able to pull up a pdf of the complaint without any trouble.

The barrister wiggled around in his chair. Mary Beth helped him pull his laptop from his leather satchel and Jensen and his minions all came around behind to see as he performed a name search.

U.S. v Old Wengo Realty Trust

The case caption appeared in the search results, but when Pomfried tried to search for documents an alert box popped up.

Files for this matter have been placed under seal by order of the Court. Please contact the Clerk's office for more information.

"What in the hell?" Pomfried said. "Under seal? For a land condemnation?"

"If it even is a land condemnation," Jensen said. "Looks to me like it might have been a tax case or something, thus the privacy. Guess we'll never know."

"Like hell," Mary Beth said. "We'll get the records from the clerk's office."

Jensen smiled. "Maybe. If you've got a sufficient basis to unseal them. But even then, I'm afraid those records sometimes have a way of disappearing."

"You son of a bitch," Mary Beth said.

Jensen held up his hands. "Hey, don't shoot the messenger. You can check with Land Use too. Send them some Freedom of Information Act requests. I'm quite sure you won't find any record of any kind of McCray County lake project."

Mary Beth instantly knew she'd been outmaneuvered. Somehow Jensen had managed to make the entire project disappear. Vanishing with it was the leverage she thought she could use to get out from under the current charges.

The room fell deathly silent, Mary Beth and Pomfried both looking at each other like: What in the hell do we do now? Their bluff had been called.

Jensen placed a pen atop the plea agreement. "The time for

games and make believe is over, Sheriff. These are your options: Either we convict you and send you away for fifteen years, or you plead guilty and help us catch your brother. Now what's it going to be?"

Mary Beth looked to Patrick, but he was still staring out the window, brooding like a little bitch. She turned to Pomfried again, but there was no help to be had there either as he turned up his meaty palms.

"Oh, Jesus," Mary Beth said.

It had been a good try. A good plan. And against a less shrewd operator, it probably would have worked. But she needed to admit that Jensen was holding all the cards. Mary Beth couldn't risk a fifteen-year sentence. If she went away that long, Sam would be nearly as old as she was now by the time she got out. She'd miss his whole life. All the big milestones. College graduation. Wedding. Grandkids.

Mary Beth snatched up the pen. "God help me." She scratched out the M of her name.

"Stop."

Everyone turned to look at Patrick. "Don't do it, Mary. Don't sign it," he said.

Jensen turned so red-faced, he looked like he might have an aneurysm. "Connelly, what in the hell are you doing?"

"Coming clean."

"The hell you are. In fact, you shouldn't even be in here. You're excused from this meeting, Connelly. Go wait in the hall."

"Just hold on, now," Pomfried said, snatching the pen from Mary Beth. "I want to hear what he has to say."

Jensen grabbed Patrick by the arm to try and usher him out but Patrick pulled away. "It's all true, about the lake project," he said. "I can attest to it."

Jensen slapped the table hard enough to make everyone jump. "Goddammit, Connelly. You cross me and I will fuck you up good. You really want to throw away your whole career, everything you've worked for this...this—" Jensen was pointing angrily at Mary Beth.

"Watch it," Patrick said. "I think the word you are looking for is: sheriff. The sheriff who saved all our lives. And you're damn right I'm willing to risk it."

Mary Beth felt all the chills. She had always laughed at old movies where women would swoon over a man, but right at that moment, watching Patrick risk it all for her, if she hadn't already been sitting, she might have caught the vapors herself.

"It will be your word only," Jensen said. "There's not a shred of paper to back it up."

"Wrong," Patrick said. "I kept copies. Of everything. Just in case you tried to burn me."

Jensen pounded the table again. "You fucking idiot."

Princess asked, "Will you go on camera, Mr. Connelly?"

Patrick looked uneasy about it but said that he would.

"I'm thinking we should make it a dual interview," Pomfried said. "The Sheriff and the Assistant U.S. Attorney. We can also tell them about how Jensen pushed this bogus prosecution of my client to try and cover it all up."

"I think that's a good idea," Princess said. She looked at her watch. "If we're going to get it ready to air this evening I'd like to go ahead and get started."

Pomfried crossed out the "M" Mary Beth had written on the plea agreement and slid it back to Jensen. "Guess, we'll see you court," he said. Then Pomfried stood, struggling again to free himself from the armed chair, and motioned for Patrick and Princess to follow him and Mary Beth out the door.

Jensen stopped them. "Wait."

Mary Beth watched the prosecutor intently, waiting to see what he'd do next. His demeanor was smoldering, but also defeated. After a brief moment of reflection, he gestured to one of his associates and said, "Go, draw up the dismissal."

It took about twenty minutes before the document exonerating

Mary Beth was drafted and signed, and the lauditory press release agreed to. Once that was done, Princess gave Jensen her word that the lake story would never see the light of day.

"Guess that's it then," Mary Beth said. She stood to leave.

"We'd still like your cooperation in catching your brother," Jensen said.

Mary Beth couldn't believe he had the audacity to ask. She put her floppy brimmed Stetson on and said, "Tell you what, John. If Sawyer shows up at the next family reunion, I'll be sure to give you a call."

Jensen grumbled something indecipherable, and stormed past Mary Beth with his minions following behind. She caught Patrick by the elbow. "Can you hang on a sec?"

"Sure."

Mary Beth then said her goodbyes to her team, starting with Princess.

"I owe you big," she told her.

"Yes, you do," Princess said. "I'm thinking my husband could use an extra week of vacation."

"Princess, make it two weeks."

The women hugged for the first time ever in their cool relationship. "I'm glad it worked out for you, Sheriff. You deserve it."

Alexander Pomfried was next, standing with his leather bag slung around his shoulder, loosening his bow tie.

"Guess this is it, then," Mary Beth said. "Next time we see each other, we'll be on opposite sides again."

"Sugar, I look forward to it."

Mary Beth smiled.

"I'm gonna let you get away with that one because you helped me out. But the next time you call me, Sugar, I'm gonna kick you in the ass. You know that right?"

Pomfried winked at her. "Y'all be good now," he said, waving to Mary Beth and Patrick as he took his leave.

Then it was just the two of them. Mary Beth and Patrick. So much to say, and neither knowing where to begin.

"Thank you," Mary Beth said, finally. "Thank you for what you did just now."

"You're welcome."

There was another awkward silence, then Mary Beth said, "Why'd you do it?"

Patrick ran his hands through his hair, looking like he was asking himself the same question. "Did you ever do the test?" he asked. "Like a DNA test?"

Mary Beth's knees suddenly felt weak. She took a seat at the table "No," she said. "No, I never did."

"So you don't know for sure. You don't know that Sam's my...." Patrick didn't finish the sentence.

"Sam got a perfect score on the SAT," Mary Beth said. "In the *seventh* grade. He learned to read when he was three. Trust me, that didn't come from me or Bill."

Patrick sighed and brushed back his hair again, holding it there, exposing his widow's peak. "You know, I spent hours last night going through all his social media. Facebook, Instagram, Twitter. Looking at every photo I could find of him. Sam really does look a lot like you."

"Yes, he does."

"Has the strawberry blonde hair, not as curly as yours, but wavy. The fair complexion. High cheekbones. Everything except his nose."

"I know," Mary Beth said. "He's got your schnoz."

Patrick ran a finger down his nose that was still slightly crooked. "Well," he said. "What my nose looked like before you popped me."

"He takes after you in other ways, too. He's sweet, sensitive, but also competitive. Sees the world differently than most people, like he's always thinking on another level. Sometimes he can get so inside his mind he gets tunnel vision. Book smart but not real practical. He's a good kid, though. A good young man."

"You must have done a good job raising him."

Mary Beth smiled. She liked to think that was true.

There was another long silence, then Patrick said, "So what now?"

Mary Beth kissed him on the cheek and said, "Now, I need to go catch my shithead, fugitive, brother. We'll have time to talk about the rest, later."

45

AS SOON AS MARY BETH was liberated from her ankle brace-let, she called Sam to tell him the good news. They made plans to celebrate that evening, just the two of them, Sam even offer-ing to make dinner—something he normally did only once a year on Mary Beth's birthday. After that, the sheriff made the two-hour drive from Charleston and went straight to the office. She needed to organize the search for Sawyer but got waylaid by hugs and high fives and then Izzy, who was still on leave, showed up with a couple bottles of champagne, and it soon turned into a party. Sawyer had already been in the wind for days, Mary Beth figured one more wouldn't hurt. She'd swallow her pride and reach out to the feds in the morning, see where they were with things, and have her guys start scouring the woods of McCray at first light.

She cut out of the office a little after five, before she'd had too many toasts to drive. She took her time on the way home, cruis-ing through town, past the railroad tracks and an old timey drive-in diner with waitresses on roller skates.

When she got home, Sam's silver Prius was parked in the

driveway. Mary Beth went inside where she immediately smelled the spaghetti sauce cooking, loaded with garlic, just the way she liked. Then she heard her brother, Sawyer, tell her to put her gun down on the table.

For a second, Mary Beth thought her heart had stopped.

"I know you heard me," Sawyer said.

She was standing in the foyer, perfectly still, next to a ceramic vase full of dried cattails. To her left was a sitting room that almost no one ever went in. That's where the voice came from. Mary Beth slowly shifted her gaze. An oval shaped wooden coffee table with a glossy veneer was in the center of the room, a love seat along the front wall, and two high, wing-back chairs in the corners. Sawyer sat in one of those chairs, pointing a gun, not at Mary Beth, but at her son, Sam, who was in the chair opposite him.

Both men looked like hell. Sawyer dirty and haggard, in mud-covered clothes, looked like he hadn't showered in a week. Meanwhile, Sam's face was red and swollen, with a trickle of blood running down from his nose.

"What's going on?" Mary Beth asked.

Sawyer said, "Gun. Table. Now."

"Okay. Okay. Just relax." Mary Beth undid the leather safety strap and slowly removed her pistol, then placed it gently on the coffee table.

"The other one, too," Sawyer said. "That little fucker you keep down in your boot."

Mary Beth didn't like giving that one up, but she didn't have much choice. She unsheathed her hummingbird and sat it on the table, then took a step back.

"Thought you'd be sitting on a beach somewhere tropical by now," she said.

"No," Sawyer responded. "No, since last night I've been getting hunted through the woods like a fucking animal—by my own mother's men. Would you know anything about that?"

Mary Beth shrugged. "You've become a liability to her, Sawyer. Bad for business."

"You meddling little bitch. Finally Mom's favorite, huh, is that it?"

"Oh Sawyer," Mary Beth said. "Sweetie, you were never her favorite. You were just the only one dumb enough to listen to her."

Sawyer fired a shot at Mary Beth's feet that made her jump.

"Ha!" he shouted. "This is fun, isn't it? All of us being together like this."

Mary Beth trained all her attention on Sawyer's gun, waiting for an opportunity to go for it without endangering Sam. "Mom will eventually get you, Sawyer" she said. "Or the feds will. Either way, you'll likely end up dead. Why don't you let me take you in? Keep you safe."

Sawyer smiled, showing off his chipped front tooth. "No, I don't think I'll be going anywhere. I like it here. Been having too much fun catching up with my nephew." Sawyer smacked Sam on the knee. "We've been having ourselves a little strength competition. I won, of course." Sawyer held up his gun, some kind of Ruger, sleek and black. "Before you got here I was actually about to fire one into little Sammy's foot—same way you did me. And you know what this pussy did? He cried, MB. Ain't that the most pathetic fucking thing you ever heard? I tell ya, I don't know how big old Bill Cain ever had an effeminate little bitch ass boy like this. Your dad must be rolling over in his grave, son."

"Don't talk about my Dad." Sam's voice and hands were shaking. "Ffffuck you," he said.

Sawyer cackled. "Ah, shit! You hear that, Sis? I think I just heard his balls drop."

Sam lunged at Sawyer, who was ready for him. He backhanded Sam so hard the boy fell into his chair and flipped it over. But Mary Beth had sprung into action too. She leapt over the coffee table, pouncing on Sawyer like a mountain cat, landing on his back and wrapping him in a choke hold.

Sawyer dropped his gun and charged backward, slamming Mary Beth into the wall. Framed pictures crashed to the ground but Mary Beth managed to hang on. She wrapped her legs around Sawyer's waist, and clamped down harder on his throat. Sawyer came forward and slammed her back into the wall again, this time smashing all the air from her lungs.

Mary Beth slinked, limply to the ground and Sawyer jumped on her like a UFC fighter ready to ground and pound. She curled into a ball, trying to protect her head with her arms, while Sawyer wailed away at her back and sides. The blows felt like sledge hammers. Fast and furious. Mary Beth's ribs were about to break.

Then a gunshot exploded and shook the room.

Sawyer stopped punching. They both looked over at Sam who was holding Mary Beth's Glock 22, having just fired a round into the ceiling. He lowered the gun on Sawyer.

"Get off my mother."

Sawyer stood, slowly. "Now what do you think you're gonna do with that?" He reached out a hand. "Hand that over."

What happened next, seemed to be in slow motion. Long enough for it to occur to Mary Beth that, though she and Sam were as different as could be personality-wise, there was one characteristic they had in common: marksmanship.

It was the one physical pastime she and Bill had been able to interest Sam in, starting him off with a BB gun at age six. The memory of all the time mother and son had spent together at the range flashed through Mary Beth's mind as she watched her son steady his grip with two hands and squeeze off three rounds, grouped right in Sawyer's chest. Center mass. Just like she taught him.

Sawyer collapsed to the ground with a thud. He looked down at the smoking holes in his chest like they confused him. "I didn't think you had it in you," he said before his head slumped forward.

Mary Beth snapped out of her state of shock. She seized Sawyer's wrist and checked his pulse. There was none.

"Oh God." Mary Beth looked back to Sam, who dropped the gun.

"Oh shit," he said. "Oh shit, shit, shit."

Mary Beth rushed to Sam and held him in her arms the way she used to when he still was a little boy, waking up from a bad dream. "It's okay, Sammy."

He started shaking all over. "I shot him. Oh, my God, mom. I shot him."

"No." Mary Beth pushed Sam's chin up, forcing him to look her in the eye. "I shot him, Sam. Look at me. Are you listening? I shot him. It was me. You got it?"

Sam shook his head, No.

"Yes, I did, Sammy. I want you to picture it for me, baby." Mary Beth kissed him on the forehead. "Visualize me lying over there. Sawyer's standing over me. Can you see it?"

Sam nodded. This time, in agreement.

"Okay. Now take me out of the picture and put yourself there. You are lying on the floor, Sam. Right where I was. Now look up at Sawyer. Are you looking at him?"

Sam closed his eyes. "Yes."

"Good. He has a gun in his hand, doesn't he, Sam?"

Sam opened his eyes. He looked at Sawyer's gun on the floor, near where he'd been sitting.

"That's right," Mary Beth said. She pulled her sleeve down over her hand and used it to pick up Sawyer's gun without leaving any fingerprints. She moved it across the room and placed it just inches from Sawyer's dead right hand.

"That's the gun he was holding. Now hear the blasts as he falls back, and you look over at me. I was right here. Right here holding my gun. My gun, Sam. The one I used to kill him with, right? I had no choice, did I? He was going to kill us both if I didn't, wasn't he?"

"That's right."

Mary Beth kissed Sam's forehead again. "That's right, baby. Everything else happened exactly the same. Except when you came off the chair at him, you two ended up over there by the wall." As she spoke, Mary Beth picked up the chair Sam had knocked over. "You two fought. Then I fired a warning shot into the ceiling. Then Sawyer turned the gun on me, and that's when I put him down. You got it?"

Sam nodded.

"I want to hear you say it."

"I got it."

"Good. Just keep seeing it in your mind. Play it over and over again until it becomes real."

"Okay," Sam said.

Mary Beth squeezed her son's bicep. "Now run to the bathroom and wash your hands, Sam. Scrub them like you've never scrubbed them before. Then do it again at least three more times. I'm going to call my people. We'll control the scene. But just in case the FBI gets involved somehow and insists on a gunpowder residue test, I want to make sure it will come back negative."

"What about you?"

"Don't worry about me. I'm the sheriff. And this was an intruder in my home, a felon on the run. Trust me. If I'm the shooter, this won't be a problem."

Sam still looked worried but he did as his mother instructed and went to the bathroom.

As soon as he was gone, Mary Beth picked up her gun. She carefully wiped it down to remove any of Sam's fingerprints then got herself in the same position her son had been in before firing the fatal shots. Mary Beth imagined it from Sam's vantage point, picturing Sawyer standing there. She mimed firing off three rounds in his chest, then tilted her aim a little higher—a miss as Sawyer fell—and fired a round into the wall. That way if any residue tests were run, it would confirm she'd fired the weapon.

Sam came running back in.

"It's okay," Mery Beth said. "You just keep washing your hands. Wash it all away, Sam. I'm going to make the call."

Mary Beth dialed the station and Deputy Skipwith answered.

"I just killed an intruder in my home. Get someone out here right away."

Mary Beth hung up while Skipwith was in mid-question, then she called Patrick.

"Mary?"

"Yes, it's me. Listen, I just need you to come over to my house right away. My deputies will be here soon and I need a witness to their investigation who the FBI will trust."

"Investigation? Mary, what's going on?"

"I'll explain everything when you get here. But Patrick, just you, okay? No Jensen. No FBI. Just you."

"Okay, but can you just tell me what this is all about?"

Mary Beth looked over at her dead brother slouched against the wall. His vacant blue eyes stared back at her, minus the mischievous twinkle she was so used to seeing there.

"Let's just say that you can call off your manhunt."

46

PRINCESS GOT THE EXCLUSIVE, telling the story about the Moonshine Messiah's death in a segment that was picked up and aired across national news. After that, no one ever seriously doubted Mary Beth's account or suspected Sam was the actual shooter in a killing that was deemed justified, without much ado. Sawyer was buried the following Saturday at the old homestead, next to his father, in a private ceremony held in secret and attended only by family, minus Mary Beth and Sam, for obvious reasons, and of course Uncle Jimmy, who was still officially presumed dead, though some believed he was still out there somewhere, living off his bushcraft.

Then on Monday, McCray County was officially laid to rest, as well. The annexation into Jasper was finalized, making Mary Beth sheriff over all of it. A combined area of nearly one-thousand square miles of some of the roughest country and residents a person could ever hope to find. Her first official act was to set up a substation in what used to be McCray, where she planned to keep three permanent deputies, and would visit personally at least once a week. The building was a bit of a fixer upper but "had good bones" according to the real estate agent—whatever that meant—and was close to the highway, making for easy access. The only downside was the view, since it overlooked one of those God-awful Mountain Flowers' billboards claiming its well-endowed dancers as West Virginia's "Second Greatest Natural Resource."

Mary Beth was at the new office during its first week of operation, still unpacking boxes with Izzy and two other deputies, when she received one visitor she'd been expecting and one she hadn't. Mountain Mamie had been invited and surprised her daughter by bringing along Jason Bailey as a housewarming gift, complete with a signed confession over the killing of Elwood Gray.

"That was our deal, remember," Mamie said. "Anyone gets killed, then I turn them over to you on a silver platter. Well, here you go."

Mary Beth read over Jason's statement while Izzy and the other deputies took him into custody. The document completely insulated Mamie, of course, not mentioning her at all.

"So, I guess we'll be seeing a lot more of each other now," Mamie said.

Mary Beth looked her mother dead in the eyes. "No," she said, "we won't."

"Why, whatever do you mean, dear?"

Mary Beth sat down behind her new desk and kicked up her feet. "I'm talking about our deal, Mama. I'll accept Jason Bailey's scalp as payment for Elwood Gray. But what about the others that died? At the courthouse, and up at Old Wengo."

Mamie looked confused. "Those militia men are all in jail now. And your brother clearly paid the price, so you can't honestly expect—"

"I'm talking about your role in all that, Mom. Unless you're here to turn yourself in, then I'd say you've breached our deal."

Mamie gaped. "I'm no more responsible for Sawyer's actions than you are."

"Really? You're telling me Sawyer came up with that whole scheme by himself?"

"Of course. Why would I want all that ruckus up there? It's bad for my business, sweetheart. You said so, yourself."

Mary Beth nodded. "Let's just see what my attorney has to say about that." She pounded on the wall and Patrick Connelly appeared from a back room, wearing one of his perfectly-tailored Brooks Brothers suits.

"Good afternoon," he said.

"Mom, you remember Patrick, right?"

Mamie glanced around the room like she was expecting someone else to jump out from the shadows. "Mr. Connelly," she said. "Still courting my daughter after all these years?"

"I'm actually here on official U.S. Attorney business."

"Oh," Mamie said. "And what, pray tell, is that?"

"Follow up on the McCray Hydroelectric Lake Project." Patrick opened his briefcase and laid out several maps, showing the boundaries of the intended lake. All the lots acquired by TNT, LLC, had been outlined in green, right along the future coast, while the lots TNT was unable to acquire were shaded in red.

"There are forty-eight of those red lots," Mary Beth said, after explaining the colors' significance. "So, I got curious and decided to cross-reference the holdouts with people who were arrested up at Old Wengo. Tell her how many of them were up in Sawyer's compound ready to be blown to hell the day the shit went down."

"Forty-two," Patrick said.

"Forty-two," Mary Beth repeated. "Forty-two out of forty-eight. Including Uncle Jimmy—your own brother. You fucking muderous bitch."

"I will not be talked to in that manner, young lady," Mamie

said, making a show of being offended. "And don't you dare talk to me about brothers."

"Don't *you* dare," Mary Beth snapped. "Don't for a second try to say we're the same. What happened with Sawyer was self-defense."

"Oh, you think you've got it all figured don't you?"

"I do now," Mary Beth responded. "See, that's the piece I'd been missing, Mama. Everything else fit. I figured the feds went to Sheriff Bailey for help evicting Sawyer, which Bailey knew was a suicide mission so he went to the only person who could help: you—who he already knew because his son works for you, which means he's probably been on the take for years."

Mamie harrumphed and crossed her arms.

"So, you got Bailey an audience with Sawyer in exchange for the lake project info, and at some point, you and Bailey became partners in your little land grab. But that's as far as I got before. The thing I didn't think about was there couldn't be a lake project because Sawyer wasn't leaving that mine for anybody. And you would have known that better than anyone. So why go around buying up property, banking on a public works project that couldn't happen, unless you'd figured a way to get Sawyer out of there? And what better way to do that, than to sell him on a plan that would deliver the bloody revenge against the feds he's coveted his whole pathetic life? You even timed it to coincide with the anniversary of Daddy's death. Oh, and in the process, you figured you'd conveniently kill off the holdouts who wouldn't sell to you."

Mary Beth paused to gauge her mother's reaction.

There was none, save for a clinching of her jaw before she said, "I suppose you think I manipulated your brother. Tricked him into doing my bidding."

"That possibility had crossed my mind."

"Well, think again. Sawyer jumped at the opportunity to kill off his followers. And you want to know why?" Mamie didn't wait for an answer. "Because he'd bitten off more than he could chew. Pitching his utopian nineteen-fifties community. He never expected folks to actually come. Just thought they'd send money. But all of a sudden he had droves of hungry mouths to feed, looking to him to provide food, water, sewage...justice." Mamie shook her head. "Whenever someone who doesn't believe in government is put in charge, it never goes well, and your brother decided he'd rather burn it all down than admit to being a fraud."

Mary Beth's instinct was to come back at her mother with something to defend Sawyer in some small way, but what she'd said about him did smack of the truth.

"Well, whether that's what happened or not, Mama, it was all for nothing. Because the lake project is caput. Eighty-sixed. All those lots you bought are now worthless. Isn't that right, Patrick?"

"That's right," he said. "After everything that happened, the government didn't feel it would be appropriate to move forward."

"Yeah," Mary Beth added. "The government's decided to dedicate the land to one of those green energy projects Elwood Gray was so keen on. See if they can bring some new jobs to the area."

A familiar blaze of fury burned in Mamie's eyes. Mary Beth tensed up, expecting her mother to lash out. But the old lady collected herself. "Well, how kind," she said, exhaling loudly, then wheeling around to conceal her true reaction to news that had cost her millions. Mamie drifted toward the window and looked out at the wooded hillside where one of her strip club billboards nestled amongst the trees like a gaping wound. "The heights of your disrespect," she grumbled. "Your lack of gratitude. Do you know that I had to *walk* to the hospital? Walk! Just to give birth to you."

That was a common refrain growing up. Every time Mary Beth crossed her mother, she'd hear about the selfless trek to the emergency room, enduring labor pains the entire way, in order to bring an ingrate daughter into the world. This time, however, Mary Beth was ready for it.

"You lived right next to the hospital, Mom. Dad showed me the apartment once. He said you'd have had to walk farther to get to your car than you did to get to the ER. And, he walked with you. You never mention that part."

"That's not the point," Mamie said, turning back. "The point is, I am your *mother*."

Mamie had always been able to infuse that word with such invective, it usually hit Mary Beth like a baseball bat. But not that day. Mary Beth was determined to cut the cord, once and for all. She walked to her mother and put her arm around her, saying, "I know that, Mom. That's why I'm going to give you this one chance. You've got a week to leave the state before I bust you."

"But what about our deal?"

"You broke the deal. You arranged for people to be killed. The penalty is either expulsion or arrest."

Mary Beth expected her mother to react with anger. She was prepared for that. And even to go to fisticuffs if necessary. But Mamie actually turned misty-eyed, her voice cracking when she said, "You'd really run me out of West Virginia? Out of my home?"

Mary Beth sighed and pointed out at that monstrosity of a billboard. "Mom, you don't belong here. Cause, you don't get it."

"Get what?"

"Our greatest resource never was our coal. It's always been our people. And you never cared one drip about them."

There was another flicker of rage in Mamie's eyes as she pulled away from her daughter's embrace. "You think you're so much better than me. You think you're so different."

Such an assertion would normally push Mary Beth buttons, but she felt oddly serene. Confident for the first time in her life that she was different from her mother. At least in the ways that mattered most. "One week," she said.

Mamie stood there glaring for another moment, then huffed. "Well, I'm not going to stand here and take any more of this abuse."

"Good. You've got a lot of packing to do."

Mamie held her head high. "Good day, Mr. Connelly." She tried to look dignified as she walked, her high heels clicking loudly on the linoleum floor.

Mary Beth called out to her just before she reached the door. "Tell me one thing, though, before you go."

"What?"

"Did you fix my first election? Are you the one behind all those dead folks who voted for me?"

Mamie cranked her chin up another notch. "I have always supported my children," she said. And, with that, she turned and left. Out of Mary Beth's life—hopefully, for good.

Izzy re-entered the room having overseen the booking of Jason Bailey. Patrick started folding up his maps until Mary Beth stopped him with a point, pinning them to the table with her index finger.

"Something wrong?" Patrick asked.

"You tell me," she said.

Patrick looked confused. "What is this?" He glanced at Izzy for help but the deputy just shrugged.

"All the places in the entire country to build this hydroelectric lake, and the government just so happened to pick McCray County, West Virginia, right where my baby brother'd set up shop with his little militia," Mary Beth said.

Patrick's face turned a sickly pallor.

"Yeah, that's what I thought." Mary Beth pointed to a tiny date at the corner of the map where the engineers had signed off. "The condemnation suit, the plat maps, everything looks like it was thrown together pretty quickly after those stories came out about me in the paper and I found myself in the government's crosshairs. There's even a mistaken reference on there to a town in Tennessee. Like the lake was originally plotted for someplace else and then moved here at the last minute."

Patrick took a deep breath. "Mary," he said, "everything I've done has been to try and help you."

"Help me?"

"Yes, dammit. To help you. The government was going to come down on you and they didn't care at all about Sawyer. The only reason they offered to wipe your slate clean is because I made arresting Sawyer significant enough by moving the project to McCray."

Mary Beth put both hands on her knees and bent down to speak to Patrick like he was a truculent child. "My brother is dead, because of you. Residents of my county are dead. Federal agents are dead. All because of what you set in motion."

"But—"

"But what? You thought I thought I wouldn't figure it out?"

Patrick was speechless. Mary Beth shook her head in disgust. "No, that's not it at all, is it?" she said. "Of course I'd eventually figure it out. You just thought I wouldn't care. That I'd be that pathetic fucking chicken. So desperate for the crumbs I'd follow you anyway."

"Mary, I—" Patrick began, but Mary Beth overrode him. "Well, guess what, asshole. My brother's gone, my mother's leaving, and I'm still here. Not because I'm scared or desperate. But because this is my home. It's what I want."

"It was just a stupid story, Mary. Please, if you would—"

"Stop talking," Mary Beth said. "I'm not finished." She closed her eyes and turned her head to either side, cracking her neck, then spoke slowly, carefully enunciating each word. "I am going to give you the same chance I gave my mother. To get your meddling ass, out of my state, and never come back. Do you understand?"

"But what about S—"

"Don't," Mary Beth said, jabbing a dangerous finger in Patrick's chest. "Leave now or I'll publicize this whole thing—what you did and why you did it—and ruin you. Do you understand? Yes or no?"

Patrick looked like he had a lot more to say but thought better of it. He nodded up and down.

Izzy took him by the arm. "Come on, counselor. It's time to go," he said, and walked Patrick to the door.

Mary Beth stormed over by her desk, breathing deeply, trying to keep her emotions in check as she stared at the wall. There were so many intense feelings when it came to Patrick, but now when she thought of him, the thing that was paramount was the image of her brother's dead blue eyes. Whether it was completely fair or not, that would always be the first thing she thought about.

"I love her, Izzy," she heard Patrick whisper.

"I know," Izzy whispered back. "But don't try to talk to her when she's like this. I'll see what I can do."

They exited as Deputy Goforth was entering, carting a dolly full of file boxes.

"That all of it?" Mary Beth asked.

"Nope. Still got a whole trunk full," Goforth said.

Izzy came back in, trying to plead Patrick's case. "MB, you need to take a minute and think before you run this guy off."

She crossed her arms. "Nothing to think about."

"Sure there is," Izzy said.

"He was going to, literally, sink McCray County, Izzy. The place where I was born. That's now part of my jurisdiction."

"Just consider," Izzy said, "just for a second, all the bullshit you've looked past with your family. All the compromises you've made. Now you got somebody who may have done something wrong, but he was doing it because he really cares about you."

Mary Beth shook her head. "I'm done compromising. Done way too much of it, already. Lost my taste for it."

Izzy growled in frustration and gripped the air with his good hand. "Quit being so damn stubborn."

"I am who I am, Izzy."

Mary Beth grabbed the top box from Goforth's stack and carried it to her desk as though she was done with the conversation.

"So that's all there is to it?" Izzy said. "Nothing else to talk about?"

"No, we've got a lot to talk about." Mary Beth pulled a file from the box and held it up. "These are all the unsolved cases we just inherited from McCray."

"So?"

Mary Beth gave Izzy a leveled look. "So I suggest you forget about all this touchy-feely crap and pull up a seat. We've got a lot of work to do."

ACKNOWLEDGMENTS

BEING A WRITER can be a tough existence, especially without the ability to commiserate with those similarly afflicted. Fortunately, while writing this book, I had the benefit of two excellent critique groups: the Yonder gang of Eryk Pruitt, Scott Blackburn, J.G. Hetherton, Phillip Kimbrough, and J.M. Rasinske; and the Barnes & Noble group of Lyn Fairchild Hawks, Stephanie Moore, Becky Moynihan, and Amanda Gladin-Kramer. Thank you all for your feedback and friendship, both of which were invaluable.

Thank you to my editor father and school-teacher mother who are still my first and favorite beta readers. Special thanks to my wife, Michelle, who is not a big book person but indulges me anyway, and my kids, Dylan and Gabi, who would love to read my stuff if I'd let them--maybe when you're older.

Finally, thanks to Publisher and Editor extraordinaire, Ron Earl Phillips, and all the cool kids who make up the Shotgun Honey Hive Mind.

RUSSELL W. JOHNSON is an attorney who got so sick of billable hours he started writing crime fiction. His first story was published in *Ellery Queen Mystery Magazine* and won the Edgar Awards' Robert L. Fish prize in 2015. Since then, he's had stories published in a number of outlets and recently won the West Virginia Writers Association's Pearl S. Buck Award as well as First Place for Book Length Fiction. More information on his writing is available at www.russellwjohnson.com.

ABOUT
SHOTGUN HONEY BOOKS

Thank you for reading *The Moonshine Messiah*, a Mountaineer Mystery, by Russell W. Johnson.

Shotgun Honey began as a crime genre flash fiction webzine in 2011 created as a venue for new and established writers to experiment in the confines of a mere 700 words. More than a decade later, Shotgun Honey still challenges writers with that storytelling task, but also provides opportunities to expand beyond through our book imprint and has since published anthologies, collections, novellas and novels by new and emerging authors.

We hope you have enjoyed this book. That you will share your experience, review and rate this title positively on your favorite book review sites and with your social media family and friends.

Visit ShotgunHoneyBooks.com

FICTION WITH A KICK

shotgunhoneybooks.com

CPSIA information can be obtained
at www.ICGtesting.com
Printed in the USA
BVHW031648260523
664951BV00027B/721

9 781956 957259